Praise for *The Improbable Theory of An...*

"With perfect comic timing and outraged... *Improbable Theory of Ana and Zak* will have you cheering for the underdog."
—Robin Constantine, author of *The Promise of Amazing*

"Peppering his novel with references to delight die-hard SF fans and pop-culture aficionados alike, Katcher (*Almost Perfect*) pens a love letter to fanboys and fangirls everywhere. On the surface, the story is a lighthearted and entertaining romance, but serious undertones explore the fractured side of parent-child relationships and misfit characters desperate to find a tribe. A delightful romp for anyone still figuring out where they belong."
—*Publishers Weekly*

"This well-paced novel is an excellent combination of self-discovery and adventure. . . . Give this to fans of *Eleanor & Park* or *Nick & Norah*."
—ALA *Booklist*

JAN 17 —

$1 - 3y^2$ $S_3 = \begin{bmatrix} 1 & 0 & 0 \\ 1 & 0 & 1 \\ 0 & 0 & 1 \end{bmatrix}$

$\{6\}$

x

$\Delta t =$

$\{6\}$

$\overline{s \cdot x}$

$\frac{1}{2}b \cdot h$

$= m r^2$

$2L$

the IMPROBABLE theory of ANA & ZAK

by Brian Katcher

$\frac{\delta}{\delta x} \frac{+}{-}$

x

$(x$

$[(x$

$(x^2$

$(x-$

$1 - 3y^2$

$1 \frac{-}{5}$

KATHERINE TEGEN BOOKS
An Imprint of HarperCollins Publishers

Katherine Tegen Books is an imprint of HarperCollins Publishers.

The Improbable Theory of Ana and Zak
Copyright © 2015 by HarperCollins Publishers
All rights reserved. Printed in the United States of America.
No part of this book may be used or reproduced in any manner whatsoever
without written permission except in the case of brief quotations embodied in
critical articles and reviews. For information address HarperCollins Children's
Books, a division of HarperCollins Publishers, 195 Broadway, New York, NY
10007.

www.epicreads.com

Library of Congress Cataloging-in-Publication Data
Katcher, Brian, author.
    The improbable theory of Ana and Zak / Brian Katcher. — First edition.
        pages   cm
    ISBN 978-0-06-227278-2
    1. Contests—Juvenile fiction.   2. Science fiction—Congresses—Juvenile
fiction.   3. Brothers and sisters—Juvenile fiction.   4. High school student
activities—Juvenile fiction.   5. Academic achievement—Juvenile fiction.
6. Tacoma (Wash.)—Juvenile fiction.   7. Seattle (Wash.)—Juvenile
fiction.   [1. Contests—Fiction.   2. Genius—Fiction.   3. Brothers and
sisters—Fiction.   4. High schools—Fiction.   5. Schools—Fiction.]   I. Title.
PZ7.K1565Im   2015   2014030718
Fic]—dc23   CIP
                                                                              AC

Typography by Michelle Gengaro-Kokmen
16 17 18 19 20   PC/RRDH   10 9 8 7 6 5 4 3 2 1
❖
First paperback edition, 2016

To my mother, Connie.
Thanks for taking me to the library.

ZAK

"Zak! Hey, Zak, where are you?"

The sound of my stepfather's voice fills me with dread. My mother is gone—we are alone.

"Zak! Get out here."

I try to ignore it. Try to lose myself in an issue of *Fangoria*. For now, I'm safe in my little hiding place in the utility room. If I don't answer, maybe he won't find me. Maybe he won't make me do those things . . .

"Zak!"

I look up at the sneering face of Han Solo on the wall, momentarily wishing he were here to back me up. But no, this is something I have to face alone. Steeling

...self for what I know lies ahead, I exit my refuge.

I find him upstairs, grinning that carefree smile of his. And holding a football.

Mother of God, it's worse than I thought.

He stands there in my kitchen, wearing the fraternity sweater from a college he (probably) graduated from decades ago.

"C'mon, boy-o!" he says in that chirpy voice of his. "It's beautiful outside."

This being Tacoma, Washington, beautiful weather means it's only drizzling. I can think of a thousand things I'd rather be doing, from organizing my DVDs to chewing on tinfoil. But Mom had asked me to make an effort to spend some time with *him*.

Please, Zak. Just an afternoon. It would mean so much to me. She had the big sad mom eyes. I have no choice in the matter.

I stomp out the back door, close enough that Roger has to scoot out of my way (small mercy, no one makes me call him "Dad"). Let's just get this over with.

Rog is oblivious to my discomfort. He stands there with the ball in hand, no doubt reliving his high school days. He then passes it to me. I bobble it a few times and drop it.

"Good eye!"

"Spare me your platitudes." I grin internally as his

brow furrows over that last word. I hurl the ball back at him and only fall short by a yard. A sad showing for the digital Football Frenzy champion three years running.

We toss the ball in silence for a few minutes. I remember the chain gang prisoners from a movie and am tempted to break into a chorus of "Po' Lazarus."

"Zak?" He breaks the silence. "Your school newsletter came in the mail the other day."

"Glad to see you reading." *Toss, miss, toss, miss.*

"Says that soccer tryouts are coming up for the summer leagues. I thought maybe you'd be interested."

This comment is so ridiculous, I nearly laugh. Luckily, I remember my vow never to smile in his presence. "You thought wrong." I'm pleased with my voice. Disdain, just the slightest edge of sarcasm.

Unfortunately, Roger does not shut up. "Well, maybe not soccer. How about baseball?"

I catch the football with my chest. "I don't really know how to play."

He smirks. "C'mon, everyone knows how. Didn't your father show you?"

The ball flies from my hand. I smile inside as it pegs Roger right in the eyeball. He falls to his knees.

"Ow . . . Wow, good arm there, kid . . . ow . . . Um, that's enough for me now . . . Geez, my contact . . ."

I'm already marching back to the house . . . *my* house. I am livid.

Roger, are you really that dumb? Or are you just a colossal prick? No, my father never taught me how to play baseball. Though right now, I wish I did own a bat.

I slink down to the basement and return to the utility room. Like Superman and Doc Savage, I have my own little Fortress of Solitude. My laptop next to the water heater. My collection of movie memorabilia on the unfinished plank shelves. A mini fridge. I used to have this all set up in the den, but Roger has taken over that room. He says he needs it for his job. His job apparently includes a lot of fantasy football and buying crap on eBay.

I rummage through a plastic bin and pull out a framed photo. Me and my dad, Christmas morning. We're wearing the matching Indiana Jones fedoras we'd gotten each other. I think I was nine.

It's hard to believe I haven't seen him in six years. Some mornings, I still wake up and expect to find him in the kitchen, charring a pan of bacon. Instead, I find Roger, sprawled out on my couch, watching the sports highlights.

Sometimes I wish I was little again. That I could believe that Dad was off excavating Incan ruins in South America or something, and that one day he'd pull up into our driveway and . . .

Grow up, Zak. You know that's not going to happen.

I return the photo to its place. I don't display it. I don't want Roger looking at it and feeling superior to the man in the picture.

Two months. That's how long my mom knew Roger before they got engaged. Two damn months.

ANA

I look at my watch. It's just after three. Perfect. If I can finish things up in the library in under ten minutes, I'll have just enough time to make archery practice.

It's my fault that I didn't take care of this before school, of course, but my brother, Clayton, asked me to go over his math homework for him, and then Mrs. Brinkham stopped me to talk about the quiz bowl tournament, and I couldn't very well tell *her* no because I'll need her to write me a letter of reference for that scholarship later this month, and then lunch was a total disaster because . . .

Ticktock, ticktock.

No one is waiting at the library checkout. Perfect. Mrs. Newbold, the librarian, smiles when she sees me.

"Ana! I heard you came in first place at the—"

"Do you have the books I put on hold?" It's rude to interrupt, but I worry that if I don't get down to business, she'll keep me here for twenty minutes, just chatting.

The librarian blinks, then hurries off to find my material. I check my watch again. Two after. Still on track . . .

"*Achtung!*" The voice barks from behind me. I nearly jump over the counter.

On a table in the middle of the library, a half dozen kids have set up some sort of board game. I've seen these loud idiots here before. I thought about complaining, but there was no point. After school, the media center is always empty. I think the librarians are glad to have company.

The desk phone rings and, much to my annoyance, Mrs. Newbold answers it, my books tantalizingly clutched in her hand. I tap my foot in frustration, then turn and glare when someone at the gaming table begins to bark orders in a painfully fake German accent.

He's a tall, skinny, pasty guy in a T-shirt that says NEVER TRUST A SMILING GM. I'm disturbed to see he's wearing one of those spiked Prussian helmets. Actually, everyone at the table is wearing some bizarre headgear:

a furry Russian cap, a turban, a bowler hat. I'm intrigued enough to look at their game board. It's a map of Europe, covered with little plastic soldiers and cannons.

Boys, always playing at war.

The librarian hangs up and passes me my books. I grab them without another word. I can just make practice with a couple of minutes to spare. Not that Coach minds it when other people wander in late, but that's their problem.

After practice, I'll have enough time to change before dinner. Then I can start on my history project, before . . .

"Herr Fräulein! Bitte komen ober here, mach schnell!"

It's the guy in the plastic helmet again. He's turned toward me, standing there with one foot on his chair, grinning. His hat is about a size too big, shadowing his eyes. All I can make out is a long, narrow nose and a careless smile.

I recognize him. He's always in here running games, or in the cafeteria playing cards, or in the commons laughing with his goober friends.

"What?" I ask, annoyed. I'm running out of time.

His grin widens. It's the smile of a guy who has nowhere to go and nothing to do when he gets there. Someone who wastes all his time.

He tilts his helmet back, revealing brown eyes and

shaggy hair. He's let his scraggly sideburns and chin whiskers grow out in an unfortunate attempt at facial hair. Probably trying to look older. Someone should tell him to shave—he'd look a lot nicer. Someone should also tell him to get a haircut, buy a shirt that's not split at the armpit, and not wear a hat that makes him look like a refugee from a Berlin mental hospital.

He juts out his chin, making him look even more ridiculously self-confident. "How'd you like to help shape the destiny of 1914 Europe? Defend her soft underbelly?"

His comments are so nonsensical, I turn to his table-mates, hoping they can explain. Or get this guy to shut up.

An overweight guy in a French gendarme's cap speaks up. "What he's saying, *ma chérie*, is we're short a player. Want to be Italy?"

I turn back to Kaiser Jr., to tell him to sit on his helmet. But I notice his smile has wavered. His eyes look just slightly nervous, hopeful. No point in embarrassing him in front of the other commanders in chief. I sigh.

"Listen . . . what's your name?"

Instantly, his sheen of arrogance returns. "They call me Duke."

I look down at a binder next to the game board. ZAK DUQUETTE, it reads.

"Listen, Zak. Touched as I am that you've saved me a country that's clearly vulnerable on four fronts, I'm late."

He attempts to suavely run his fingers through his hair and almost knocks his helmet off. "Well, we meet here every Tuesday . . ."

"Maybe some other war."

I cut the conversation short by leaving the library. I'm going to be late as it is.

Briefly, I wonder what it would be like to be someone like Zak. Not that I want to waste my time on a game like that, but it would be nice to just sometimes do something I want to do. To have friends that I can be with because we're having fun, not because we're at a club meeting or working on a project. To not have to account for every second that I'm not at home or in class.

My sister, Nichole, used to be like that.

I don't have a sister anymore.

ZAK

Smeggin' hell. Blew it.

I watch, disinterested, as the Turks launch an improbable beachhead against England, bringing all of 1918 Europe under Ottoman rule.

It was that girl who distracted me. Ana, that's her name. She's in the library all the time, but I've never spoken to her. I know she's one of those smart, go-getter types—her picture is on every other page of the yearbook. Stupid me, I thought maybe she'd like to hang out with the rest of us geeks. I figured this was the perfect opportunity to introduce myself. Nope. Guess she was too good for that.

The Great War has ended. The plastic dead are swept, unceremoniously, back into the box. I grunt good-bye to my friends as they leave. Only James remains, twirling his field marshal's cap on a finger.

I pick up my helmet and put it back in the box. It occurs to me that, just maybe, there's a reason that guys don't generally wear military headgear when attempting to talk to girls.

"Intimidated by the size of my *Pickelhaube*?" I mumble, then chuckle.

"Excuse me?" asks James.

I return to reality, such as it is. "That's what I should have said to that girl, Ana."

I expect James to laugh at me, but he nods sagely. "The perfect comeback, ten minutes too late. *L'esprit de l'escalier*, as they say in France."

I smile at my chubby friend. As usual, he's wearing a mishmash of clothes that may or may not be a tribute to his favorite comic book characters. I recognize Cyclops's sunglasses, the Punisher's black T-shirt, and Archie Andrews's checkered pants. With a knowing smirk, he removes a glossy booklet from his bag.

WASHINGCON! March 2–4th, Seattle. The Pacific Northwest's Biggest, Baddest, Boldest Science Fiction, Fantasy, and Comic Book Convention!

On the cover is a drawing of our state's namesake.

The august general and president is decked out in a frilly collared tux, clutching a chain gun in one fist and lighting a cigar with the other. To the left, a buxom woman in petticoats and skirts attacks a vampire with a poleax.

"Steampunk," I say, staring at the image like a prisoner viewing an unconditional pardon. "Nice."

"Just got it in the mail yesterday," says James. "You make your room reservation yet?"

I flip through the scheduled events. "Of course. I told my mom that I'm staying in a hotel room with you and your parents."

"Funny, I told my mom the same thing."

We both laugh. For years we've been going to this con together, and not once have we worried about where we'll stay. I could always count on a friend of a friend to have a room where we could crash. Barring that, I could sneak into one of the quieter movie theaters and take a catnap. And caffeine was always my friend.

James glances at his Dick Tracy communicator watch. "So are we doing the X-fighter Turbo battle this year?"

"You gotta ask? When is that, anyway?"

"Four a.m., I think."

"Good. I hate it when they schedule it at some weird time."

James stands. "See you 'round, Duke."

"Right. Hey, that girl, Ana . . ."

He holds up a palm and shakes his head. "Forget it. Not a chance."

I am a touch offended. Ana isn't *that* hot, after all. Scrawny, flat chested, with a mane of frizzy, dark hair. She does kind of have a Barbara Gordon thing going on, though. "What, I'm too dorky for a chick on the math team?"

"You're too lazy. Trust me, that girl only dates National Merit Scholars, and she doesn't even date *them*. Take care, Duke."

Okay, so she's out of my league. I'm used to it. Very used to it, actually. That's another reason I was looking forward to the con. Whole new set of dating rules there.

I grab my things and leave, thoughts of the convention running through my head. Just ten more days.

Most years, the idea is exciting. This time . . . let's just say I really need to get out of the house. To get away from Roger and his attempts to make me into a stepson who doesn't embarrass him. Seventy blessed hours with my own kind.

I'm almost out the door. Almost outside into the dreary, late-winter day.

"Zak!"

A woman's voice calls me from inside the school. Adult. Teacher. I pretend not to hear. Just ten more steps.

"Zak Duquette!"

Too late. I turn. Mrs. Brinkham, my health teacher, rapidly approaches, awkwardly cradling a sheaf of papers. "Zak, I'm glad I caught you. I need a word."

"Ah, Mrs. B, I kind of have to get home."

"It'll just take a moment." She pauses to move a lock of dark hair out of her eye, almost causing her to lose the pile of homework she's clutching. As usual, she's a living example of entropy. She has a run in one of her stockings. There are Band-Aids around two of her knuckles. A coffee stain dots the front of her white blouse, and she's missing an earring. Though she's got to be pushing forty, she still has an awkward, confused air about her that makes her seem much younger. Last year a new school security officer asked to see her hall pass.

Annoyed, I follow her to the health room. I slump on a desk, pretending to be interested in the model of the Visible Man, as Mrs. Brinkham awkwardly sorts her papers. Not for the first time, I ponder what she would have looked like twenty or so years ago. She was probably pretty cute, and it hasn't totally faded with age.

Finally, she pulls up her chair and sits opposite me.

"Zakory, you know I'm your faculty advisor, right?"

We have faculty advisors? I guess I was vaguely aware of that, the same way I'm aware that I have a spleen. It's just not something I've ever really given much thought to.

"Yes. My advisor. Of course."

"I'm sorry I haven't spoken with you yet. I'm so busy with this class and all, sometimes it's hard to find the time."

I stifle a laugh. Health class is an absolute joke. It's a required course, but it's not like it's hard studying face washing and the importance of not shooting heroin. I cherish the fifty-minute nap her class provides me every afternoon.

Mrs. Brinkham continues. "I'd like to know what your plans are after graduation."

I shrug. "I've been accepted into Tacoma Community College."

I move to leave, but she actually wants to know more. "Did you apply anywhere else?"

"Nah. Figure I can get a job with computers with an associate's. Listen . . ."

She presses on. "What kind of job?"

"Computers," I repeat.

She shakes her head. "Zak, you're a smart boy. A talented boy. Have you given any thought to—"

"TCC. That's where I'm going." Why is everyone so down on the ju-co? It's cheap, easy, and I won't have to move.

"Do you participate in any extracurricular activities? Any sports or—"

I cut her off. "I appreciate your interest, but I'm good

to go. Let's do this again some time." I stand, glad to end the conversation.

"Sit down." Her normal, tittering, flighty voice is suddenly gone. I return to my seat, surprised.

"Was there something else? Ma'am?"

She does not smile as she passes a paper to me. I recognize it—it's my semester report on dysentery. Or diphtheria. Some *D* disease.

My Spidey-sense is tingling. "Um . . ."

"Zak, this whole essay is copied from Wikipedia." She's upset. She never gets upset. This is bad.

I play innocent. "I used it as a source, sure."

"You cut and pasted almost the whole thing. You didn't even take out the hyperlinks!"

Yikes, I thought I caught all those. Fortunately, this is Mrs. B we're talking about. Surely there's a way out. "I'm sorry. I was kind of in a time crunch myself. I'd be happy to do it over." I give her a smile.

She doesn't return it. "This is cheating, Zak. Academic dishonesty. I know most of you don't take this class very seriously, but it's a real course just the same. I'm going to have to take this to the principal."

"Wait . . ." Why was she in hard-ass mode all of a sudden? I sure as heck wasn't the only student who liberally borrowed from the internet. True, maybe I'd gotten a little lazy this time, but it's not like this was an important class. I'd completed the assignment, which was more than some of my classmates did.

"You'll receive two weeks of detention. And a zero on this assignment, of course."

"Couldn't we . . ." *What? Think, Duquette!*

"This paper was twenty percent of your final grade. And since you've blown off every other assignment in here, you cannot hope to recover from this. You'll fail."

"Fail?" As in, actually fail? As in, not pass a class?

She then adds the coup de grâce. "And since health is a required course, you will not graduate. You'll have to make it up in the summer. And you won't be able to enroll in TCC until late fall, I'm afraid. Not without a diploma."

I'm frozen in sick fear. What had gotten into her? Okay, I crossed the line. I can admit that. But not letting me graduate? Even the droolers who take PE every hour get to walk at the ceremony. Why is she singling me out?

"Isn't there anything I can do?" My voice comes out as a pathetic squeak.

"Perhaps." She smiles in an enigmatic way. For a moment I hope she's going to ask me to lock the door as she unbuttons her blouse, but I'm not so fortunate. "You know that I'm the quiz bowl team's sponsor, right?"

Huh? "Yes. I'm a big fan."

She ignores that. "We're competing for the championship in a couple of weeks. I think we have a very good chance of winning. We have a good group this year."

"Okay." *What does this have to do with me?*

"The problem is, we've lost a couple of team members recently. Kathryn Ciznack moved unexpectedly, and Leroy Cooper is no longer available."

"Because of the . . ." I take a toke from an imaginary joint.

She nods. "We have enough people for a full team, but no alternate." She stares at me meaningfully. "I thought perhaps you'd like to volunteer."

I try not to cringe. Remembering what hangs in the balance, I ask her what I'd have to do.

"We leave for Seattle on a Friday morning, and won't return until Saturday night, so it would mean most of your weekend. You'll sit in a couple of rounds to give other people a break. You will dress nicely and you will take the contest seriously."

I bite my lip, pretending to ponder. Inside, my brain is doing backflips. A day off from school? A Saturday away from Roger? This was hardly the deal with the devil I was expecting.

"And I'll get full credit for the report?"

She shakes her head. "If you rewrite it and hand it in to me by next Friday, I'll count it as complete. You'll pass this class with a C, which, quite frankly, is a gift."

"Fair enough."

We stand. She gives me a piece of paper. "That's a permission form for the competition. I need you to have a parent sign that and get it back to me tomorrow morning."

I reach for it, but she holds it just out of my grasp. "Zak, this is a one-time offer. The second you try to get out of this or don't try your hardest at the tournament, the deal is off." Her face is more severe than I've ever seen it.

I take the paper gingerly and back out of the room. Good Lord, talk about landing on your feet! Instead of getting my ass reamed, all I have to do is throw on a tie and play *Jeopardy!* And another weekend away from the intruder in my house. Maybe this will get Roger off my ass about participating in after-school stuff.

I pause at the front door of the school and glance at the permission slip. Seattle, that's a great town. I know people there. If there's any downtime, maybe I could call some friends to play a little Call of Cthulhu. When, exactly . . .

My eyes freeze on the permission slip. *No.*

No, no, no.

I stagger outside, into the pouring rain.

March second.

The same weekend as the convention. My favorite time of the year. The event I look forward to for twelve months. My Christmas.

And now I'm not going.

I fall to my knees. Raising my arms to the heavens, I shout out in impotent frustration.

"Connnnnnnnn!"

ANA

Everything in its place. My bike, parked directly between my brother's and the deep freeze. My jacket, hanging on the second peg by the garage door. My quiver and arrows, on the rack. My bow, in the corner, unstrung (wouldn't want that thing to go off accidentally).

Due to a popular book series and the movies it spawned a lot of girls have taken up archery recently. I've been doing it for years. Not really out of enjoyment, but because it makes me well-rounded. That's what the good colleges want, after all—someone well-rounded. What the scholarship committees look for. What my parents expect of me. That's why I practice archery. Why I captain the quiz bowl team. Why I volunteer at the soup kitchen, go to mass every Sunday, and never, ever get a grade lower than an A–.

I'm so well-rounded I'm almost spherical.

I brace myself and enter the house. There's no reason I shouldn't want to go in. Just my dad, cooking dinner, my mom, working at the computer, and my little brother, Clayton, doing his homework.

Just like every Tuesday afternoon for the past two years.

"You're late," says my father, looking up from slicing tomatoes for taco night.

Tuesday night is taco night. Tuesday night has always been taco night. Tuesday night will always be taco night.

I stop to peck Mom on the cheek. "Sorry, Coach wanted to talk to us about—"

"Ana." Mom smiles and waves a finger at me, but the warning is very much there. I'm to be home at a certain time, every evening. No excuses.

"It won't happen again."

Clayton, is already setting the table. I go to help him. He nods at me and smiles.

I grin back and stifle a laugh. At thirteen, he's the youngest freshman at our school, and it really shows. He hasn't started to mature, and he looks like he belongs more in fifth grade than ninth. It doesn't help that Mom still picks out all his clothes. Even at home, he wears slacks, a shirt buttoned up to his neck, and socks that are two different shades of white.

If I lived with a different family, I might offer to take him shopping for something more stylish.

Then again, maybe I'm the last person to give advice on what's cool.

Right when I lay down the last fork, the living room clock chimes five thirty. Like automatons, we march to our spots. Sometimes I entertain wild notions of switching chairs with Clayton, just to shake things up a bit.

As Dad says the blessing, I glance at the empty seat across from me. Nichole's spot. And no matter how much my family tries to pretend that she never existed, that will always be Nichole's spot.

My mind drifts back to the days when she used to kick my shins under the table to make me squeal during grace. How she used to dump salt in Clayton's drink or make vampire teeth out of her carrot sticks. How she would—

"Ana?"

Mom interrupts my thoughts. She's speaking to me. I didn't hear what she asked, but it doesn't matter. It's the same thing she asks me every single night at dinner: *How was your day, Ana?*

I rattle off my lines like a liturgist reciting a prayer. My day was fine, no trouble, I got good grades in everything, I haven't disappointed you. I'll never disappoint you. Amen.

Mom and Dad smile at me. Then their heads creepily turn toward Clayton at the exact same time, for his speech.

"Wait." I say it so quietly, they almost don't hear me. But they do. *Darn.*

"Yes?" Dad cocks an eyebrow. I'm going off book here.

"I . . . got an email today. From Seattle University. I . . . it was an acceptance letter."

Clayton smiles and starts to say something before he notices the look on my mother's face. This is not a time for congratulations.

"I wasn't aware you'd applied there, Ana." There's no anger in her voice. There's no pride, either.

I try to make light of it. "Oh, it was nothing. Just a safety school." *You know how us crazy teenagers are, going out and applying to colleges.*

"Well, good for you," says Dad, with real sincerity. "Always thinking ahead. So, Clayton—"

"It's just that . . . they have an excellent psychology program. One of the best in the northwest."

Under the table, I've bent my fork into a pretzel. But

I actually did it. I actually suggested . . .

"Ana," says my mother, in a voice that indicates the conversation was over before it began. "We've discussed this. We all agreed that going to school here in Tacoma is the best course of action, at least for your freshman year. You'll be able to save a lot of money by living at home."

I don't recall any discussion. All I remember is them telling me that I would be attending the University of Washington at Tacoma. And coming back here, night after night.

But I'm Ana Watson. I didn't spend four years on the debate team to *lose* an argument. I have a thousand reasons why going to school in Seattle is the best course of action. Besides, when it comes down to it, this is my life, my education, my decision.

Silently, I listen to Clayton rattle off an animated speech about his day.

I know better than to rock the boat. I know what happens in this family when you don't play by the rules.

That empty chair across from me is a constant reminder.

ZAK

7:30 AM

Remember that great, underrated Terry Gilliam movie, *Brazil?* There's a scene where this poor schmuck is mistaken for a terrorist and a bunch of armed goons come blasting through the ceiling, lock him in a full-body straitjacket, and hurl him into a black van for transport to the recducation center.

As I sit on the front porch, waiting for the school van to pick me up, I can relate. It's a rare sunny day for Tacoma. Mom has left for work. Right now I should be sleeping through whatever class I have first hour—some sort of English lit thing, I think—and waiting for tonight.

Kicking ass at D&D. Taking names at a round of

Magic: The Gathering. Then, who knows? A viewing of a bootlegged *Ranma ½*, complete with hilarious Japanese commercials? A spontaneous drum circle? Maybe slip into the Vampire Ball?

It doesn't matter. I'll be going to Seattle today, all right. But not to Washingcon.

All is lost.

The beautiful day mocks me. The slightly-less-gray-than-usual sky laughs in my face. I'm in a foul mood. I want to punch a hobbit.

To my right, Roger hovers above my head, cleaning out our gutters. He doesn't ask me to hold the ladder and I don't offer. Apparently, he doesn't have to go to work today. I wonder vaguely what he does for a living. I know he works with Mom down at city hall. I think he might have told me about his job, but like everything else about him, I'm desperately uninterested.

Roger returns to ground level, merry as a Cockney chimney sweep. He wipes his hands on a rag and joins me on the stoop.

"Big ol' mess up there. Probably ten year's worth of gunk packed in the downspout."

"Thank you for sharing that with me."

He starts to rise, but doesn't. "So . . . quiz bowl, eh?"

"Yep."

"Guess you have to be pretty smart to do that."

"I wouldn't know. I'm not really on the team." I take out my phone and pretend to text, but quickly put it away when I read my new messages: all from James and the other members of my BattleTech squad, accusing me of treason for bailing on them.

Roger continues to talk, unaware that I'm not listening. I hope he wasn't this awkward when he asked out Mom. Against my will, I imagine what their first date was like.

When the school's van pulls up, I'm actually relieved to see them. I quickly grab my bag and hop in.

Mrs. Brinkham is driving. She nods to me, eyes half on some printed directions. I manage to force a smile. Hopefully my face says, *Thank you for this opportunity*, rather than, *You witch—I hate you.*

I'm surprised to see that Ana, the girl from the library, is here. Maybe this weekend won't be an absolute bust after all. We'll be on the same team, so I'll have a chance to make a better impression. I smile at her. She glances up from her binder for a second. Just one second. Just long enough to let me know that she's seen me, and that she can't even bother with a simple "hello."

I wonder if she's that rude to everyone, or just me.

In the middle row, a cute, somewhat chubby girl slumps against the window, sound asleep. A gangly blond guy sits next to her, playing a game on his phone.

I'm forced to take the only available seat, in the back. If God were merciful, I would have been alone. Instead, there's a boy sitting in the window seat. He doesn't look older than ten or eleven, so I assume he's Mrs. Brinkham's son or something. He smiles up at me from behind thick glasses.

"Hi!" His voice is as joyful and irritating as Jar Jar's. "I'm Clayton!" I half expect to see a name tag hanging from a yarn lanyard around his neck.

I sit silently.

"What's your name?" He continues to stare at me, his face split into a plastic clown's grin. Only when I actually see him blink do I start to relax.

"Duke."

"Is that really your name?"

"Look, um, Clayton? Maybe you'd be more comfortable sitting up there with your mom."

For a moment, he looks perplexed, then laughs. It sounds as if a kitten is being stepped on. "Mrs. Brinkham? Oh, no, she's not my mother. I'm on the team."

The logical side of my brain tells me to shut up, but I ask anyway. "Aren't you a little young?"

He stomps on the kitten again. "I'm thirteen. I skipped the second grade. Now my sister and I get to go to the same school again." He gestures to the front of the van. After a moment I realize what he's saying.

"Ana's your sister?"

He nods again. There's a slight resemblance, but it's clear who got the looks in the family.

Clayton pulls out a tome so big and musty, I mistake it for the *Necronomicon*. "World history. That's my weak subject. Do you want to quiz each other?"

The blond guy in front of me bends to get something out of his bag. Our eyes meet.

Tough luck, pal, he wordlessly communicates.

"Or do you want me to quiz you? Here's an easy one. Xerxes was the king of: a) Macedonia, b) Persia . . ."

I stare, longingly, at the rear door of the van. We're only going about forty. If I rolled just right when I hit the street, I'd only break a few bones.

"Clayton, please stop. Please. I'm not interested." I pause, then lower my voice so Mrs. Brinkham won't overhear. "I'm not even really on this team. I'm not even supposed to be here today!"

"You sound like that guy from *Clerks*."

I'm a little shocked that he got that reference, but not enough to mention it. "Look, Clay, I had to skip something very fun to come here, and I'm not in a great mood." I glance up to make sure Mrs. Brinkham isn't listening, but she's at the wheel, texting.

We sit in silence for about ten seconds.

"What are you missing today?"

"A convention I go to every year. Seriously, Clayton . . ."

"Last year I had to miss archaeology camp to go to the scholars' academy."

Great Zarquon.

"It's a con. A science-fiction convention. Washingcon, you ever heard of that?"

He tilts his head. He then raises his hand in the Vulcan salute. The guy in the seat in front of me laughs.

"It's not like that, Clayton. It's . . . it's kind of magic." Realizing how lame that sounds, I continue. "It's like, you never know what's going to happen. Last year, some engineers built a functioning AT-AT out of an old motorcycle. Year before that, the SCA reenacted the Battle of Hastings. Eight people wound up in the hospital. They're supposed to do the Battle of Badon Hill this year."

The guy in front of me has turned around and is listening.

"I got to drive one of the original Batmobiles once. I met George Takei, the only man I'd ever switch teams for. I met Gilbert Shelton and I think I got high just from shaking his hand. I saw the guy who played the original RoboCop, and he's uglier without the mask."

"I always liked that movie," says Clayton.

The girl in front of me yawns, stretches, and looks in my direction. Everyone on the bus except Ana is listening to me. I pour it on, only exaggerating a bit. "Two years ago, the Lovecraftians tried to summon Hastur in the boiler room. And when they turned the lights back on, *one of the guys in the circle was gone!*" I don't mention that two purses and a laptop vanished with him.

"One time this guy proposed to his girlfriend with an alien that ripped out of his chest. And she said yes! And my friend James swears that Bill Murray cornered him in a hotel hallway, yanked the pizza he was carrying out of his hands, said, 'No one will ever believe you,' and walked off."

Blond Guy looks impressed. "So why did you come here instead?"

I ignore him, continuing to spin tales, many of which sort of happened at one time or another. The catfight between a Lady Galadriel and Harley Quinn, versus another Galadriel and a female Pippin. The time I had to share a bed with Sailor Moon (her boyfriend slept between us, but still).

Eventually, we begin to slow down for the Seattle gridlock. Everyone returns to their seats. Clayton still stares at me. His eyes are wide. I hope I've managed to shock him just a little bit.

"Duke, where did you say this event was?"

"Right here in Seattle. At the convention center."

I lean back in my seat and put in my earbuds to end

the conversation. Just as the narrator begins chapter seventeen of *Snow Crash*, I hear Clayton mumble something.

"Fascinating."

ANA

1:30 PM

"Seventeen over negative pi," says Clayton. He has not touched the scratch paper in front of him.

"Correct," replies the judge, trying to hide the slightly shocked edge in his voice. Another ten points for Meriwether Lewis High School.

"Which exiled Russian leader was assassinated in 1940, in Mexico City?"

Landon buzzes in excitedly. "Who is Leon Trotsky?"

"Correct. And may I remind you once again, you do not have to answer in the form of a question."

"Sorry."

For our opponents, the ending buzzer must sound

merciful. We're ahead by nearly one hundred points. They mutter their congratulations and ashamedly gather their things.

I smile at my brother. "Great work, Clayton."

He blushes and ducks his head. "It was a team effort," he mumbles.

I glance at my two other teammates as they take sips of bottled water and prepare for the next round. It's true—we are pretty formidable. Landon, the history and government expert. Sonya, who knows everything about the life sciences and language. Me, with my decent handle on the humanities and arts. But Clayton . . . science and math were his strong points, but honestly, he could probably take on any team single-handedly. I give him a playful punch on the shoulder, nearly knocking him off his stool. If it wasn't for him, we wouldn't have a team.

Across the room, I see the one weak link in our chain: Deadweight Duquette. Instead of doing some last-minute cramming like the other alternates waiting in the audience, he's found another lazy person and is playing cards with him. Their game has all the sleazy dignity of a backroom poker game.

I walk over to his table to grab my phone. (That's one thing we can trust him to do: watch our bags.) I know my irritation with him is pointless—after all, he's only an alternate. Still, I don't like the idea of someone on this team who was obviously here against his will.

Just as I fish my phone out of my purse, Zak's opponent wanders off. He instantly turns to me.

"Hey, Ana, good show there."

"Yes, Zak."

His eyes narrow. I remember how he'd introduced himself as Duke. I hope that using his real name annoys him.

"Your little bro was kicking some ass up there. He's like a mini Brainiac."

I turn on my phone. "Yes."

"I'm serious. The way he does math in his head, you ought to get him to try out for Stupid Human Tricks."

Yes, there's nothing I'd like better than to see my brother paraded around like some kind of genius freak. He gets enough of that already.

As if on cue, Clayton has joined us. His cute little smile is back. I almost return it, but then realize, much to my disgust, that he's grinning at Zak.

"Hey, Duke."

"Hey, C-Dawg. Nice play on that physics question."

Clayton's grin widens. And . . . good grief, he's blushing. Actually blushing.

Zak fans his strange cards out on the desk in front of him. "You got a few minutes? Wanna play a round of Mazes and Monsters?"

"Sure! Um, I've never . . ."

"Real easy. The goal is—"

Okay, it's time to nip this in the bud. "Clayton, get back up there." I point to the front of the room. My brother immediately stands.

"Hang on," interrupts Duquette. "This'll only take like, three minutes."

Clayton glances at me, and I shake my head. No distractions, not today. As soon as he's out of earshot, I sit down next to Zak.

"I appreciate you making an effort to include him . . . ," I begin.

Zak shoots me an obnoxiously offended look. "He's not a baby. I just wanted to play cards. It gets a little boring out here in the studio audience."

Poor little baby. "Sorry, Zak. But the rest of us are here to win a tournament. We've been working for this all year, and I don't need you distracting Clayton right now. You two can play when we get to the hotel. But leave us alone during the competition."

Zak's eyebrows squish together until they form a single fuzzy caterpillar on his brow. "Leave *you* alone? Excuse me, I thought I was part of this team too."

I am *so* not in the mood for his drama. "You sure didn't act like you wanted to be on this team when we were in the van this morning."

Zak's lips retract into an angry little pucker, which is kind of hilarious. "No, Ana, I didn't. I'm missing something very important to me right now. And all I've done today is sit around with my thumb up my butt. So why the hell *am* I here?"

I start to explain how each team is required to have four members, and we needed him along just in case someone got sick. He's like a spare tire. I've captained this team for two years. I've worked hard to get us here. Someone like Duquette wouldn't understand that.

Before I can think of a way to explain, Mrs. Brinkham rushes over, distractedly digging through her purse.

"Ana, did I give you our registration forms or did I leave them in the van?"

Okay, maybe our team has *two* weak links.

"You never gave them to me."

Mrs. Brinkham continues to remove wads of old Kleenex and other trash from her bag. "I need to turn those in." She looks back up at us. "Could you run down to the parking lot and get them? They should be on the dashboard in a purple folder."

Duquette just stands there. Perhaps the instructions were too difficult.

"C'mon, Zak," I prod. "Straight down the stairs. We parked next to the big fountain." I try to nudge him forward with my palm.

"Actually," interrupts Mrs. Brinkham. "I was talking to you, Ana. Go stretch your legs. Maybe get a snack."

Well, maybe our sponsor has forgotten the schedule, but fortunately I haven't. "I'm sorry, Mrs. Brinkham, but the next round is in"—I check my watch—"six minutes."

"I know." She clears her throat. "Take a break. Let's let Zak have a round."

Zak's face breaks into a stupid grin, which he quickly swallows when he looks at me.

"Mrs. Brinkham," I begin, trying to sound calm. "If we win this round, we're through for the day. I really don't think this is the time to play shorthanded. Um, no offense, Zak."

He shrugs.

Mrs. Brinkham, however, pointedly hands me her keys. "We're up against a new team, mostly freshmen. Zak will be just fine."

I'm beginning to lose my composure. "I don't think—"

Zak reaches for the keys. "Hey, I'll go get the papers, I don't mind."

Mrs. Brinkham holds up a hand. "Get up there, Zak. It's almost time."

Zak stands. But he doesn't leave. He looks at me. Expectantly.

If I tell him to stop, he'll stay here. Lord knows why, but he won't take my place, not unless I say it's okay.

They both stare at me. Mrs. Brinkham dangles the keys.

If I insist on participating, Zak won't argue. If we both stand up to Mrs. Brinkham, then she won't force the issue.

"Zak?"

"Yeah?"

"Don't . . . don't buzz in, unless you're really, really sure."

I snatch the keys from Mrs. Brinkham's outstretched hand and storm out, returning a minute later to trade the house keys she gave me for the van keys. I make it to the lobby before I begin to shake with rage.

Mrs. Brinkham wasn't the one who led us to this tournament. She wasn't the one who convinced my mother to let Clayton try out for the team. She wasn't the one who talked Landon into dropping out of track so he could come to our tournaments. It wasn't her who confirmed our tournament dates and registered our team. She didn't bring us here.

And in the end, I didn't argue with her. I let Duquette take over, rather than fight about it. I've captained this team for three years. I ought to march right back up there. I ought to tell her . . .

No, Mrs. Brinkham is probably right. At this point we

could stick a sock monkey in my seat and we'd still win. I'm no longer needed.

I storm off to the van and locate the folder, not at all where our sponsor said she'd left it. I notice the clock on the console. If I run, I can make it back with two minutes to spare.

And then get told I had to let Zak have a turn. Because it was only fair.

Except life isn't fair.

I pull out my phone and send a text.

Please call me after three.

I blow my nose, gather the papers, lock the van (which Mrs. Brinkham had forgotten to do), and return to the building.

Though it is frowned upon to enter a room during a session, I silently slink in. I want to watch, to make sure everything is running smoothly.

Something is wrong. Something is very wrong.

Clayton is breathing hard. He does that on the rare occasions when he is confused. Landon and Sonya look sick. In the front row, Mrs. Brinkham crumbles a piece of paper in her fist.

Zak, curse him, sits there with his head on his elbow, hardly awake.

"Carbon fourteen," says an opposing player.

"Correct."

The scoreboard adds another ten points to our opponents' score.

We're down by thirty. And according to the timer, we have less than two minutes to go.

Sonya catches my eye. Even from this distance, I can see the accusation.

We are losing. Because I left Do-Nothing Duquette in my seat. Because I didn't stand up to my coach. Because I felt a little sorry for our alternate. I've let everyone down. We are going to lose. It is all my fault.

I fall into a chair. We will sink into the losers' bracket because of this loss. That means more rounds. More chances to screw up. We're falling down a hole from which we may never emerge.

The moderator relentlessly pounds on. "Which country was the first to officially use fingerprinting as a crime detection tool?"

A boy at the opposing table hits his buzzer. "The United Kingdom."

"Incorrect."

At my table, Clayton is almost hyperventilating. Sonya and Landon exchanged baffled looks. Landon's hand hovers indecisively over his button.

The buzzer sounds, but it's not Landon.

"Argentina," mumbles Zak, as if speaking from a dream.

"Correct. Which fictional character had an older brother named Mycroft?"

C'mon, Clayton, you know this.

"Sherlock Holmes." Zak again. Both tables turn and stare, like he's a parrot that unexpectedly said something profound.

"Which Dutch painter . . ."

"Vincent van Gogh."

In less than half a minute, Duquette has tied the score. My hands leave sweaty prints on the desktop in front of me. I want to smile at him in an encouraging way, but his eyes are still half-closed.

Down to the wire. Last question.

"What is the largest Commonwealth nation in the world?"

"Australia!" shouts an opposing girl, without buzzing. She quickly hits her button and repeats her answer.

"Incorrect."

Both teams turn toward Zak, like weathervanes in a windstorm. For a moment, I think he's not going to answer. Then his thumb twitches like a vegetative patient's.

"Canada."

"Correct."

And the timer dings. Game over. We've won.

Our table goes wild. Landon embraces Zak, which

startles him fully awake. He's even more shocked when Sonya plants a kiss on his cheek. Mrs. Brinkham rushes up and ruffles his hair.

I slowly join them while the other team bitterly nods their congratulations as they leave.

He did it. That loudmouthed slacker actually pulled it off. Saved everything. The game, the competition, our hope for victory.

I stand next to Zak. Before I can thank him, Clayton steps between us.

"Great work, Duke." He shakes Zak's hand, while looking at him with an expression of childlike hero worship.

Zak smiles back. He's proud.

And it's then that I realize I cannot do it.

I cannot congratulate this interloper, no matter how much he did for us.

I know it's immature. I know it's petty. But Duquette is not a real member of this team. This is not his victory.

And Clayton sure as heck is *not* his brother.

ZAK

2:31 PM

I have to admit, that was kind of cool. Me, jumping in at the last second, saving the day. Mrs. Brinkham all impressed. Sonya using it as an excuse to kiss me. If it had been any other weekend, it might have been a nice feeling.

But this isn't just any weekend, I reflect as we all make our way into the hotel lobby. In a few hours, I should be walking into the convention center. It is always an inspiring sight, seeing that sea of cosplayers in their finery. Everyone from A-ko to Mr. Zzyzzx. Some people work all year on their costumes. James said he was going to have something especially impressive this con. Too bad

I'll only see it on Tumblr.

Dad loved the whole freak show aspect of it. He was never much into fandom, but the couple of years that he took me, he really seemed to enjoy himself.

Landon nudges me in the side. Mrs. Brinkham is speaking.

"All of you should be very proud of yourselves." Is it my imagination or is she looking at me? She begins passing out room cards. "You're on your own now. Make good choices. I'll be by to say good night around ten. We'll meet here in the lobby tomorrow at eight."

Suddenly, my depression fades away. We're on our own? The center is only a half hour from here by bus. Quicker, if I want to spring for a taxi. I could actually be at Washingcon *earlier* than most years! Duck back here for check-in, sneak out for the night, drag my ass back in time for the morning meeting . . .

"Zakory? Do you have a moment?"

Dang. Mrs. Brinkham. I force a smile.

"Zak, I just wanted to thank you for what you did today. You really impressed everyone."

"Thanks. Well, see you tomorrow—"

"Hang on." She touches my shoulder. "I mean that. You really did great. And I heard you talking about how you had other plans this weekend. I just wanted you to know we're all really glad that you're here."

I fight it . . . fight it with every ounce of my being, but it's useless. I'm touched.

"Thanks." *Gee whiz, ma'am, t'weren't nothin'.*

"Also, I appreciate you talking to Clayton. The other team members kind of ignore him, so thanks for stepping up."

"What about his sister?"

Mrs. B bites her lip. "She seems so distracted recently. At any rate, could you keep an eye on him tonight? Maybe have dinner together? I hate to think of him sitting around in the room alone."

She knows. Somehow, she knows I'm planning to sneak off.

"I don't know. I was kind of thinking about taking some time on my own."

She shakes her head. "Remember our agreement, Zakory. You're here for one reason, and one reason only. I'm going to need you to hang out with Clayton tonight. If I find out you've gone farther than . . . let's say four blocks from here, then there's going to be trouble."

I consider my options. It wouldn't be hard for me to take Clayton out for a Happy Meal, then dump him off at the hotel in time to catch the Spinal Tap cover band tonight. But I have a mental image of Clayton knocking on Mrs. Brinkham's door at nine o'clock, dragging his teddy bear and asking to be tucked in.

That scenario would not end well for me. I sigh.

"As you wish."

As I climb the stairs, trying to locate room 237 (dear God!), I'm cornered by Sonya. She's changed out of her uptight tournament clothes and into jeans and a top that was designed for a slimmer girl. Her belly strains against the fabric, while the sleeves dig into her round little arms.

She unexpectedly places her hand on my shoulder and her curves suddenly are not so unpleasant.

"Zak, you were incredible today!" She's grinning and doing that head ducking thing girls do when they're nervous. "We would have lost if you weren't there."

She's still touching my shoulder and I have difficulty responding. "Oh, um, well . . . just doing my part."

"You really were amazing. I wish you'd joined the team earlier this year." There's a long pause. Neither of us speak, yet we don't break eye contact. After a second, she lowers her hand.

"So do you have plans for dinner?" she asks.

Holy crap, is this evening going to work out after all? True, I was stuck taking Clayton to Chuck E. Cheese's, but maybe I could arrange a group outing. Then, after Clayton is in bed, Sonya and I can adjourn to the hotel's hot tub.

Just as I'm opening my mouth to be suave, Landon comes thundering down the stairs. He nods at me. And then kisses Sonya.

Of course he does.

"You ready to eat?" he asks his girlfriend-which-was-obvious-in-retrospect.

She giggles. "Sure. Zak, do you want to come with us?"

Over her shoulder, Landon bites his lip.

"Um, no. Clayton and I are going to go find a whiskey bar or something. You guys have fun."

They descend the stairs, talking and laughing. Meanwhile, I have a date with a thirteen-year-old boy.

Golly gee, I'm having a good time.

ANA

2:35 PM

I have the beginnings of a glorious headache. I splash some water on my face at the bathroom sink. Sonya has already left with Landon. Mrs. Brinkham is probably in her room, decompressing. Duquette is doing whatever the hell he does. And me, I'm standing here, gripping the porcelain, my stomach tying itself in knots.

Today should have been simple. We should have glided through every round, especially against that last team. Instead, we almost blow it, because I'm not there. Because Brinkham decided we're in kindergarten and everyone gets a turn. Even Duquette. Thank God he has half a brain.

I shake my head. No time to think about that right now. Tomorrow, we have a chance to advance to state. That's going to look phenomenal on a scholarship application. But only if we pull it off. And let's face it, Clayton and I are going to be the ones to do it. I can't let down the team again, not even for one round. Not even tonight. We have work to do. I run a brush through my stubborn hair and leave to find my brother.

Landon is just leaving the boys' room, wearing that stupid smirk he gets whenever he might be alone with Sonya. Clayton sits on his bed. Thankfully, Duquette is nowhere around.

I sit down next to him. He's removed his dress shirt. Underneath he's wearing a gaudy promotional T-shirt from my dad's work. It's a size too small. I'll have to remind Mom to take him clothes shopping soon.

"Great job today, Clay," I say.

He seems distracted. "Oh. Yeah."

"You look tired. What do you say we grab a bite to eat?"

No response. Maybe he needs a nap.

"There's an Italian place near here. I'll treat you to some panini bread. Then maybe we can quiz each other. Bet I win!"

He turns and looks at me with an odd expression. For the first time, I notice the trail of fuzz on his upper lip. "Ana, I think I'd rather eat with the guys tonight."

I smile at the idea of Clayton hanging out with "the guys." "I think Landon has other plans."

"Well, maybe Duke wants to do something. You know, just the boys."

My brother's attempts to act cool are cute, but it's time to be serious. "You're not doing anything with Zak."

To my surprise, he wants to argue. "You mean Duke."

"I mean Zak. Clayton, you don't want to spend time with a guy like that."

His brow furrows. "He certainly pulled our butts out of the fire today. What's your problem?"

He's getting upset. This isn't good. I need him in top form tomorrow. "Clay, I'm sure he's a great guy. But he's not serious about the team. He spends all his time playing cards and games. That's a guy with no future. You're better than that."

This doesn't appease Clayton. "You're acting like I'm in love with him or something. Jeez, Ana, I just want to have a little fun for once!"

He's angry, but I'm terrified.

My memories are yanked back several years. It was a Friday night. Mom was out of town, Dad was asleep. And I caught Nichole sneaking out for the night. To see Pete again. After our parents told her she wasn't allowed.

I told her not to go. Told her she'd end up in trouble.

She just shook her head and looked at me with that amused expression.

"Calm down, Ana. I'll be back in a couple of hours. I just want to have a little fun for once!"

I didn't stop her. I let her go.

I need to explain this to Clayton. How one bad decision ruined Nichole's life. And mine. And if he's not careful, he'll be next.

Unfortunately, Duquette chooses this moment to barge in. He sneers at the room and tosses his bag onto the couch. I'll have to finish my talk with my brother later.

"Get some rest, Clay. I'll be back around five."

"'Kay."

As I pass Duquette, I make up my mind to thank him for stepping up today. He did really come through earlier, and who knows, he might be useful again in the future. But then he smiles that stupid, careless grin, the one that seems to say, *Nothing at all matters.* I picture him on the deck of the *Titanic*, scooping broken iceberg pieces into his drink.

I shove past him without a word.

ZAK

2:45 PM

I stand there a moment, watching Ana close the door behind her. What the turlingdrome is her problem? I save the team and she treats me like I'm some feces-throwing chimp.

Just another reason why today sucks.

I survey the room. Clayton sits on one bed, Landon's bag is on the other. Typical. I drop my duffel onto the couch and pull out a change of clothes. I'll force Clayton to trade beds with me later.

"Hey, Clay? Any idea why your sister is treating me like I just ran over her puppy?"

He's staring at the door, as if she's still standing there.

"Clay?"

He comes back to himself. "Oh, don't let Ana bother you. You know, it's that time."

Eww . . . her brother knows?

Fortunately, he elaborates. "College applications, scholarships, that sort of thing."

I nod, but I don't believe him. There's something about me that rubs Ana the wrong way. She's probably intimidated by my manly looks. I run my hand over my chin. The goatee is coming in nicely.

I start to remove my tie, but quickly check myself. It had belonged to Dad, and he knotted it for me when I was eleven. I never learned to tie one, so I've preserved the knot all these years.

"Hey, Duke? That convention you were talking about . . . how long have you been going there?"

Talk of Washingcon brings me down. "Since I was ten. This is the first year I've missed." And the last year I'm ever going to miss.

"Wow. Your parents let you go there that young?"

Parents. Thanks for mentioning that, Clayton. If you could just bring up Roger, you'll win the Duke's Painful Memory Triple Crown.

"Yeah. I didn't spend the night until I was twelve, but yeah. They . . . they trust me."

"No shit?"

From anyone else, I wouldn't have noticed. But Clayton going all PG-13 on me causes me to take a closer look. He's standing by the wall, his brow wrinkled, his tiny fists clenched, his jaw working.

"Clayton?"

He jumps, startled, like I'd just caught him playing with himself. "Nothing. I mean . . . are you going to go tomorrow? It's a two-day event, right?"

"No," I growl. I'd asked Mrs. Brinkham about this earlier, trying to see if she'd just let me stay in Seattle after the tournament on Saturday and find my own way home. No dice. This is a school event, and I'm not to be out of her sight until they drop me off in front of my house in Tacoma on Saturday night.

Clayton doesn't know when to let up. "Too bad. It's probably not even that far from here."

"Maybe five, ten miles." So, so close.

"Yeah, over at the . . ."

"Olympic Convention Center." Sweet wretched hive of scum and villainy.

"And do you—"

I don't want to talk about this anymore. "You want to eat, Clayton? You like Mexican?"

He doesn't answer for a moment. "I'm actually not

too hungry. You can go without me, if you like."

Tempting. "We'll go later, then. I'm going to hop in the shower."

"Yes. Okay. Yes. Take your time."

He says this so pointedly, I'm afraid he's going to beat one off while I'm in the bathroom. I get my toiletries case, the one that still has my dad's old razor in it.

Clayton is looking at something on his phone. He's staring so intently, I ask him what he's looking at.

"Um . . . just looking up how to play that card game of yours."

"Mazes and Monsters?" I point to my bag. "The deck's in the top pocket if you want to look at the directions. We can play a couple of rounds later."

He continues to mess with his phone. "Yeah, Duke. Let's do that."

I close the bathroom door and blast the hot water. Right now I could be sharing a hotel room with ten or twenty of my closest friends, instead of hanging around with Boy Wonder and his sniping sister.

"Hey, Duke?" my roommate shouts. "How much does it cost to get into Washingcon?"

"Thirty for one night. Why?"

There's no answer. Wearily, I climb into the shower.

ANA

3:01 PM

And now, everyone is mad at me.

Clayton is mad because I won't let him go off and get in trouble with Duquette.

Duquette is pissy because he's missing his stupid little fairies and Martians club.

The rest of the team is mad at me for not being at the helm during that last round. They didn't say anything, but I could just tell. I should have been there. I should have insisted. I let them down.

And Mom and Dad . . . they're always disappointed in me. It's not that I don't do well, it's that I don't do well enough. It's like I have to be perfect just to be average.

Nichole was the one who screwed all that up. And now Clayton and I have to play catch-up all of our lives.

Guys like Zak can go out and have fun—heck, they can take it for granted. They don't know what it's like to have to beg to go out for pizza with the debate team. To not be allowed to go to a friend's house unless it's school related. To have to tell guys you don't date, rather than you aren't allowed to date.

Focus, Ana, focus.

But that's something to think about later. Right now, I need to take a shower, change, and grab some food.

My phone rings. I'm surprised—normally Mom wouldn't call to check up on me until later in the evening. I glance at the screen.

Domino's Pizza.

Gleefully, I answer. It's not the pizza place, of course, but when your parents are in the habit of checking your phone records, you don't want any strange numbers arousing their suspicions.

"Nichole?"

"Hey, girl."

Instantly, the stress of the day fades away. I sit on the bed and close my eyes. I can almost imagine it's like before, with Nichole and I sitting in her room, just talking. Just talking like sisters. As long as we want to.

I can't believe I haven't seen her in almost two years.

"Ana, I got your text. Are you at school? Everything okay?"

"Yeah." I make an effort to keep my voice firm, in control. "I'm at a quiz bowl tournament. Just wanted to talk to you while I could."

There's silence on the line. I instantly regret my choice of words. *While I could.* While Mom and Dad aren't around. So they won't know I'm talking to you.

"So, did you win?" she asks eventually. Nichole was never one who was really focused on school, but she was always proud of me. She still is.

"Yeah. Thanks to Clayton."

"How's . . . how's he doing?"

"Phenomenal, as usual. Last week he got the top score on—"

Nichole interrupts, her ADD kicking in. "And how are *you* doing?"

"Oh, just fine."

"Listen, Ana, I can tell when you're upset. I have to leave for work in a couple of minutes, but if you need to talk, I can call in."

"No, no. I'm great. Really. It was just a long day."

"Ana . . . I know when you're lying. Now, when are you coming up to visit us?"

I hold the phone away from my face for a couple of seconds as I try to keep my voice even. "Soon, Nichole. Soon."

"Yeah." Nichole packs a lot of cynicism into that one syllable.

"I promise! I've just been really busy, with speech and quiz bowl and—"

"I have to go, Ana. Please. Try to get up here some weekend. I'm on a regular schedule at work now, so we could have the whole time together."

"Nichole, you know it's not that easy for me to get away."

"Try."

She hangs up.

I don't cry. I don't. I stand there, mentally reciting my informative speech from last month's debate tournament.

I am strong. I am strong.

I am a pathetic little weakling who won't visit her only sister.

I am strong. I am strong.

I am a bad sister. I won't argue with my parents. I won't stand up to them. I won't demand to visit Nichole.

I am strong. I am strong.

Because they kicked her out. They disowned my sister because she broke the rules. And they'll do the same to me. They will.

I am strong.

Enough of this. I have a couple of free hours. Enough time to change clothes, take a short nap, and do a little studying for tomorrow.

As I start to unbutton my white blouse, I catch a glimpse of myself, reflected in the rain-splattered hotel window. I smile, wryly. To be honest with myself, it's not like I have to explain the dating ban to a *lot* of guys.

Nichole used to say I was cute. But then, that's a pretty girl's prerogative. She never had to deal with steel-wool hair, a pointy chin, and a complete and total lack of a chest.

Good old Ana, straight As in everything . . . including cup size.

I stand in profile, trying to imagine what I'd look like with curves. And do I really want that? I'd probably just end up attracting morons like Duquette . . .

Who is that out there?

I lean into the window and wipe away the condensation. Outside, one story down, I see someone walking away from the hotel. A kid. He's standing in the middle of the street, in the drizzling rain.

I can't make out his features but I know who it is. Only one person would be wearing that glaring tangerine-and-red T-shirt.

It's Clayton. He's leaving the hotel alone.

I watch, helplessly, as he hails a taxi and climbs inside.

* * *

I storm down the hallway, ready to kill the first person I see. And I'm making sure that the first person I see is Zak Duquette.

What was that cretin thinking, letting Clayton go off in a taxi somewhere? He's only thirteen, for goodness' sake! Where does he need to go now that he needs a cab?

Oh, if my parents find out about this, I'm so dead.

I arrive at the boys' room. Taking a deep breath, I smooth my top, focus my energy, and attempt to drive my fist through the door.

There is no answer for a minute or so. Maybe no one's there. But just when I've decided to go find Mrs. Brinkham, I hear Duquette shouting from inside.

"Hold your horses! What, did you lose your key or . . ."

He opens the door. I take a step back when I realize that he's been in the shower. His hair is covered in shampoo and he's wearing nothing but a flimsy hotel towel that he holds around his waist, revealing his pale, damp torso.

"Ana?" He squints through the suds.

I quickly make eye contact. "Where did my brother go?"

"Huh?" He points to the empty room, where the TV

plays loudly. "I thought he was in here. Maybe he went to get a soda."

I shove my palm into his hard, wet chest and force him back into the room, shutting the door behind us. I then realize that Duquette might misinterpret a gesture like that, so I cut to the chase.

"Clayton just left this hotel in a taxi. I saw him but couldn't stop him. Do you have any idea where he's going?"

Zak wipes soap out of his eyes with his wrist, his other hand still holding up the towel. "I dunno. You know, I was right in the middle of a—"

"Think!"

He opens his mouth, then pauses. "That little punk," he mumbles.

"What?"

"He must have gone to Washingcon! He kept asking me about it. I thought he was just curious."

I clutch my face in my hands. This cannot be happening. My little brother, running off to Duquette's world of drunken trolls and spacemen and God only knows what else. Oh, this is bad. So very bad.

And then Duquette laughs. Like this is funny. Like it's a joke.

"Wow. Clayton decided to break the rules. Didn't see that coming."

I don't need this. I turn to leave.

"Awesome."

That does it. I twirl around to give Duquette a good smack across the cheek to pay him back for putting this moronic idea in my brother's head.

At least, that was the plan. I come up short and crack him across his big old nose. It must have hurt, as he yelps and clutches his face.

His towel lands on my feet with a wet *plop*.

ZAK

3:33 PM

Our taxi driver is having a loud argument with his dispatcher in Russian. I'm thankful for this. It gives me time to lean back, enjoy the ride, and think of how absolutely, utterly screwed I am. I cannot believe that little geek left the hotel. First chance he gets, he runs off to have fun at *my* con.

It's exactly what I would have done, of course. The kid has moxie. Moxie that is going to get me kicked off the team and straight into summer school. I'll be spending June taking tooth-brushing lessons with the mouth breathers. Plus, my hair is still wet, I'm wearing dress slacks and a stained T-shirt, and I'm pretty sure Ana got a view of everything when I had my wardrobe malfunction. And it had been *so* cold back there in the hotel room . . .

On the seat next to me, Ana repeatedly attempts to phone her brother, pausing only to scowl at me when the call goes to voice mail.

Eventually, I'm forced to break the non-Cyrillic silence. "I don't think he's going to pick up."

She turns to me, and for a moment I fear she's turning into the She-Hulk. After a second, I realize that her eyes are just really green, kind of like two angry Life Savers.

"Thanks, genius. Now, be quiet, I'm trying to think." She says it in a sarcastic, superior tone. The same tone as when she blew me off in the library the other day.

"You know, this isn't my fault." *And maybe you could mention that to Mrs. Brinkham . . .*

Ana grabs an elastic thing and forces her frizzy hair into a ponytail. If I wasn't so bloody irritated with her, I might mention she looks better with her hair loose. Less uptight. "Zakory, thanks to your stupid stories about your stupid convention, my brother is out wandering around Seattle. So unless you want me to tell Mrs. Brinkham what you've done . . ."

And there she crosses the line. I am willing to accept a little ranting, but if she thinks she is going to narc on me, it's time to go on the offensive.

"Excuse me? No one forced Clayton to leave, okay? I was in the shower, and I wasn't going to invite him in there with me. And you know what? He's thirteen, not eight. I've been going to this con since I was ten. I think MegaMind can handle himself for one night."

Ana rolls her eyes farther than I think the optic nerve can stretch. "Just show me where this convention is. Then, if you want to leave, fine. Tell Mrs. Brinkham whatever you want. Good Lord, I can't believe she wanted *you* on our team."

I shouldn't let her get to me. What do I care what she thinks? But for some reason, I need to defend myself. "You don't know me. You . . ." And then I go blank, unable to think of that perfect, cutting comeback. What had James called it? *L'esprit de l'escalier.*

Ana has her phone out again. "I know one thing, Zak. You're a guy who only cares about number one. I'm concerned about my brother, while you're probably still pissed that you're not playing cards dressed like an elf right now."

I am having difficulty staying civil. "You know what? Have fun looking for your baby brother. You're going to wander around all night, and when you find him, he'll probably be drinking a soda and watching a movie. I mean, what the hell do you think is going to happen?

C'mon, everyone gets in trouble now and then. He just wants to have a little fun for once."

Okay, maybe Ana's a little too high-strung to find that calming. But I am unprepared for my companion's reaction.

"Stop this cab!" she bellows. Her face has gone stark white. For an instant, I'm afraid she's going to take a swing at me.

Rasputin brakes hard, to the accompaniment of angry honking behind us. Without a word, Ana jumps out onto the sidewalk.

I sit there, stunned. I know my comment was stupid, but I hadn't expected her to bolt like that.

Oh well, her problem. It was her job to find Clayton, not mine. Not my concern.

Right. Like hell it isn't.

With a resigned sigh, I jump out after her. I then dive back into the cab to pay the screaming driver the fare.

It's drizzling like Silent Hill out here and it takes me a moment to locate Ana, storming off down the street in the wrong direction. I rush to catch up.

"Hey, Ana!" She doesn't turn, but she stops. I expect to find her with tears streaming down her face, alone and needing a friend. Instead, I'm greeted with the most wrathful and contemptuous expression I've ever seen. But I hold my ground.

"Ana, c'mon."

She snarls at me. Literally snarls. "Just go away."

"C'mon. I want to help."

"That's a laugh."

I fight against the dark side rising within me. "Where do you get off judging me? If you need a hand, well, I'm here, all right?"

She wipes a stray hair off her forehead. "You wouldn't understand." Those words are final, carved in granite. I have been dismissed.

Luckily, I never know when I'm defeated. "Try me."

She juts her sharp chin at me, and I prepare myself for a lecture about responsibility and being a good little boy. But suddenly, her entire rigid frame collapses. Her shoulders slump, her head lolls, and her arms dangle limply. For a ghastly moment, she reminds me of a corpse on the gallows.

"Listen, Duquette—Zak." She's staring at her shoes. "You're a guy who can go out and do whatever he likes. Whatever."

I start to object, but before I can think of a rebuttal, she continues.

"It's not like that for Clayton and me. I don't want to get into it, but . . . I can't let anyone find out he wandered off."

"C'mon, Brinkham's a softie—"

"I'm not talking about her, Zak. If my parents ever knew I lost track of Clayton, it would be . . . bad."

For a moment, I think I see her green eyes glisten, but it might just be a trick of the light. I stand there, uncomfortable, wondering what she means by "bad."

She runs a hand over the bridge of her nose. "So I have to find my brother before anyone realizes he's gone. Could you just get me to the center? Then you can go back to the hotel, or stay there or whatever. I know this wasn't your fault. Mostly."

Yeah, like I'm going to go off and leave her after that. I try to mold my face into an inspiring smile.

"Listen, Ana? I may have kind of exaggerated about how crazy things get at Washingcon. Really, it's just a lot of geeks like me. I know that place inside out. I'll help you find your brother. It might take a couple of hours, but we'll track him down. And if Brinkham suspects anything, just tell her we all went out to eat and lost track of time. She'll believe you."

She looks at me for a moment. The humidity has caused her hair to frizz out like a poodle's. It's strangely adorable. And just for a second, the side of her mouth tics upward.

"Thanks, Zak."

We begin walking north. She doesn't make an effort

to stand close to me, but she's not actively trying to lose me, either.

"Hey, Duquette?" She's not looking at me.

"Yeah?"

"Today at the tournament . . . you really sucked a lot less than I was expecting. One might almost say you weren't a total pathetic embarrassment."

The sarcastic, backhanded compliment cheers me up a bit. As we approach the convention center, the sun begins to come out.

ANA

4:10 PM

I so desperately want to blame all of this on Zak. To point my finger and denounce him as the conspirator who led my poor little brother astray. To make him take the heat for what's shaping up to be an enormous catastrophe.

Of course, I can't. Tempting a target as he is, all Zak is guilty of is shooting off his mouth. Clayton ran off of his own free will. And I was the one who let him do it. At least I will be in my parents' eyes.

Good grief, if I had just let him go out to eat with Zak, maybe he would have stayed. All I was trying to do was the right thing. That's all I ever try to do.

Zak walks alongside me, merrily whistling. I wonder if he'll ditch me the second we arrive at the convention or if he'll really help me find Clayton. If he does, I'll owe him big time. I shudder, picturing myself wearing one of his war hats.

Zak suddenly reaches out and grabs my arm. I'm creeped out until I realize he's just guiding me around a water-filled hole in the sidewalk that I was too distracted to notice. When it's clear I'm not going to step in it, he removes his hand.

I shake my head. This guy has enough faults to fill an aircraft hangar. But he's here with me now, looking for my brother. I guess that should count for something.

I remember how he accidentally dropped his towel in the hotel room and how I pretended I hadn't seen anything.

Lord, the first time I see one and it belongs to Duquette, of all people.

"So what are these things like, Zak?" I ask, in an effort to dispel that mental image. "A bunch of people playing those war games?"

He smiles at me in an odd way. "There's a little more to it than that. And call me Duke."

"Oh, you guys also watch movies, right, Zak?"

His grin widens. "You'll see. Here we are."

The Olympic Convention Center lives up to its name;

it's the largest in the Pacific Northwest. Above the gaping entrance doors hangs a huge banner welcoming everyone to Washingcon. Below that, a towering painting of a cybernetic General George Washington mows down an army of zombie redcoats with what appears to be a coal-fired machine gun. There's no one outside, probably due to the foul weather. With an elaborate bow, Zak ushers me inside.

Okay, maybe my impressions of a science fiction convention were based on Duquette and his friends. I knew there'd be a lot of people here, but I was expecting something much more low-key.

I was not expecting a sixty-something woman dressed like Smurfette. That's a lot of blue cleavage.

The lobby is huge, hung with giant banners of watershed moments in U.S. history, as portrayed by robots. Smaller, handmade signs, dot the walls:

CTHULHU FOR PRESIDENT: THIS TIME, WHY
CHOOSE THE LESSER OF TWO EVILS?
LEST WE FORGET: DONATE TO
THE RED SHIRT MEMORIAL FUND
REPRODUCE AND POPULATE THE EARTH

But the people . . . dear God. There must be over a hundred conventioneers there already, snaking out in two long lines from the registration tables. Dozens of others mill around, talking, laughing, dueling with light-sabers. And many of them are in costume.

I recognize the octopus guy from Spider-Man, eating a doughnut with one hand and holding a soda with the other, a slice of pizza with the other, and a box of popcorn with the other. There's one of those *Doctor Who* robot things, dispensing beer from a keg somehow mounted in its chest. Near the snack bar, a well-endowed woman has attracted a circle of admirers. She's wearing a corset and not much else. I squint to see what is written or tattooed on her shoulders: BEAT ME UP, SCOTTY.

"Impressive sight, no?" Zak raises his eyebrows devilishly.

"It's like something out of a Hieronymus Bosch painting."

"Um . . . yeah, my thoughts exactly. Too bad we can't go to the masquerade tomorrow night, that's when you see the really impressive cosplayers."

I look back at the crowd, wishing briefly that I could see what he meant by "impressive." I notice a lot of the conventioneers are dressed almost normally, in T-shirts and jeans. I turn to ask Zak if he ever dresses up, but he has his back to me, waving at someone.

"Hey, asshole! Asshole!"

Across the lobby, a man in a jumpsuit and huge white helmet waves at Zak.

"Go ask your friend if he's seen Clayton," I order.

Zak looks at me strangely. "I don't know that guy."

"But you just . . ."

He laughs. "Oh, I see. No, he's dressed like Major Asshole. You know, from *Spaceballs*?" He looks at me expectantly, as if he's not speaking total gibberish.

"Zak, let's go page Clayton, okay?"

"They won't page anyone here, unless it's a desperate emergency."

"But Clayton's just a kid."

He shakes his head. "It really pisses them off when people use the con as a babysitting service. If we tell them the truth, they're going to want to call your mom and dad."

I picture my parents being summoned to pick us up in this madhouse.

"I see. Okay, so what do we do?"

"You got a picture of him on that phone? I know a lot of people. We'll ask around."

I start to press forward, but he gently restrains me.

"Whoa. One does not simply *walk into* Washingcon."

I think my angry glance startles him, because he quickly continues. "Seriously. They won't let you into most of the venues without a badge." He cocks a thumb at the registration table. "Tell 'em I sent you."

I ignore his smug grin. "Zak, thanks for . . ."

He's already distracted. "Hey, Zoltan! I haven't seen you since Con-dumb!"

As Zak talks to a guy(?) in Joker makeup, I begin to have a panic attack. What if he accidentally-on-purpose wanders off? This thing was a big deal to him, after all. I don't like the idea of stumbling through this sea of semi-humanity, hopelessly trying to find Clayton.

I wait for him to say good-bye to his friend, all the while rehearsing my little speech about how important it is for him to stay focused. I touch his arm.

"Zak?"

"Yeah?"

And then, suddenly, I think of the perfect thing to say. I just pray I get the line right. "Help me, Obi-Wan. You're my only hope."

Zak's face breaks into a grin. Not his usual cocky one, but a big, goofy, puppy-dog smile. It's somewhat of an improvement.

"Go register, Ana. Let me see what I can find out."

I shake my head and join the line. I'm surprised to see that the girl in front of me has a longbow strapped to her back. It's only when I see the picture of the flaming bird on her shirt that I make the connection. That one book, which has made archery suddenly seem cool. Unlike this girl, however, I actually know how to shoot one of those. I notice that this bow has been strung incorrectly. The string is about to slide off the wood.

The line moves quickly. Just before it's her turn, I tap her arm. "Excuse me? I noticed you have a little problem there. If you like . . ." I reach out to adjust her bow.

She shoves my hand away. "Here's an idea," she snaps. "How about you keep your hands to yourself?" She stares at me as I try to think of something to say, snorts, and then turns back to the registration table.

The logical, dominant side of me wants to dismiss her as a jerk, someone below my contempt. But I was only trying to help. I don't know what her problem is, but it just drove home the fact that I don't belong here.

But I can say that about a lot of places, can't I?

It's my turn. I shuffle forward.

"Hey, don't let her get to you," says a pleasant, female voice. The registrar is a girl about my age, very slender and pretty, dressed in a ragged T-shirt, with black lipstick and dangling earrings. And bald. Her head has been shaved down to the skin.

"People are touchy about their costumes," she continues. "But she was just rude."

"Oh, um, thanks." My hurt feelings vanish. I cannot stop staring at this girl's scalp. It's like her head has been polished.

"One night or two?" she asks, politely.

I come back to myself. "Just one."

"And what name would you like on your badge?"

"Ana Watson."

"C'mon, no one uses their real name here."

"Ana Watson, please."

"Fine. Now, how will you be paying for this?"

I glance at a price list. Thirty bucks for just one night. Yikes. I remember what Zak told me. Knowing full well I'm about to be laughed at, I follow his instructions.

"Zak Duquette sent me."

Cue Ball snaps to attention. Her eyes grow wide, and she runs a hand across her forehead, as if adjusting her hair. "Duke's here?" she gasps.

"Um, Zak Duquette . . ."

"Yeah, Duke. Oh, wow, I haven't seen him since Contamination. Wow. We played Tank Battalion for like, six straight hours. That man is a *machine.* Do you know if he's going to the Vampire Ball tonight?"

This girl's reaction is both adorable and creepy. Mostly creepy. "We're just passing through, actually."

"Oh. He's here with *you.*" She passes me a laminated ID badge. "Well. Any friend of Duke's. Enjoy your stay." There's an edge to her voice now.

"It's not like that—we're just hanging out," I feel compelled to say. In fact, I really need to say that.

She instantly brightens. "In that case, tell him to give Gypsy a call, okay? No, wait. Tell him I'll text him. No . . . um, tell him I'll maybe see him . . ."

"I'll tell him you said hi," I reply, cautiously backing away from this madwoman. Good lord, were things so upside down here that Duquette was some kind of legend? Baldy wasn't bad-looking, and yet she was all atwitter over Zak. Well, I wasn't going to relay her message. I needed Zak to concentrate on finding Clayton. I wasn't going to let him be distracted by Miss Look at Me and My Hipster Shaved Head . . .

My thoughts are broken by a hideous female scream. I turn to see the rude girl from the line collapsed on the floor, clutching a bloody, possibly broken nose. Beside her sits her unstrung bow, which has snapped apart with the violence of an uncoiling spring.

A crowd gathers around her. Someone helps her to her feet and leads her away, sobbing tears, blood, and snot.

The odds certainly weren't in her favor.

I slyly pick up the weapon and restring it correctly, enjoying a bit of malicious glee. It's a fine wooden piece. Not tournament grade, but something you could have fun with. I'll turn it in to lost and found.

Later.

Across the room, the bow's owner is lying on a bench. Some guy brings her a Baggie of ice, which slips out of his hand and falls onto her nose. She moans.

Zak was right—this place is kind of fun.

ZAK

4:23 PM

I've never been to Washingcon this early, because of—what do ya call it?—school. Thanks to Mrs. Brinkham and Clayton, this year I have a chance to sign up for the good slots for Paranoia and Warhammer. And maybe sit in on the annual blessing of the con. I think it's the Cargo Cultists running things this year.

But I see Ana over there in line, looking confused and a little out of sorts. That must be kind of weird for her. She's usually so on top of things. This deal with her brother obviously upsets her, and if I should come swaggering in to save the day, she just might be thankful enough to . . .

To . . .

I dunno, talk to me like I'm a human being. Act like she's not so put out when she has to interact with me. Put on a chain-mail bikini. Something like that.

But I said I'd help her, and I'm not going to let her down. True, I'll be doing nothing more than playing Gollum to her Frodo, but sometimes that's not a bad thing. Especially when Frodo has green eyes and frizzy hair.

I edge my way to the preregistered table. I'm pleased to see James is running things, playing hooky so he can volunteer here and get in for free. He's dressed like Teddy Roosevelt, complete with wire-rimmed glasses, a U.S. Cavalry lightsaber, and a REMEMBER THE MAINE tattoo.

"Nice getup."

"Duke! Didn't think you were coming." He shoots a questioning glance at my quiz bowl slacks.

"Ana and I escaped. Thought I'd show her a good time." Nothing wrong with a little harmless exaggeration.

James reapplies his mustache. "If it was anyone else, I'd think they were making crap up. With you, I'll flat out say it."

"Bully for you. Listen, have you seen this thirteen-year-old kid around?"

"John Connor?"

"No, Ana's brother, Clayton. We're, um, supposed to meet up with him."

"Sorry." He hands me my badge. "But I'll keep an eye out."

A piercing, female scream cuts through the center. People rush toward the middle of the lobby, but I can't see what's going on. By the time I gather my registration packet, everyone's gone.

Ana taps me on the shoulder. I ask her what happened.

"Oh, some girl just got a nosebleed," she says.

I suddenly realize she has this big-ass longbow slung across her back. "Where'd you get that?"

"Sherwood Forest. Now, are you through messing around? I keep forgetting that I'm still pissed at you."

I chuckle inside. I'm beginning to realize that Ana has a real obnoxious, sarcastic, cruel side. All traits I admire. And if I were to find her brother, maybe she'd think there was something likeable about me, as well. Aside from my handsome face, of course. I'm glad I decided to grow out my beard this year.

"So, where do we head first?" she asks, elbowing someone out of the way.

"Well . . . there's not a whole lot that's really open just yet. Let's try the dealers' room."

The Washingcon sales area is in a huge showroom that in duller times would hold insurance booths or dental supply demonstrations. Today, it's the marketplace in *Neverwhere*. Aisle upon aisle of things that don't exist anywhere else. Things that probably shouldn't. Anything that was ever pulled out of a school library, forbidden by a dress code, confiscated by airport security, or quarantined at the border has found a home here. For eleven months a year, this stuff sits unnoticed in the back of gaming stores and bookshops. But when con rolls around, you can find it here, and only here. For good reason. There ain't a lot of folks who'll pay good money for a pizza cutter shaped like the *Enterprise*, a bong shaped like a sonic screwdriver, or that recalled Harry Potter broomstick.

Best of all, if you don't see it for sale, these people know where to get it. This is where James adds to his creepy collection of pre–Comics Code magazines.

Ana whistles. "It's like the Walmart of the damned."

"So what's your pleasure? Bootlegged Japanese movies? German broadswords that couldn't cut butter? Pornographic tarot cards? A lacy, backless straitjacket? A whole bunch of self-published books?"

"How about finding my brother?"

I look longingly at a pile of musty, yellowing paperbacks. "Fine. You want to circle around and meet me by the Android's Dungeon display?"

"No, just stay with me."

A hint, just a hint of nerves there. Maybe I'm imagining it, but I'll pretend she prefers my company.

We haven't gone twenty feet when the female shopping gene takes over. Ana stops at One-Eyed Jack's Armaments and buys a set of blunt, headless arrows in a cardboard quiver. She seems pleased.

"You really know how to shoot one of those things?"

"I got second place in the archery regional finals earlier this year. I actually know how to handle a weapon," she says, glancing at a man struggling with a battle ax twice his size.

The words are snippy, but the tone is not. I think she's feeling somewhat out of place. I try to put her at ease.

"All you need are some leggings and a Bavarian cap, and you'll look like one of us."

"Yes, before you know it, I'll stop bathing and everything."

That annoys me. "Why you gotta hate? You know, you could have a good time here if you wanted. Costumes are only a small fraction of what goes on here. There are panels and dances and films . . ."

She's only half listening as she scans the room for her brother.

"Look, Ana, what *do* you like to do for fun?"

She shrugs and continues to walk. "I don't have a lot of free time."

"C'mon. I know you like archery. What else?" I worry that I'm going to come across as nosy and obsessive, but it's an honest question and it wouldn't kill her to talk to me for thirty seconds.

"Speech. Quiz bowl. Youth group."

"No, I mean for *fun*."

She stops walking. "Duquette, not everyone has free weekends to spend at places like this. Not everyone has time to play board games for hours." I can't tell if she's regretting her lack of free time or looking down on me for being a man of leisure. Either way, I feel like a loser. I try to talk about something intelligent.

"So where are you going to college?"

"University of Washington. I don't think Clayton's in here. What's in that next room?"

"U Dub? Really?" Somehow, I never pictured her staying in Tacoma. I had her pegged for the University of Seattle or even some big-name out-of-state place.

Ana doesn't respond, nor does she ask about my post–high school plans. Or my hobbies. Or anything about me.

"C'mon, Ana, let's try the movie rooms."

I trot ahead, but she pulls at my sleeve. When I turn,

I'm surprised to see her looking me in the eye.

"Zak, I'm not trying to ignore you, but I only have one thing on my mind right now. Once we find Clayton, you'll have my full attention." I see the ghost of a smile on her lips. It cheers me up.

"Okay. Hey, Ana—"

"Let's split up. Meet me at the exit."

I watch as she jogs off down an aisle.

ANA

4:38 PM

I am hell-bent on finding my brother, but that's not why I refused to talk to Zak.

It was his question: What did I do for fun? Something you'd ask anyone.

How was I supposed to answer that? How was I supposed to tell a guy who probably doesn't have a curfew, a guy whose parents would probably just shrug if they knew he'd left the hotel, that I have pretty much no free time? That I never get to just screw around like he does every day? That I'll have to go to college close to home so my mom and dad can keep an eye on me?

I take a deep breath and try to remind myself that

I'm working for a greater good. That my grades mean I'll probably get to attend college for free. That all my extra-curricular activities will look phenomenal on a résumé. That my watchful parents will always keep me from getting in trouble like Nichole did. Always.

Usually, this mantra buoys me a little. Today, nothing. Maybe it's because I know that if we don't find Clayton soon, all my years of good behavior will be at risk. Or maybe it's because I'm surrounded by people having a fun time while I'm not.

This place is like a maze. A hot, crowded maze that stinks of fast food and BO. Every time I think I've been everywhere, I spot an unfamiliar section. I'm jostled by elaborately costumed conventioneers poked with weapons, and nearly trip over someone's tail. After colliding with an almost-naked Tarzan, I pause to collect myself.

A couple of chubby girls in tunics look at me and snicker as they walk by.

Once again, I'm the outsider.

"The outfit says Pepper Potts, but I'm not sure about the bow."

I look up. The man sitting behind a T-shirt stand is smiling at me.

"Excuse me?" I back away slightly.

"Your costume. The business suit and weapon. I can't place it." He's about twenty. He's just the heavy side of overweight, with the scruffy beginnings of a beard and a Miskatonic University shirt.

"It's not a costume," I reply sharply. "I'm not even supposed to be here. I just have to find my brother."

He nods. "Just out for a walk with your longbow, are you?" He smiles and I can't help but return it. I guess I am overdressed.

"It's a long story."

"I'd love to hear it." He's leaning over a pile of shirts, grinning. And I have to say, he's not entirely bad looking. But I have other things on my mind.

"Sorry, I have to go."

"Oh. Yeah."

He sounds a little hurt. Clearly he's bored or desperate to make a sale. I pause to glance at his wares. They're all T-shirts sporting slogans and logos I don't recognize. Just as I'm about to politely leave, I spot a comfortable-looking shirt with Asian writing.

"What does this say?"

"Roughly translated: 'A fifteen percent gratuity will be automatically charged to parties of five or more.'"

"I beg your pardon?"

He grins, which doesn't hurt his overall appearance. "Got it off a takeout menu. I love watching hipsters going around thinking it says something about the code of the samurai or whatever I tell 'em."

I have to laugh at that. "How much?"

"Twenty."

Might as well be a hundred. "Um, maybe next time."

"Hang on." He folds up the shirt and hands it to me. "You're a small, right? Trust me, that size never sells out here. You'll be doing me a favor."

I seriously doubt he's only trying to get rid of unwanted stock, but it would be really nice to change into something less formal. Taking the shirt with a smile, I duck into a changing booth. There's no mirror, but with my new shirt and longbow, I have kind of a geek-chic thing going on. I'll blend in, like someone who came here because she wanted to. I return to the sales floor.

"Thank you . . ." I glance at his name tag. "'Arnold Fagg'? What awful comic book did you get that one from?"

His grin fades.

Whoops, guess I'm not the only one here using my real name.

Desperate to change the subject, I hand him my folded blouse, the one my mother repeatedly warned me not to stain. "Could you hold on to this for me? It may be a while before I find my brother."

"Sure. I'm here till nine."

I start to go. He clears his throat.

"And after nine . . . I dunno, when you're done with

family business, I'm running a panel." His smile is back, but it's nervous. "It's at nine in room one fifteen south."

"What sort of a panel?"

"Make your own T-shirts. It's kind of my thing. Thought you might be interested."

"We'll see. Thanks again."

I wander off, trying to focus on finding Clayton and not on unfortunately named Arnold. He clearly doesn't give away merchandise to everyone. And making my own shirt would be a lot more fun than looking for Clayton or hanging out at the hotel.

For just a brief moment—just a second—I contemplate returning to his stand and talking some more. Just a little. Just to talk. And maybe find out if he ever makes it out to Tacoma and *what the hell am I thinking?*

Yeah, my parents would really permit that. A date with some older guy I met at a comic book convention.

They won't even let me visit my own sister.

It's clear Clayton isn't here, so I stomp off to find my guide. I half expect Duquette to be long gone, but I see him talking to a tall, strange-looking man. At first I think the guy is dressed like Frankenstein's monster, but then realize he's just really ugly. I'm about to interrupt when Zak raises his voice. I can't make out his angry words, but the man shoves him in the chest, hard enough that he stumbles. The creepy guy storms off.

I rush to Duquette to berate him for clowning around and wasting time.

"Are you okay, Zak?" I hear myself say.

Duquette looks up, surprised to see me here. "It was nothing."

Then get your ass in gear, we have to find Clayton, not stand around . . .

Once again, my mouth interrupts. "Are you sure? He hit you kind of hard."

He won't look at me. "That was Cyrax," he says, as if that explains something. He begins walking quickly.

"Zak, what was that all about?" my mouth insists on saying.

"Just a guy," he says, his voice squeaking nervously. "There was some unpleasantness at Con-viction last year."

"Go on." *I really need my mouth to shut up soon.*

Zak rubs the back of his neck. "Well . . . it was just one of those things, I guess. It was late, I went out to pick up some supplies, and Cyrax and some of his friends . . . they jumped me."

We've walked in front of an empty table. I grab Duquette by the arm to stop him. "Are you kidding? Why?"

He shrugs, a hurt, embarrassed look on his face. "It's hard to say with those guys. I was alone, weak. Took all my money, left me out of commission for a few days."

I'm utterly horrified, both at the senseless attack and Zak's blasé way of talking about it. "Did you call the police? I can't believe they even let him into this place!"

He won't look at me. "What could they do? These things happen. At any rate, he's never let me forget it. Every time I see him, he reminds me." He hisses through his teeth. "Frack, just like it was yesterday, lying there on the road, too weak to get up, not even a potion of healing on me . . ."

I am reaching out to give him a comforting squeeze of the hand when I realize what I'm hearing. "Duquette? When he beat you up . . . was it in a video game?"

"No, of course not." He paused. "Dungeons and Dragons. You see, James was the dungeon master and—"

I hold up a palm, trying to think of the best way to demonstrate what I'm now feeling. "Duquette, despite your best efforts, I find that you don't disgust me as much as previously. But I don't have time for your imaginary world, and your imaginary pain."

"What's that supposed to mean?"

I remember watching my sister walk off into the foggy Tacoma evening, knowing somehow that I'd never see her again. "It means that some of us have enough real pain in our lives that we don't need to invent more. You don't know what that's like."

I'm not prepared for his reaction. His eyes narrow. That funny smile, that devil-may-care grin vanishes. And suddenly I'm looking at the most angry teen I think I've ever seen. And he's angry with me.

"What did you say?" The words come out as a slow hiss, deadly as a gas leak.

"Zak . . ."

Our eyes lock, and just for a second, I realize there's something more to Zak Duquette than the guy who never stops laughing and never takes anything seriously. God knows why, but there's real pain in his face.

Just as I'm about to apologize (though I'm not sure for what), it vanishes. The smiley, goofy expression returns, like a mask dropped over his real features.

"C'mon. I know a guy. He's on the Washingcon board. He might be able to help us find Clayton." He shoots me a thin smile, then takes out his phone and sends a text.

I nod, relieved that I haven't offended him so much that he won't talk to me. And a little curious.

What sort of pain have you experienced, Zak Duquette?

ZAK

4:54 PM

Imaginary pain? Ana Watson tells me my pain is imaginary? Oh, that's rich.

Unbidden, the memories return. The demons that show up at random times. The reason Roger keeps finding me playing video games at four in the morning.

Dad, joking about his chronic toilet problems.

Mom and Dad, explaining to ten-year-old me how he'll need to have some surgery soon. I'm more impressed by the X-ray they've brought home. The one with that vague mass in the intestinal area.

Dad, ever the optimist, pretending he's going to buy a toupee. And that he'd finally found a diet that worked.

"Sorry, Zak, looks like I can't make the camping trip this year."

And those awful last weeks, when he'd lost everything, when there was nothing left for him to do but lay on the couch and wait for the inevitable, he'd still hang out with me. We'd sit there and watch entire series, epic things like LOTR because he was too sick to even talk, and I'd hold his hand and even then I didn't really believe I was going to lose him because, after all, he was my only daddy and . . .

And suddenly I'm back at Washingcon, storming down a corridor, with Ana by my side. And she's looking at me with what I'd almost believe is real concern.

Cool it, Duquette. It's not her fault. Everyone thinks they're the only one who's ever been hurt.

I receive a text. "That was Warren," I tell Ana. "He says to meet him in the Pacific Ballroom."

Ana nods but doesn't say anything. It's hard to read her. She's always so snippy and pissed off, but sometimes she almost acts like she's enjoying being around me, just a bit. If this gamble with Warren pays off, she might actually lose her contempt for me.

Evening is falling. The rooms grow more crowded as guests begin to trickle in from the cubicle farms and computer help desks around the city. Soon the events will start: autographing, panels, games, and movies.

"So, do you guys rent the entire complex?" Ana asks out of nowhere.

"Pretty much. We don't need all the space, but the convention center learned early on that it's best we do what we do without any outsiders. Especially after what happened four years ago."

She sighs. "You clearly want me to ask about that, so tell me what happened."

I snort, wishing she'd show a little fake enthusiasm. "The Seattle Square Dancing League held their annual barn dance here. Quite a sight, seeing an octogenarian cowboy in polyester pants almost throwing down with an Asian Anakin Skywalker. It's hard to say who was the bigger group of freaks."

"Spoiler alert: It was you people." Ana is smiling, so I let it pass. I have the uncomfortable feeling that I'd let a lot pass, just to keep that smile pointed at me.

"At any rate, Warren's in here." We've arrived at the ballroom. Its doors are closed, and a sign reads PRIVATE EVENT.

"Shall we knock? I've seen enough of this place that I don't want to barge in on anyone."

I chuckle, remembering the time I stumbled upon a square dancer getting very friendly with a Ghostbuster half her age. "It's cool. Warren's one of the con organizers.

He told me to come on in." I remember something. "Hey, Ana, when you meet him . . . don't mention it."

"Mention . . . what?" she places her hands on her hips and looks at me sternly.

"Nothing weird . . . well, maybe it is." I've known Warren so long, I've grown used to his peculiarity. Maybe Ana will find it endearing. "It's just . . ."

She's not listening. Her gaze is fixed on something behind me. I turn but don't notice anything, other than a dozen or so people milling around in front of a room, waiting for a presentation.

"Zak! Look at the guy in the Iron Man helmet."

I let out a world-weary sigh. "Ana, that's Boba Fett. Can you honestly not tell the difference?" I mean, the directional range finder is a dead giveaway.

And then I realize what she means. The bounty hunter is not wearing armor. Instead, he has on a blinding orange-and-red shirt, one so clashing that it hurts the retinas from fifty paces.

I know that shirt. Clayton was wearing it, last time I saw him. So ugly, even I noticed it.

I grin. "Dr. Kimble at last. So, how do you want to do this? Good cop, bad cop?" I start to walk toward him.

"Wait." Ana looks uncharacteristically indecisive. I wonder what happened to the bossy team captain, but

I don't miss her. "Zak, maybe you should go talk to him alone."

"Just me? Why?" That smacks of duty and effort. And why would he listen to me over his sister?

"The thing about Clayton is, he always does what he's told. I mean always. But tonight, we got in kind of a fight. I think he's angry with me." She looks over at her brother, but he's still mingling with the crowd.

I wonder if Clayton is really that obedient, or if he's just better at getting away with things than Ana. "What did you fight about?"

She gives me a cockeyed look, with just a slip of a smile. I have the strange feeling that she's implying something I'm too dense to catch.

"Just talk to him, Zak. Clayton likes you. Try to get him to go back to the hotel, at least by bed check, okay? He doesn't have to go with me, but maybe you could keep an eye on him?"

Story of my life. I try to impress the girl, and end up hanging out with her little brother. But damn, her green eyes . . .

"Duck into the ballroom, Ana. Let Warren know I'm on my way. I'll have a word with your bro."

She gives me a one-armed hug. I'm so taken aback, I forget to return the embrace.

"You're an okay guy, Zak Duquette," she says, and releases me.

"Please, call me Duke."

Ana opens the ballroom door. "Good luck, Zak. Hey, how will I recognize Warren?"

"Trust me. You'll know him when you see him."

She shoots me a questioning look, then vanishes into the room.

Well, it's all down to yours truly. If I can convince Clay to hang out with me and come back to the hotel before lights-out, Ana will be most grateful. First-date grateful. Maybe.

I guess I'll confront him, man to man. Just remind him that it'll cause a lot of trouble for a lot of people if he goes AWOL.

I slip into the crowd. Remembering how he said he enjoyed *RoboCop*, I decide to break the ice with a line from the film. "Come with me, citizen," I say in a monotone as I firmly grab his arm.

The results are impressive. Clayton spins his mask toward me, then yanks out of my grasp and goes darting down the corridor, elbowing people out of the way.

I'm too pissed to be diplomatic. "Get back here, you little . . ." He's sprinting like a jackrabbit. I rush after him.

There's no way I can catch him in a mad rush—there are too many people, and I think he's faster than me.

Luckily, I have an encyclopedic knowledge of the convention center. I duck into an EMPLOYEES ONLY door, dash down a maintenance hall, nod hello to a surprised guy taking out the trash, and emerge in an empty kitchen. I crack a door and wait. Sure enough, he comes walking by, trying to adjust his facial armor. I yank him by the collar and pull him into the food prep area.

I'm furious. "Knock it off. You know what I want."

Even under the helmet, Clayton looks terrified. His whole body is shaking, knees knocking, breasts heaving . . .

Uh-oh.

Boba Fett hurls the mask to the ground. Underneath is a shorthaired, fine-featured girl of about nineteen or twenty. Her eyes blaze with rage and fear.

It's going to take a very, very delicate touch to extricate myself from this situation. I take a deep breath.

"I—"

Her petite fist snakes out (how could I have missed the nail polish?) and drills me right under the eye. I stagger back into a counter.

"Ma'am, I'm so sorry. I thought you were someone else."

She replies with an uppercut, smacking my jaws together with a tooth-rattling clunk. My vision goes blurry.

"My friend's little brother. Believe it or not, he has a shirt that same—"

Her blow to my solar plexus cuts my apology short. I stand there trying to suck in air with a stunned diaphragm.

"Just . . . a . . . mis . . . under . . ."

I think she realizes I'm not fighting back. I hope she'll end the onslaught, but hell hath no fury, and so forth. I don't see the foot coming, but I sure feel it as it connects between my legs. I collapse to the floor.

My feeble voice spurts out in six-point font, "So . . . sorry."

She's not kicking me, so either she's decided I've had enough, or is searching for a rolling pin. I lay there in the fetal position, staring longingly at an industrial fridge and its probable contents of numbing ice.

Boom. Boom. Boom.

Something is coming.

BOOM. BOOM. BOOM.

Something is near. I don't want to look.

BOOM.

I can't help but think of the classic horror movie, with the tied-up woman, the ominous approaching shadow, and the islanders all chanting *"Kong!"*

I slowly turn my head.

He's huge. Tall, and very wide. He's shirtless, wearing

nothing but furry leggings and a Viking helm. And hair. Lots and lots of hair. All over.

I remember him. He was standing near Boba Fett when I attacked her. His lips fold into a snarl. He cracks his knuckles. It sounds like artillery fire.

Ruh roh, Shaggy.

ANA

5:15 PM

I have no idea what to expect when I enter the ballroom. Zak says there are weird subcultures at the con, and I fear I might walk in on something that cannot be unseen.

I'm pleasantly surprised to realize that the room is being prepped for a wedding. A half-dozen well-dressed people unfold chairs, arrange flowers, and string balloons. An easel near the door proclaims this to be the Horowitz-Danvers wedding and reception.

Suddenly, I'm frozen in horror. *This is a wedding.* Right here. Freak show central. I thought Zak said the con reserved the whole center, but he must have been mistaken. This couple obviously has no idea what they've signed up for. I picture the look on the poor bride's face when a bunch of drunken Wookiees stumble in during the vows. I have to warn someone to get some kind of security detail in place. Where is Zak's friend?

"May I help you?"

He's a very handsome man in his thirties, with brown, slightly receding hair, steely eyes, and no costume.

"Warren?"

"Er, no, I'm John. Ma'am, this is a private event."

"That's what I need to warn you about. Do you have any idea what's going on out there?"

He looks concerned. "What?"

"A comic book convention! I don't know if anyone told you, but there are some very strange people here this weekend. You might want to consider having someone watch the door."

He blinks, then laughs. "You scared me there for a minute. Trust me, I know about the con. My fiancée and I met here two years ago."

And that confirms my theory that these people have no social skills. This guy convinced his poor girlfriend to get married at the geek parade. Maybe she pretended it was a good idea, but there's not a woman alive who'd be enthused about this idea. I give the marriage two years. Maybe four—he *is* cute.

"Miss? Are you looking for Warren? He'll be back in a minute."

"Thank you. And a piece of advice. Buy your wife flowers every day for the next year or so."

Someone joins us. "I'd rather get chocolates."

He's a big, somewhat tubby man, with a full beard and a graying ponytail. John smiles.

"This is my fiancé, Mark." They both smile, as if daring me to have a problem.

Little foot-in-mouth action there. Nice one, Ana.

I shake Mark's hand. "Congratulations to you both." I notice that someone has labeled the two sections of chairs FEDERATION and REBEL ALLIANCE. They obviously deserve each other.

I start to walk away, but pause. I know it's not my concern, but these two guys seem so *normal*. I have to know why they're holding their ceremony here.

"Could I ask you guys a personal question?"

They both kind of laugh. "You want to know why we're getting married at Washingcon?"

"It's not my business . . . but yes. Doesn't this seem like a silly place for a serious event?"

"Wow," says Mark, "That's exactly what my sister said."

John chuckles. "Maybe it is kind of odd to have the ceremony here instead of somewhere more formal. But this place has a lot of happy memories for the both of us. You know, for years now, I've been called a freak, a pervert, a deviant, a weirdo." He pauses. "It's been even worse since I came out as gay."

Mark rolls his eyes. He's obviously heard the joke before.

John continues. "But not here. At the con, there's one hundred percent acceptance, no ifs, ands, or buts. This is the one place where anyone can go and not be judged. And that's why we decided that this would be the ideal spot."

Out of John's line of vision, Mark subtly shakes his head and cocks a thumb at his fiancé. I swallow my giggle.

"Good luck to both of you." I attempt to give the Vulcan salute, but my fingers don't go that way. "May the force be with you, and all that . . ."

My phone beeps. I excuse myself to read the text.

It's from Zak.

THAT WAS NOT CLAYTON. STAY WHERE YOU ARE.

Great. Now what?

"Ana?"

I turn around. A tall, well-built black man stands behind me. He's dressed impeccably, with creased trousers, a starched shirt, and a perfectly knotted tie, complete with clip. His shoes are polished, and his ebony hands are so delicate I think they may be manicured.

And he's wearing a mask. An alien mask. Not that unusual around here, I suppose. But this thing is all battered and faded. Most of the paint is missing. It's like something you'd find in your parents' basement, kept only for sentimental reasons.

"Warren?"

"Yes. Duke texted me that you're having some difficulty locating your brother?" His voice is deep and smooth.

"Um, yeah. He's not supposed to be here, but we're kind of hoping to, you know, avoid trouble."

Warren chuckles. His laughter is warm, comforting, and *why in the world is he wearing that stupid mask?*

"I'm a Washingcon official. I may be able to figure out where your brother—what's his name?"

"Clayton Watson."

"Where Clayton might be headed." He gestures to a table. Propping my bow against the wall, I pull up a chair as he opens a laptop from an expensive-looking carrying case.

"I'm not really supposed to be doing this," he says as it boots up. "But Duke said it was an emergency."

I'm in love with this guy's voice. He's like a radio announcer. It's killing me that I can't see the whole picture, but Zak warned me against asking about Warren's oddity.

"Thanks for your help."

"Please, don't mention it." He's typing into his computer. "So, are you enjoying the con? Something tells me you're not a regular."

"No. Things are kind of . . . crazy."

He nods. The dead, opaque eyes of the alien reveal nothing. "Well, there are certainly a few unusual characters about. I've learned not to notice."

"You don't say."

"Hang on." Warren peers at the screen. He actually lifts the mask a bit for a better look, but he's bent forward and I can't see any of his features.

"Your brother did indeed register here about two hours ago. One night, all access. Paid cash. Minor badge."

"That doesn't give me much to go on."

"Well, let's keep looking . . . yes, here we go. Hmm. Looks like he signed up for the Mazes and Monsters card tournament. Five thirty, convention room B three. If you hurry, you can make it."

I breathe a sigh of relief. As soon as Zak gets here, we can track down my brother, beat him savagely, and then all go back to the hotel.

There is a loud thumping noise from somewhere in the room. In the middle of the center aisle, part of the floor begins to rise. Some sort of maintenance trapdoor. It flips open with a bang. Filthy and disheveled,

Duquette climbs out from somewhere under the floor. The wedding planners give him a cursory glance and go back to what they're doing.

Zak looks exhausted as he flops down on a chair next to me. His shirt is stained with grease and the knees of his trousers are gone. He sits there and grimaces for a minute, as if in pain. Finally, he lets out a long sigh.

"Evening, Warren." He then turns to me and nods.

"What the hell were you doing under there?" I blurt, horrified.

"Under where?" He then smiles, tiredly, and chuckles. "Underwear."

"Zak?"

Zak tents his fingers and regards me through narrowed eyes. Though he's smiling, it's a tight, uncomfortable, almost angry smile.

"Here's a fun little fact, Ana. The promotional giveaway shirts for that *Operation Anarchy* movie are the same color as that one your brother was wearing. I chased some poor girl halfway across the building before I realized *your* mistake."

Behind his mask, I hear Warren make a *tsk*ing sound. I replay the scene in my mind. Zak's right, I was the one who first mistook her for Clayton.

"Was she angry?"

He chuckles, humorlessly. "Yes, she really hammered

that point home. As did her boyfriend, who promised to break every one of my bones. Fortunately, he actually fell for that 'your epidermis is showing' gag and I escaped through the maintenance tunnels." Zak pauses, just long enough for the silence to become awkward. "And how have you been?"

"Warren found out where Clayton is." My effort to change the subject falls flat.

"Well, jolly good. I hope you can take care of it. There's a rather unpleasant Viking fellow I'm trying to avoid."

Warren clears his throat. "Duke, would you like me to call security?"

"That won't be necessary." He stands. Slowly, as if something aches. "As soon as we collect our stray sheep, we're leaving. I've had enough of this crummy day." He nods. "Warren."

I try to say something, but Zak's distracted by the sight of the grooms. "John! Mark! You two finally tying the knot?" He walks over to them.

I turn to Warren. "Well, that's that, I guess." After we get Clayton, we'll go back to the hotel. Crisis averted.

Warren stares at me with his blank eyes.

"Oh, don't look at me like that."

"Sorry. Is this better?" His expression, of course, doesn't change.

"Very funny."

"So . . ." He looks down at his perfect nails. "How do you know Duke, anyway?"

I look over at Zak. He's standing with the grooms, juggling some party favors. All three of them are laughing.

How do I know him? He's the moron who got forced onto my quiz bowl team and then saved the day. He's the jerk who convinced my brother to run off and the guy who nearly got killed trying to rescue him. He's a complete and total geek who people automatically like. And I've seen him naked.

"He's a friend." I don't look at Warren. Even with the mask, I can feel his eyes boring into me.

He clears his throat. "Someone told me Duke wasn't coming to Washingcon this year. I'm glad to see he made it—it wouldn't be the same without him."

"Yeah." *Too bad he can't stay.*

I stand up to collect Duquette. He meets me halfway across the ballroom. His mood seems to have improved.

"I need to get Mark and John something before we leave town. They're registered at Crate and Barrel, Target, and Rock Bottom Comics."

"C'mon, Zak, let's get Clayton."

He frowns and bites his lip. "Yeah."

"Zak . . ." I take a breath, preemptively regretting what I'm about to say. "Thank you for coming out here.

I know you'd rather be with your friends. And if we find Clayton soon, maybe you could show us around for a little bit or something. We've got a couple of hours before curfew and I . . . owe you."

Zak's face slowly molds into a smile. It's not cocky— it's actually kind of warm. Nice. "Thanks, Ana."

I turn away and grab my bow before I can return the smile. "C'mon, let's get Clayton. We'll still have an hour or so before we should go back. And I mean, it's not like we're doing anything wrong, right? Mrs. Brinkham said we could go out to eat, and they have food here, right? So really, we're not doing anything that bad. I mean . . ."

I'm babbling. I sound like an idiot. In front of Duquette. Fortunately, he doesn't laugh at me.

"Let's go, Zak."

He holds the ballroom door open for me. "Call me Duke."

"No."

"Then how about Eddie Baby?"

"No."

"Renaldo?"

"No."

"Peaches?"

"Stop talking now."

"Okay."

Side by side, we walk down the corridor.

ZAK

5:36 PM

Things just got interesting.

I like to think that Ana is finally warming up to me, seeing me as something other than the geek who can help find her brother. But that's probably just wishful thinking. More than likely, she just realized that her parents aren't here and she can cut loose for once.

Ana walks next to me, clutching her bow nervously and looking over her shoulder every time someone screams. It's easy to forget that *I'm* the one who has a hit out on me.

I have to think of something fun for us to do in the next hour or so. Something low-key and not too bizarre.

Someplace where I won't run into Attila and his girl (my manhood can't take any more abuse). I have one shot at this.

A dance? Too date-like.

A film? Somehow, I doubt our tastes mesh.

A game? She'd be bored.

The Furry fiesta? Dear God, no.

"Ana, would you . . ."

She suddenly stops dead in her tracks, a look of sheer panic on her face. I turn, expecting to see the Viking barreling down on me. Instead, she reaches into her purse and pulls out a ringing cell phone.

"It's my mom," she whispers, her green eyes wide.

I'm not sure how to reply to that.

A very loud group of bronies advances down the hall.

"I need to go somewhere quiet!" she hisses as the phone rings again.

I quickly reconnoiter and guide her into an empty conference room. She sighs, leans her bow against the wall, and answers her phone.

"Hi, Mom." Her voice is shaky. I start to duck out to give her some privacy, when her hand snakes out and grabs my wrist. She's not making eye contact, but her grip could almost be described as painful. Either she's holding me captive or just wants moral support. Whatever the reason, I'm not going anywhere.

"Things are going great," she says into the receiver, her speech rapid and uncomfortable. "Yeah, we did really well . . . yes . . . oh, Landon and Sonya and, um, Landon and Sonya. Yes."

Her grip tightens. Her tiny little fingers manipulate my wrist bones in directions they're not supposed to go. My hand turns pale as the circulation is cut off. Only my manly pride keeps me from wrenching out of her grasp.

"Clayton? Oh, he's fine . . ." Ana's voice rises an octave. "He's . . . he's . . . he's . . ."

C'mon, Ana, easy lie here. He's in the bathroom. Taking a shower. Picking up a pizza with Landon. Talking to Mrs. Brinkham. Say something!

"He's, uh . . ." Her emerald eyes are huge. My joints are starting to snap, crackle, and pop. She's about to panic. I can read it in her face. She's just a few seconds away from blurting out everything.

I snatch the phone from her hand. She releases my wrist in surprise.

"Hello, Mrs. Watson?" I make my voice as loud and friendly as possible.

"Who is this?" asks Ana's mother. She is loud and not at all friendly.

"This is Zak Duquette, the newest member of the Meriwether Lewis High School quiz bowl team. Did Ana tell you how amazing she and Clayton were today?

I mean, the whole crew was on fire, but your kids, wow! You should be proud as anything."

There's a slight pause. "Um, yes. Now, Clayton . . ."

"Yeah, he's bunking with Landon and me. Hope he doesn't mind snoring—some nights I rattle the darn windows." I break into a volley of fake laughter. Ana is staring at me like I've just pulled the pin out of a grenade. "At any rate, we're all going out to dinner in a minute. Clay just stepped into the bathroom."

"I've tried to call Clayton—" Mrs. Watson begins.

"Yeah, poor guy left his phone in the van. I'd laugh, but I did the same thing once. Left it in a McDonald's in Gig Harbor, came back a week later and it was still there, believe it or not."

"I—"

"So I'll let him know you called. It's gonna be an early night, so he'll probably call you back in the morning. Hey, maybe you could settle something for me. The first governor of New York was Elihu Johnson, right?"

"I—"

"Thanks! Landon was trying to tell me it was Roscoe Conkling, if you can believe that. Anyway, it's been nice talking to you. If we go to nationals, I hope you can come and watch us. Go MLHS!"

"Wait, put Ana back on—"

"How's that? Sorry, I think we're breaking—"

I hang up and hand the phone back.

Ana is catatonic. Only the twitching of her eyelid reveals that she has not slipped into a coma.

"Lots of words real fast," I tell her. "That's the secret to a good lie. They're not sure what you said, and blame themselves when they get confused."

Her phone rings again.

"Don't answer that. Your battery just died."

This seems to snap her out of the trance. She pockets her phone, picks up her bow, and leans toward me.

"Thanks, Zak. I went blank there. Glad you were here."

I try to shrug it off. "No big deal. Heck, James and I once drove out to Eugene for the weekend. Had my mom convinced I was in the basement the whole time."

"It is a big deal, Zak."

Much to my surprise, Ana gently takes my hand in hers and intertwines our fingers. Her eyes have a warm, flirty look.

"Try something like that again and I'll kill you."

She smiles at me again and we walk out of the room together.

And just for a few seconds, just for a moment, she continues to hold my hand.

ANA

5:50 PM

We've arrived at the conference room where Warren directed us. Zak has spent several minutes conferring with various people. Their badges all sport ribbons and pins, so they're evidently some kind of con authorities.

While he talks, I think about the stunt he pulled with my mom. It probably will end up making her furious. But . . .

Furious at the obnoxious kid on the phone. Not at me. When I get back, I'll just tell her how the jerk team alternate thought he was being funny. Blame any confusion about Clayton on Zak. Make it all his fault. No problem.

Except I'd have to paint Zak as some sort of idiot slacker. And after spending a couple of hours with him, I know that's not really the case. Mostly.

And here he is, standing in front of me, a sheepish expression on his face.

"Here's the thing, Ana."

I instantly wince. Any explanation that starts off with those words is going to end in bad news.

"Yes, Zak?"

He taps a sheet of paper he's holding. "Clayton is here. Warren was right, he's in the Mazes and Monsters tournament, and he's already advanced to the second round. I bet the little weasel stole my cards, that's how he's doing so well."

I sigh with relief. "Where is all this?"

"Through those double doors."

I'm already moving. Zak clears his throat.

"Duquette, I have a feeling you're about to piss me off."

He shrugs. "You can't go in there during gameplay. No spectators." He points to a balding, potbellied man in a white uniform slouched near the entryway. A rent-a-cop.

"Are you kidding me?" I finger my bow. The guard makes such a tempting target.

"Calm down, William Tell. They're playing for a

three-hundred-dollar prize. They don't want any audience members helping out their friends."

"How on earth could they do that?"

Zak apparently doesn't understand the concept of a rhetorical question. "Well, one year some guys rigged up a primitive fiber-optics network . . ."

My headache is returning. "How long will this game take?"

"Depending on how well he does, maybe two hours."

I glance at a clock on the wall. If we wait for Clayton, then have to hang around to find a taxi, a half hour ride back . . . that's cutting it way too close. Plus, what if he gives us the slip again?

"Can't you go in as a player, Duquette?"

Zak won't meet my eyes. "Ana . . ."

"Out with it." I set my bow on a table so I can place my hands on my hips.

"Last year . . . there was some unpleasantness. I was sort of kinda asked not to return. In a very official sense." He tries to smile, but I think my expression kills it.

"Wonderful. So there's no other way in?"

He shakes his head. "We're going to have to wait him out. Are you hungry?"

I don't answer. I have a feeling that if we don't corner my brother right now, we'll lose him forever in this crowd. I'm already picturing Mrs. Brinkham, knocking on the door to the boys' hotel room. She's beginning to panic, not knowing where half the team is. She takes out her phone and calls my parents . . .

"Last call!" I'm jolted back to reality. "Last call for the Mazes and Monsters competition. Sign up now or be lost forever."

Zak kicks at the bench leg like a bored ten-year-old in church. There's only one thing for me to do.

"Sign me up!" I snap the clipboard from the announcer's hand and scrawl my name. According to the sheet, we begin in five minutes.

My companion is stunned. "Ana, um, you don't know how to play."

I sit back down, cross my legs, and smile. "Teach me everything you know. You have three hundred seconds."

The conference room where we'll be competing is filled with portable tables. Dozens of competitors are wedged into chairs, and I get the feeling that not all of them are familiar with the concept of soap. I scan the area for my brother, but I don't think he's here.

"Excuse me," I ask a normal-looking middle-aged man. "Where are the people who competed last round?"

"Um, I think they have the winners in a private waiting area until their next turn. Hey, nice bow, are you dressed like—"

"No."

Drat. Looks like I'm going to have to try to find Clayton the hard way. Once I've lost, then I'll have Zak round up some space marines to raid the winners' circle.

Meanwhile, I have no choice but to fumble my way through this game. While I have been provided with a foil-wrapped package of Mazes and Monsters cards, Duquette tells me I won't stand a chance. Players apparently spend years building their M-and-M decks. He claims he knows people who have spent over a thousand dollars on their cards, but what kind of loser would do that?

"Ana Watson! Did not expect to see you here!"

I squint at my opponent. "Do I know you?"

He leans forward. "It's me, James. Zak's friend. I didn't know you were into gaming. How come you never joined us in the library?"

"It's a recent interest." I almost ask him why he's dressed like President Theodore Roosevelt, but stop myself. He might tell me.

"Actually, James, I'm only here because I'm trying to track down my brother, Clayton. I've got to make it to the next round, and idiot Zak apparently was banned for cheating."

James looks surprisingly grim. "Not quite, Ana. Last year, he was one round away from being champion. And he threw the game." His voice has the somber tone of a PSA on the dangers of meth.

"Why?"

"Well, Duke denies it, but he lost on purpose so his opponent could impress his girlfriend."

I open my cards and pretend to shuffle them, trying to imagine a girl who'd be impressed by the champion of this game.

Probably as unlikely as finding someone who'd be impressed by a quiz bowl champion.

"Gentlemen!" barks the cyborg referee. "And, um, lady." He nods in my direction. "You all know the rules. You may begin at your leisure."

I try to remember what Zak told me. A troll beats a wizard, a wizard beats a gnome . . . a red card trumps an orange and so on down the visible light spectrum . . . spells are worth two . . . no, five . . .

"James? I don't suppose you'd like to impress *me*?" I bat my eyes.

"Sorry, Ana. At the game table, it's all business." He removes his wire-rimmed spectacles and replaces them with a large pair of mirrored sunglasses. He then fans his cards in front of him, inches from his nose.

Mirrored sunglasses.

I can totally see the reflection of his entire hand. All his cards.

I swallow, shuffle my cards, and commit his hand to memory. "I open with a red . . . make that an orange troll. And I bid five hundred manna."

I gather my cards and my bow. James sits, dejectedly, unable to process how he lost to such a newbie. The worse the game went for him, the closer he held his cards to his face. I'd have to warn him about that. Later.

"Thanks, James. Sorry it didn't go well for you."

He half smiles. "*C'est la guerre.*"

The winners' room mirrors the original venue, only smaller. About twenty guys mill around, snacking, reading, and talking. One man strums a guitar. Clayton is not among them.

This is no time for manners. "Has anyone seen a thirteen-year-old boy?" I yell without preamble. "Blond, glasses?"

"Clayton?" asks someone. "Yeah, I played him in the tiebreaker round. Came down to the wire, but I won."

"What? You mean he's gone already? Did he say where?" *I played this stupid game for nothing?*

"He said he was going to check out the SCA event."

Another meaningless series of letters. "Where's that?"

He stares at me as if I'm the one not making any sense. "The courtyard. Hey, you can't leave now!"

I'm already moving toward the door. "Unless the Sixth Amendment has been repealed, yes, I can."

Someone blocks my path. A tall guy. When I look up at his face I suppress a scream at his hideous mask. Then I suppress another one when I realize he's not wearing one.

It's Zak's nemesis, Cyrax.

Up close, he's quite hideous. Nothing I can put my finger on, but there's something about his face that gives me goose bumps. The dark circles under his eyes, his thinning black hair, his liver-colored lips, and his crooked nose . . . in a sea of unattractive people, Cyrax still stands out.

"Going somewhere, young lady?"

His breath isn't bad, but it has a weird, musty quality, like when you turn on the furnace for the first time in the fall.

"I have to go. Family emergency." I try to squeeze around him, but he leans to the side.

"In the middle of the game? But I'm to be your opponent. Surely you can finish the round."

I can see why Zak doesn't like this guy. "I forfeit. You win. Get out of my way."

He doesn't move. "I'm afraid it doesn't work like that"—he glances at my name tag—"Ana. This is the winners' circle. Either we see this through or there's no victor."

I glance at the spectators. The guitarist nods in confirmation.

Cyrax cracks a smile. I can hear it cracking. "Come, Ana. I've worked too hard and waited too long to quit now." He extends a bony arm. "Let's play."

While I of all people can appreciate the sweat and sacrifice that comes with being a champion at something, now is not the time. This may be my last chance to head Clayton off, and I'm not going to waste it talking to this overgrown ghoul. I attempt to force my way past him.

He grabs my arm. His knobby fingers tighten around my wrist.

"We play."

Oh, hell no. I throw back my arm and drive my fist into his gut. Not as hard as I can, but enough to let him know that no one grabs me like that. Ever.

It's like hitting a scarecrow. My knuckles bury themselves in his shirt, but encounter no resistance. I may as well be striking a bag of leaves. I throw another jab with no effect. He does not let go of my arm.

He begins to speak as if I hadn't just slugged him. "You're a friend of Zak Duquette's, are you not? Yes, I remember. That must be why you're so anxious to quit. Because you're preprogrammed to lose. Just like Zak. Am I right?"

I attempt to wrench my hand away, but he may as well have me in cuffs. I'm starting to get scared. I could yell for help, but James is gone and I somehow doubt these card players would do much.

"So will you play or continue to be a loser like your boyfriend?"

Well, I tried to get away. I did my best. I have no choice. I have to stand up for myself. And for Zak, I guess.

"Well, if you won't let me leave . . ."

Cyrax's mouth expands, revealing his gray teeth.

"Then *everybody* leaves."

With my free hand, I reach out and yank the fire alarm.

A blaring siren fills the room, just like I expected.

Cyrax lets go of my arm, just like I planned. Clutching my bow, I make for the door.

Then the sprinklers activate. Streams of chemical-green liquid rain down on the room, drenching everyone's very expensive cards.

I did not see that coming.

ZAK

7:09 PM

I'm a nervous pacer, and Ana's continued absence
doesn't help. I've made the circuit to the snack bar and
back so many times that the guys playing speed chess are
starting to look annoyed.

How embarrassing to have to send Ana into the tournament. I should have been the defending champion,
but last year Nealish had looked so sad and hopeless, I
had to give him a chance to look cool in front of that girl
he liked. And now they're dating and I have a lifetime
ban for throwing the game. So much for selfless sacrifice.

I wonder what's taking Ana so long. She's probably

found Clayton and is struggling to drag him out by his nose. I hope they don't end up knocking over a table.

"Psst!" Someone is loudly hissing on the other side of the food court. I glance over. It's a short person, dressed entirely in a black hooded cloak. I can't make out any features, not even their face.

But the longbow and little black pumps are kind of a giveaway.

Ana hisses again and jerks her shoulder at me. I join her.

"It is indeed a balmy evening for a Friday," I say with a thick Italian accent.

Ana ignores my attempts at intrigue. "Clayton's left the tournament," she whispers. "He's gone to something called the SCA. What's that?"

"The Society for Creative Anachronism," I mouth back. "They do reenactments of the Middle Ages. What's with the cloak? And why are we whispering?"

She shakes her hood. "I'm not sure why you are. *I'm* whispering because they wouldn't let me leave the tournament early and I kind of caused a big scene."

I get an uncomfortable feeling in my gut. "Uh, Ana? Did it have something to do with those sirens I heard earlier?"

"Let's just say I'd really like to get out of here as soon as possible. Which way is the courtyard?"

"Straight down the end of this hall."

She gathers her bow and moves forward. "God, I'm so sorry I came here."

I mean to keep my mouth shut. Honestly I do. It's not like I expect überserious Ana Watson to suddenly start having fun at Washingcon. Or having fun with me.

But there's no point in saying anything. She's scared, uncomfortable, and wants to leave. My feelings aren't important.

But somehow, a little yelp escapes my mouth. A sad little yip, like a puppy whose tail you just stepped on. Totally involuntary.

She hears me, and turns.

I can't make out her face under that hood. But a trick of the light allows me to see her eyes. They glow green in the shadows, kind of like a gorgeous Jawa.

And for a moment, those eyes smile at me.

She turns away, and I follow. Of course.

"So wait," I abruptly ask. "Why are we going to the courtyard?"

"Someone said the SCA meets there. So what exactly do they do again?"

"Costuming. Pageantry. They're a fun group." Usually. Almost always. Except for once or twice a year. I wish I had a schedule to refer to. It suddenly occurs to me that Clayton may be in trouble.

Ana is talking. "So if this is a courtyard, he won't be able to give us the slip, right?"

"Well, it's more like a vacant lot, but if luck's on our side, we should be able to corner him." *Please, please, please let luck be on our side.*

Ana seems greatly relieved. "Thank goodness." She smiles at me.

I'm too worried to smile back. Surely it's not tonight. I rack my brains. The program said Saturday night, right? Not Friday?

I breathe a little easier when we reach the center's rear lobby. A young mother passes us, holding hands with an adorable little princess decked out in crepe paper and cardboard. Behind them, two young gladiators run by, dueling with plastic swords.

Thank God. The SCA is doing children's costuming tonight. I have nothing to worry about.

We navigate around the tables where two middle-aged hippies are cleaning up the last of the glue and glitter, and pass through the double doors into the cold evening air.

And onto a battlefield.

Behind the convention center sits a massive vacant lot. It's the size of a city block. Construction of an office building was supposed to have started two years ago, but some lawsuit has prevented that, and it remains an empty, muddy field.

A field filled with two hundred warriors, about to enter into brutal hand-to-hand combat.

It's not quite dark, but it's overcast. Distant lightning illuminates the combatants in random, eerie bursts.

They stand in rigid ranks, two armies, separated by a football field of bare earth. Every combatant that existed from the fall of Rome to the Age of Enlightenment seems to be standing at attention, ready to kill. Bare-chested Aztecs. Swiss guardsmen in full papal regalia. Conquistadors. Ninjas. Vikings. Crusaders. They hold their weapons aloft and ready. In the darkness, it's easy to miss that every sword, club, and ax is made of padded PVC pipe.

The air is heavy with moisture and sweat. There's an expectant tension the air, as if each side is just waiting for the other to make the first move. Everyone seems to breathe in unison.

Ana's hand grasps my shoulder. "Zak? What's happening?"

"The annual battle. Badon Hill this year."

"They're just play fighting, right?" Her hand tightens.

I point to a tiny group of spectators, huddled against

the building. "See Hannibal Lecter and Professor Moriarty over there? They're emergency room doctors in real life. They're here for a reason."

"Do you see my brother anywhere?"

The armies continue to stand there, as if waiting for a signal.

I notice a pirate with a spyglass. "Can I use that for a second, matey?" I stand on an AC unit and with the borrowed eyepiece, I scan the crowd, hopelessly trying to locate my quiz bowl buddy.

"Over there, Zak. Under that streetlight."

I focus. Yes! He's lost his glasses, but it's certainly him.

"Bingo. Wow, what are the odds that there are two shirts that color?"

"I'm going to get him." She marches off toward no-man's-land.

"Whoa!" I hop down and jump in front of her. I don't want her out there when the teeth start flying. "Let me get him."

"Okay." She agrees so quickly, it's slightly insulting. "Go grab him before . . ."

A lone, eerie note from a bagpipe splits the night. Two black-clad torchbearers emerge from the darkness, followed by an enormous, shaven-headed man in a loincloth. His body is covered with tattoos. His only other adornment is an eye patch, which I don't think is part of his costume.

In a low, guttural, and yet clear voice, he begins to recite the battle ode. The words never fail to stir me, and I barely even speak Orkish.

"Too late. I'm going to have to do this the hard way." I quickly scan the area. I grab an abandoned, two-handed sword that is leaning against the building.

The orc's words reach a crescendo. People begin to stir.

"Zak? Is this such a good idea?" Ana looks genuinely worried.

"I'll be fine." *Gulp*.

She suddenly smiles. "Of course you will. I bet you do this every year, right?"

I grin. "Yeah." *No. Not once. Too scared*. I still remember signing James's cast from the one time he participated.

A female dwarf passes a horn to the orc general. This is it. "You get out of here, Ana. But how about a kiss for luck, first?"

She drops her hood and for a moment I think my ploy actually worked. But she just smiles. "Not on your life. You be careful. Come back in one piece, Zak."

I hike to join the nearer army. "Call me Duke! Everyone else does!"

I can barely hear her above the loud blast on the horn. "Not everyone."

Some of the SCA members have ignored the 900 to 1600 AD timeline. I wedge myself between a Greek hoplite and a World War I doughboy. We march forward.

At first, there is no sound but the unsettling cadence of shod feet marching in time (and the inappropriate strains of "Wipe Out" from a car on the next block). No one seems eager to be the first over the top. I entertain the unworthy idea of sneaking around the building and capturing Clayton from the rear.

A scream pierces the night. "FREEDOM!" A dark figure rushes toward us from the opposing forces, the duct tape of his weapon gleaming.

Within seconds, everyone rushes into the fray. Battle cries split the air.

"FOR SCOTLAND!"

"ALLAHU AKBAR!"

"SPOON!"

"THERE CAN BE ONLY ONE!"

"VIVE LA FRANCE!"

I heft my weapon and shout the only thing I can think of.

"MERIWETHER LEWIS HIGH SCHOOL QUIZ BOWL TEAM!"

I put my head down and rush forward. I'm elbowed

and jostled by the crowd, but I clear the neutral zone without anyone challenging me. A Germanic berserker attempts to take my head off with a very real-looking war hammer, but I duck just in time. I leap over the groaning form of a Teutonic knight and hurl myself behind the enemy lines.

Hand-to-hand combat has begun in earnest. The gruesome sound of plastic against flesh fills the night. I nearly trip over a sprawling longbowman and wince as somebody's flying retainer hits me in the eye. Luckily, no one has singled me out yet.

In the distance I see the streetlight where Clayton had been standing. If I could just make it there . . .

"Banzai!" A samurai leaps in front of me, his katana arched over his head. He's bleeding from both nostrils, but doesn't seem to notice.

Fortunately, I know him. "Hey, Paul, now's not a good time."

He responds by bringing his sword down on my head. It bashes into my skull with cracking force.

"Argh!" I stumble backward. He swings again. Pure instinct allows me to parry with my own weapon. I'm falling back in full retreat.

Something blocks my path. Some idiot has illegally parked his car in this lot, a decision he will certainly regret in the morning. I scramble, butt-first, onto the hood. Paul misses, his sword striking with such force that the side-view mirror is knocked loose. I take the opportunity to land a blow of my own. This only seems to make him angrier. He leaps, flat-footed, onto the hood. I shuffle onto the roof to the accompaniment of cracking windshield glass.

Paul lunges forward, determined to gut me. I do what comes naturally and dodge. Momentum carries him forward and he teeters perilously, three feet off the ground. I swing my sword into his ribs and he goes flying.

Though I really should just run, I have to see if he's okay. He lies in the mud, not moving. I climb down beside him.

"Paul?"

He comes to life, unsheathing a short sword from his belt. This one is metal. I'm about to beg for mercy when he rips open his tunic, places the blade against his bare belly, and begins what sounds like a prayer in Japanese.

Good luck with that. I rush to the rear of the dwindling battle.

No one is near the lamppost. I search desperately for Clayton, but my head is still swimming. Is that him over there? Yes! He has a set of nunchaku and is flailing away at an overweight Cossack.

"Playtime's over, Clay." I stagger toward him, tapping my sword in my palm. It then falls to the ground as two mammoth, hairy arms engulf me in a bear hug from behind.

"I yield! I yield!" I manage to squeak.

It makes no difference. I kick and struggle like a three-year-old, and still my captor drags me into the secluded trash area behind the convention center. He roughly deposits me against the nonedible grease receptacle.

I jump up, facing my attacker directly in the chest. I crane my neck to see his face. He leers down at me from under his Viking horns.

Oh, dear.

"I have to hurt you, pal. Nothing personal."

I'm giddy with panic. "Actually, I think that would be quite personal."

He flexes his shoulders. "You grabbed my girlfriend. I can't let that go."

Where's a Roman legion when you need one? "It was all a misunderstanding. I thought she was a little boy."

Probably not the best thing to say. He takes me by my shirt, but most of it tears away in his hand. He compensates by grabbing me by my hair. He cocks his ham-size fist. I wrench at the fingers clamped down on my skull, but they're not going anywhere.

"Try to think of something else," he says with real compassion. "I hear it helps."

An odd sense of peace fills my body. I close my eyes.

Tell me about the rabbits, George.

And suddenly, I'm being hugged. Hugged? He's wrapped his burly arms completely around me. Is he going to let bygones be bygones, solidifying our truce with an awkward bro hug?

Nope. He's crushing me. My ribs begin to rearrange themselves as his arms clamp tighter and tighter. My eyes pop back open—and somewhat out of their sockets—as Conan methodically narrows his grip, relentless as a boa constrictor crushing a goat.

He's grinning at me, but the image goes gray as my diaphragm can no longer flex and my oxygen supply is cut off.

Now would be the perfect time to say something funny and cutting, something to make my tormentor realize the error of his ways and release me.

Urrrrgggggghhhh.

The gray fades to black. I'm going to die.

I knew the risks. All part of being on the quiz bowl team. Not everyone makes it back alive.

Suddenly, a pained scream fills the air. And I don't think it's me. I'm surprised to discover that I'm no longer being murdered, but am leaning against the building. The Viking clutches his head and howls.

A Valkyrie stands there at the entrance to the alley.

Seven feet tall and bare-chested, she towers above us, her flaming sword held aloft.

I shake my head and the whole vision melts away to reveal Ana, brandishing a PVC mace, which she has neatly broken over Conan's skull.

He clutches his bruised forehead and proceeds to make a noise that no human throat should be able to make. The sound the Tunguska blast must have made. Stunned and terrified of what he'll do to Ana, I lurch forward.

She's quicker. With a deft motion, she grabs something from behind her and lunges.

For a second, I think she's stabbed him in the face. It's only when his battle cry reverts to a howl of pain that I realize what's happened.

She's taken one of her arrows, one of the blunt arrows she bought in the dealer's room, and shoved it up the Viking's nose. As far as it will go.

It's a highly ludicrous sight as he bounces from foot to foot, yelping in pain, flailing his arms about like Curly Howard, with two feet of plastic shaft protruding from his nostril.

"Uh, Duquette?" Ana tugs at what's left of my shirt.

Right. We must flee. Fortunately, my years of friendship with the many smokers around here are about to pay off.

"This way!" We round a corner, and as usual, someone's wedged a kitchen door open so they can duck out and enjoy a quick cigarette. We hurtle through and I kick the rock away. The monster is already bearing down on us, snorting like a bull through his bloody nose, but he won't make it in time. And the door locks from the inside.

Just as the door swings shut, I catch a glimpse of a lone figure. He's standing on a low perimeter wall and is cast into sharp detail by one of the security lights.

That stupid orange-and-red shirt.

As the door slams in my face, Clayton looks in my direction. And salutes me.

ANA

8:13 PM

Zak sits on a bench in some sort of access hall for the kitchens. He's been staring at the opposite wall without saying anything for about ten minutes.

I'm starting to get worried. When I first led him here, I thought he might have been pissed off. Maybe I violated the rules of battle or something by helping him. But he's still not talking, and not responding when I say his name. I didn't think that big guy hurt him very much, but still. Mom showed me this magazine article once where this kid got hit in the head with a baseball and seemed fine, and then keeled over dead two hours later from a hemorrhage.

What if Zak's really hurt? Should I call 911 or see if the con has some kind of nurse on staff? Wait, didn't Zak say there was a medic at the battle?

Paralyzed with indecision, I buy a Coke from an empty employee break room.

"Zak? Try to drink this."

He doesn't look at me, but he takes the cold can and presses it against the small of his back.

More silence. He must be hurt. I didn't think he was capable of shutting up for so long.

"Ana?" He breaks the silence, but doesn't look at me.

"Yes, Zak?"

"Are you Catholic? You were wearing a crucifix earlier."

My joy that he's speaking again is overcome by my concern that he's now babbling. "Um, yes, I am. Why?"

He's quiet for a moment. "I'm Methodist. But don't worry. We can raise the kids in whatever faith you like." He then turns and gives me a full-on puppy-dog smile. He's okay.

"Glad to see you're not brain damaged, Duquette. I mean, more than usual."

He's still bearing down on me with that smile. "So when do I get to meet the parents?"

"Knock it off, you're not that punch drunk." *And stop smiling like that.*

"Ana, I just saw you pull off the greatest con bad-assery I've seen in years. It was like—"

"I just took a swing at him when he wasn't expecting it. It was nothing."

"Nothing? Ana, you saved my life! Or at least some of my ribs. You took out an ogre at close range. That's incredible. Take a moment and reflect on how awesomely awesome you were."

Yeah, well. Okay, he's right, that was kind of cool. Maybe even a little . . . badass. And now Zak thinks I'm some kind of legend. I can live with that.

"Zak? Are you feeling well enough to keep looking for Clayton? Everything okay?"

He pulls the soda can out from his shirt, pops it open, and slurps the fizz off the top. "Yeah, I'll be fine. But listen, Ana, I've been thinking. You and I, we didn't do anything wrong tonight. That's kind of a new sensation for me. But think about it. Clayton was the one who ran off and lied. It's all him."

I think I see where he's going with this. "Yeah?"

"So, well . . . maybe we ought to let him take his lumps. I mean, I don't want him to get busted, but I don't really want to take the fall for him, either. And I don't see why you should. You've never been in trouble, and if Brinkham catches me here, then I'm going to fail her class."

I'm shocked. "You're failing *health*?"

"Yes. I had a deodorant tutor and everything. But my point is, why are we going to catch hell for what Clayton's doing? Who knows, maybe when your parents find out he isn't perfect, they'll go a little easier on you."

His argument is valid, but like his comic books, the story only makes sense if you know the backstory.

"Zak, my parents, they . . ." I freeze, remembering that awful night, the last time I saw Nichole. My only sister. "You wouldn't understand."

"Try me. Sometimes it helps to talk."

There's something about the way he says this that makes me look at him. Maybe it's because this is the first time I've heard him say anything that wasn't a joke or a complaint.

He's still sprawled on the bench, leaning against the wall, looking battered and exhausted. His brown eyes are barely open, but still he doesn't stop looking at me, his lower lip just twitching into a smile. I suddenly break eye contact and look down. The Viking has ripped away part of his shirt, revealing his pale chest. I remember again the scene back at the hotel, when he dropped his towel.

"Right," says Zak, mistaking my silence for irritation. "None of my business." He doesn't seem hurt, just very tired.

I'm tired too. Tired of running around at this stupid convention. Tired of Mrs. Brinkham, my parents, Clayton the wonder kid, and Nichole, who always acts like none of this is her fault.

I lean back on the bench, next to Zak.

"Clayton and I . . . we have an older sister. Nichole. She used to be kind of wild. Always wanting to have fun, make a joke, just barely doing enough to get by."

I suddenly freeze in horror. I'm describing Nichole . . . but I'm also describing Duquette. Eww.

"Go on."

"Well, one day she went too far. Way too far. Ended up pregnant her senior year of high school." I realize this is the first time I've ever shared this story with anyone.

Zak makes a painful hiss with his teeth. "Ouch. How'd that turn out?"

"Not well, Zak. When my parents found out, they . . ." I trail off. *What I'm about to say cannot be unsaid. Do I really want Zak to know?* "They threw her out. Bang."

Zak's eyes go wide for a moment. I fear he's going to start talking, but he stays quiet and listens.

"She never came home again. My parents never met their grandson." *Neither have I.* "At any rate, that's why tonight is such a big deal. I'm in charge of Clayton. I can't just call up Mom and Dad and say I let him wander off. You don't get a second chance at my house, Duquette. I learned that two years ago."

It seems weird to say this all out loud. The whole scenario would be laughable, if it hadn't really happened.

Duquette is staring at me again. And he's smiling. I swear, if he cracks a joke or quotes a movie, I'm going to kick him in his busted ribs.

Instead, he stands. Slowly, like some horror movie mummy.

"C'mon, let's find Clayton."

I rise. "Do we have a chance? You said—"

"I say a lot of things. The night is young, and I'd like to think the two of us can outsmart a freshman."

Zak's exhausted confidence is slightly contagious. Maybe we actually will find Clayton. Maybe we'll do it without getting caught. Maybe we'll win tomorrow. Maybe.

He turns to me and takes my arm. No, not my arm. He kind of just grabs the loose sleeve of my cloak. "Ana, listen. I—"

"Duke!" A man in a three-piece suit, black hat, and sunglasses comes strolling down the corridor. He has a pack of forbidden cigarettes in his hand, apparently ready to sneak a smoke in what he thought was an abandoned area.

Zak bites his lip. Whatever he was going to say will wait. "Hey, Elwood."

They do that weird male hug thing with just their palms and shoulders. As they engage in brief conversation, Zak glances at me and winks.

Man, that boy is cocky and annoying. But I remember what he went through outside. He did that for me, which is more than anyone else has done since Nichole left.

I'm starting to not dislike Zak Duquette. I'm actually starting to really not dislike him.

ZAK

8:29 PM

The con usually reaches critical mass between eight and eleven. Everyone who's going to come is here, and the people who aren't spending the night haven't left yet.

The building is now so packed that it's hard to move. Each gaming room is filled with caffeine-addled players hunkering down for all-night marathon sessions. The corridors are brimming with conventioneers, talking, singing, and really beginning to drink. Most have shucked their complicated costumes for casual clothes. The air is stale with sweat, BO, and the fumes of the cheap beer that's provided to anyone with an adult name badge. Many of these people aren't completely on top of traditional social cues and stand talking in the middle of the passages, blocking pedestrian traffic.

I press through the crowd, undaunted, with Ana close behind. I am determined to ferret out Clayton, even if I have to poke through every movie theater, gaming session, and room party in this building. I'm as brave and determined as Christopher Columbus.

I'm just as hopelessly lost, too. There's no way we're going to find Ana's brother in this mess. Not if he wants to stay hidden.

I glance behind me. Ana is still wearing her cloak, the bow and quiver strung across her back. She's as silent as an elf assassin.

I remember what she told me about her sister. Jesus. I know that getting pregnant is a big deal, but to kick your own kid out of the house . . . No wonder Ana had such a stick up her butt. I would too, if I knew my first mistake could be my last.

It makes me really want to find Clayton. Just so she could stop worrying. And maybe be a little impressed by me.

"Zak?" Her voice barely carries in the loud hallway.

"Yeah?"

"We're just wandering around in circles, right?"

I could lie, but she'd see right through it. "I'm sorry, Ana. I'm . . . kinda running out of ideas."

Her stern, almost angry demeanor doesn't change. But just for a second, I see a flash panic ripple across those green eyes. I don't think I would have noticed that earlier today.

I sigh. Nothing left but the nuclear option. "Maybe it's time we call in an amber alert. Let security find your brother."

She shakes her head. "You said they'd call my parents. Or call Mrs. Brinkham."

Which is very true. But we're running out of time. "Ana, I don't know that we have much of a choice. I mean, wouldn't your parents rather hear about this now, from you, rather than later from Mrs. B?"

I'm unprepared for her response. "Are you hungry? I'm hungry!" Without waiting for an answer, she grips her boney fingers into my arm and drags me into a little hole-in-the-wall pizza joint.

A waiter informs us that they'll be closing in ten minutes, but takes our orders for a couple of personal pies.

We sit across from each other in awkward silence.

"Ana, what was that all about? You've been acting kind of weird since the card game."

She toys with a cheese shaker. "Um, remember how I said I kind of caused a scene when they wouldn't let me leave?"

"Yeah."

"Well . . ." Suddenly, she laughs. "I pulled the fire alarm. Cleared the whole room. That's why I can't ask security for help. I think they may be looking for *me*."

I'm horrified and delighted by Ana's confession. I picture the chaos she must have caused, with the ear-splitting sirens and the scattered cards. I'll have to ask James about it later.

"Is that why you're wearing that cloak? So no one will recognize you?"

She nods.

"You rebel. But seriously, I don't think anyone's going to be too pissed about a false alarm."

"Well, it wasn't just a bell—" begins Ana.

We're interrupted by the voice of HAL 9000 singing "Daisy, Daisy." I check my phone.

"Sorry, just my mom saying goodnight," I mumble.

"Is it just you two, you and your mother?" she asks as I return the text.

"Yeah." And then I remember the invader. "Well, and Roger I guess."

Thankfully, the waiter brings out our two warmed-over mini pizzas, so I don't have to explain.

Ana takes a fistful of napkins and begins sopping up the pizza grease. "So is Roger your stepfather?" she asks.

Great. "Let's not call him that. Let's call him the guy

who swooped in last year and married my mom when she was vulnerable."

She looks at me. I assume. Actually, I still see nothing but her hood. "Do you spend much time with your real father?"

It's like I've been slapped. How could she ask that?

Wait. I never told her. She thinks my parents are divorced.

"No. I never see him."

"Ouch."

Ouch indeed.

"So what's this Roger like?"

If we were outside, I'd spit on the ground. "Big dumb jock. Always trying to get me to play football, be a starting quarterback or something."

Ana laughs, hard and loud. I glare at her. She doesn't apologize. Her teeth grin at me from the cavern of her hood.

"So is he really that big of a jerk?"

I roll my eyes. "I used to come home and I could relax in my own house. Now Roger won't leave me alone. He's always like . . ." I make my voice cartoonishly stupid "'Hey, Zak, wanna toss the pigskin around? Hey, Zak, wanna go shoot some pool? Zak, the regional bullfighting championships for Finland is on, wanna watch with me?'"

Ana has picked every pepperoni off her pizza. One

by one, they vanish into her hood. "Doesn't he realize you aren't into that sort of thing?"

"Hell if I care. All I know is, Mom only knew him a couple of months before he moved in. Why would she invite him to do that?"

Ana shrugs. "Because she's a woman."

"Of course she's . . ." And then it hits me. What she's implying.

"Ana!"

"Hear me out, Zak." She tosses off her hood. Her voice takes on that slightly bossy tone that irritated me back at the tournament. "I know you don't like to think of her that way, but it's true. You're just going to have to accept the fact that your mother needs a man in her life."

She had a man in her life. One who loved her more than anyone. Not like Roger.

Ana continues. "Now, I take it it's been a while since your father left? You'd really do yourself a favor by acting grown up about—"

"My father is dead, Ana!"

I said it. I almost never talk about that, but I said it. And now Ana's staring at me, stunned. Too late to stop now.

"He died a few years ago. Cancer. It was real slow and way too fast. And that's why I can't stand Roger. Yes, I know Mom needs him, but I don't care. She loved Dad.

She'd still be with him if . . . you know. You understand what that's like, Ana?"

Those few sentences took a lot out of me, physically. I almost never talk about my father, except in hushed, reverent tones with Mom. And Ana just sits there gaping at me and my attack of TMI.

Good one, Zak. Plop your dead father out on the table. That'll make this evening even more uncomfortable.

And then, much to my shock, Ana Watson reaches out and takes my hand in both of hers. Startled, I look up.

She's smiling at me. It's a sad kind of smile. She continues to grasp my hand. Not in what you'd call a romantic manner, but it's comforting just the same. We look into each other's eyes for a long moment, and it's . . . it's nice.

"Zakory? I'm sorry about what I said earlier, about you not knowing what pain is. You . . . hide it well."

Her smile widens and I return it. "You know me, always good for a laugh."

Ana lowers her eyes. "I don't know what it's like to lose your dad. But I did lose Nichole. So . . . I kind of understand where you're coming from. I mean, I know it's not as bad—"

I place my free hand on top of hers. "Loss is loss, Ana. I miss my father, you miss your sister. But listen. Just before we lost Dad—I mean, that very last week—he told me something that always stuck with me. Something that kind of helps me get through the rough patches."

Her hand tightens on mine. "What was it?"

A cardboard takeout box plops on the table next to us.

"We're closing up here, guys," says the waiter.

I release her hand. "I'll tell you later."

ANA

8:58 PM

The metal security gate closes on our heels as we leave the restaurant. I readjust my cloak as Zak texts someone.

I'm haunted by the look in his eyes when he told me about his father's illness. I would have bet money that nothing tragic had ever happened to that boy. I wonder how he buries it so well.

Same way I do, I suppose.

"Zak? It's almost curfew. Are we sunk?"

His face breaks into a confident grin. "No. Almost, but not quite. Just let me—"

"Oh, Huckleberry!" someone shouts from across the lobby.

I take no notice, but Zak has such a look of terror on his face, I think he must have spotted that Viking again. I follow his gaze, but all I see is some girl of about fifteen approaching us at a fair clip. She's very short, with hair dyed crimson and forced into pigtails. She has on a gingham dress and white-and-green-striped tights. She's painted large freckles on her cheeks and is wearing badly applied cherry-red lip gloss. A cloud of fruit-scented perfume surrounds her.

"Oh, Huckleberry!" she cries, in an affected falsetto. "You never called meeee!"

Duquette stands there like he's been Tasered. "Oh, um, hello, Jen."

Her eyes grow wide. "Tee-hee, who is Jen?" She jabs her index finger into her cheek and gouges a dimple into her jawline.

Zak swallows hard. "Sorry. Hello, *Strawberry*. Um, this is my friend Ana." He physically grabs me by both arms and positions me in front of him.

The girl curtseys. "I'm so *berry* pleased to meet you, Ana Banana! I can tell we're just going to be extra-special friends!" She then turns back to Zak. "You told me you weren't coming this year."

He glances at me, but I just adjust my hood. "Um, it was a last-minute thing."

"I'll never forget the pinkalicious time we had at

Con-demnation, Huckleberry. I was so berry blue when you never called me." She rubs a fist at the corner of her eye.

Zak doesn't say anything—he just stands there, repeatedly swallowing, his eyes round and terrified. While I find this whole spectacle hilarious, and while I'd really like to know the full story here, I decide to rescue him. I'll make fun of him later.

"Um, Strawberry? We hate to run, but Zak, er, um, *Huckleberry* and I have to find my brother. He's lost."

Strawberry clutches her hands to her chest and tilts her head. "Oh, golly, such gloomy news! How dreadful! Can I be of help?"

Any other girl, I would assume she's being sarcastic. Strawberry, I decide, is merely insane. I turn on my phone and find a picture of my brother. "Have you seen him?"

"Clayty Waity!" she shrieks, much to my utter shock.

"You've seen him?" asks Zak, equally surprised.

"He was in the karaoke room. We sang 'Summer Lovin'' together. I had such a pepperminty good time!"

That was Clayton, all right. He loved that movie. What a stroke of luck.

"Do you think he's still there?"

Strawberry shakes her head, releasing a cloying burst of fruit-flavored pheromones. "That was this afternoon.

But he said that he'd meet me at . . ." She suddenly stops.

"Yes?" Zak prods.

Strawberry's smile fades. "You know what I want, Duke." Her voice is now lower, normal. Almost sultry.

Duquette glances at me with the air of someone about to do something shameful. He then straightens his spine and smiles at Strawberry.

"You're as wonderful as a smile made of rainbows made of ice cream. You're as pretty as a daffodil in a field of gumdrops. You're as adorable as a kitten dressed like a bunny."

She pinches his cheek. "You're darling. Clayton said he was going to go to the Vampire Ball tonight."

"Thanks, Strawberry."

"Zak?" She's frowning now. "Call me, okay? Seriously." There's a touch of hurt in her voice.

He nods. "I will. I promise." He actually sounds sincere.

I clutch Duquette by the shoulder and lead him away. When I glance back, Strawberry grins at me and waves with her fingers. I don't wave back.

I wait to speak till we pass into a little alcove where a man sits selling CDs with his own picture on the case.

"Huckleberry?"

"I was lonely," Duquette mumbles. "I don't want to talk about it." The slight, dopey smirk on his face shows that he's willing to at least *think* about Strawberry.

What on earth was up with this place? First Baldy, now this. Were the rules in this place so backward that Zak was some kind of Adonis?

"So, when is this Vampire Ball?" I ask. "Wait, let me guess: midnight."

"You're catching on. Do you want to wait that long, or should we go get Warren to send out an APB?"

No, I can't get security involved, not after I pulled that fire alarm. Zak still doesn't realize that I triggered the sprinklers. Maybe I should make a full confession.

And suddenly Zak's head explodes in a haze of red mist. For a stunned moment, I think he's been shot. It's only when the plastic cup hits me on the shoe that I realize someone's dropped a drink on him from above.

One floor up, a mezzanine runs the length of the hallway. A girl with a bandage across her face stares down at us with fire in her eyes.

"What the hell!" barks Zak, squinting through the sticky syrup.

"You stupid bitch!" calls the girl, but not to Zak. "You almost broke my nose, dicking around with my bow! You still have it! Get back here! That's mine! Hey!" She's rushing for the stairs, but I'm already off and running. Zak's trucking after me, though at the moment, I only care about escape.

* * *

The men's room is every bit as noxious as I expect. Lines of guys snake behind the urinals, grunting and twisting as they unfasten their plastic body armor. No one seems to notice me by the sink.

Duquette has his head stuck under a tap. The water is red from Slushee residue. It's in his hair, his ears, his shirt, everywhere.

That was meant for me.

He turns off the water and sticks his head under the hand drier. It refuses to turn on. Sighing, he begins to dry his hair with paper towels.

"I must say, Ana, you have a tremendous knack for making friends. First Boba Fett, then the Viking, now death from above."

Don't forget a dozen pissed-off card players. "Sorry, Zak."

He removes his shirt and begins soaking it in the sink. I'm shocked at how pale he is, even for Washington in March. Again, I remember earlier when I saw him without his shirt. Or pants.

Zak wrings out his top, then holds it up and looks at it sadly. Wet, stained, and torn to shreds, there's not much left. He forces a chuckle.

"Maybe I should just go topless tonight. Give the ladies a treat." He flexes, his grin growing bigger. He has no real muscles, but he has, like, zero body fat. And he's not scrawny like a lot of the guys here, either, just lean. I wonder how he got that scar on his stomach.

"Ana? I was just kidding."

I suddenly rip my gaze away, embarrassed by how I've been staring. This con is doing strange things to my head. I try not to watch as Zak slides his mangled shirt back on, only to have it tear straight down the back.

"Great."

I scoot closer to him as someone comes over to wash his hands. "Don't you know anyone who could loan you something to wear?"

He shrugs his not-quite-broad shoulders. "Sure, but I'd have to find them and then go back to their room. Do we have time to mess with that?"

Time? That gives me an idea. I glance at my watch. "Actually, I may know someone who can help you. Where's the south wing?"

ZAK

9:47 PM

I don't see how Ana could possibly know anyone here, let alone well enough to loan me clothes. But after getting some directions from me, she leads me to a conference room where a panel is just ending. I read the schedule: *Silkscreen Your Own Shirts.*

"Ana! You came." The stocky guy who was packing up his equipment stops, his face lighting up at the sight of Ana.

How does she know this guy?

Ana pulls me roughly into the room. "Hi, Arnold. This is my friend, Zak."

He turns to me and studies my ragged, stained clothes.

"*Walking Dead?*"

"No, just tired, thanks."

He turns back to Ana. "I still have your blouse, you know."

What the holy hell?

"Thanks, Arnold. Do you think you could find a shirt for Zak?"

He looks at me with an intense dislike. I smile, trying to look macho and possessive of Ana, without coming off as a jerk and not too overboard, because I really do need a shirt. Luckily, I've practiced that expression like a zillion times.

"I'll see what I can do," Arnold replies with forced politeness.

Ana doesn't notice—she's looking at her phone. "Thanks. Hey, Duquette, we've missed curfew. I'm going to call Mrs. Brinkham, make up some excuse."

"What are you going to tell her?"

Ana's foot begins to jiggle as she thinks. "Um . . . we took a taxi to visit the museum of art, but he had a flat tire and we had to wait for a tow truck, and then the cab driver got in a fight with the tow truck guy—"

I cut her off with a raised palm. "A good lie is always the simplest. Tell her I took you and Clayton to a Japanese movie at that art theater near the hotel. It turned out to be a longer director's cut, so you're calling from the lobby to say we're running late."

She turns to Arnold with a shake of the head. "This guy makes lying an art form. And thanks for the shirt." She retreats to the back of the room to make her call.

When I face Arnold, he's looking at me like something he'd like to squish through his silk screen. I don't know how he knows Ana, but it's clear that his plans with her did not include me.

"You're an extra small, right? Now all my shirts cost thirty dollars."

"I got six bucks."

"Then I guess you're SOL."

We glare at each other for a long moment. Then, slowly our necks turn until we're both looking at Ana, who's having an animated phone conversation in the corner. Arnold mumbles something under his breath, and pulls a T-shirt out of a box.

"Here." He throws it at me. It's designed to look like a fiery red tuxedo jacket. Gratefully I pull it on.

"Thanks, pal. And if it makes you feel any better, I've been totally friend-zoned."

He smiles slightly. "She's taking you clothes shopping. Always a good sign."

I'd like to brag, but I know things are hopeless. "She's out of my league. I don't predict much luck on that front."

Arnold continues to pack up his equipment. "Yeah, well, they said we'd have moon cities by 1990. And no one predicted the internet or digital cameras. Sometimes the best guesses turn out wrong, and the most improbable theories come to pass."

I nod a thank-you and go to join Ana. He roughly clears his throat. When I turn around, he's holding his palm out to me. Sheepishly, I hand him my last six dollars.

Ana sits on a folding chair, staring at her phone. Arnold's theory on incorrect predictions aside, the look on her face does not foretell good news.

"Ana?"

She raises her head. "I talked to Mrs. Brinkham. My grandpa Watson just had a massive heart attack. They've taken him to the hospital here in Seattle."

Was this entire con cursed by God? Was it possible for two people to have such terrible luck?

I sit down by her side, trying to think of some consoling words. But, strangely, she doesn't look sad.

"The thing is, Grandpa Watson died ten years ago. And my other grandfather lives in Miami."

"Wait . . ."

She looks off in the distance. "It seems Clayton called Mrs. Brinkham earlier. Said that they rushed our grandfather to the emergency room, and that you

172

helped Clayton and me catch a taxi. Apparently you're such a gentleman that you're staying there with us until my parents can arrive. Mrs. Brinkham's very impressed with you."

I feel my hands ball into fists. "Little brother has been busy."

Ana nods. "Trying to work out an alibi for all of us. He saw you at the battle, didn't he? He knows we're here."

I stand and begin to pace. "That's a terrible cover story. Way too complicated. What if you'd said the wrong thing? Or what if Mrs. Brinkham calls your parents?"

Ana stands. "Well, she's buying it for now. Thanks to Clayton, we're safe for a bit."

"Remind me to thank him."

Ana lets out a long yawn. "Well, don't thank him too hard. At least not in the face."

My phone rings. It must be Brinkham. I pause to do some quick character development. I'm in a hospital waiting room, worried, overcaffeinated, and exhausted.

That actually won't be much of a stretch. I answer the phone, but it's not my teacher. It's James.

"Duke! Did you piss off some lunatic dressed like a barbarian?"

"Um . . . today? Let me think . . ."

"Don't be a douche. He's here in the hospitality suite, drinking a bunch of mead. He knows who you are, and he's ready to rip your arms off."

Oh, goody. "I've had worse."

"Duke! He's got friends with him. You have to leave the con before he finds you. Or lay low for a couple of hours. You can use Jerry's hotel room."

I thank him and hang up.

"Ana?"

She looks at me with her prim smile and her wide green eyes. And tempting as it would be to take her to a hotel room, I don't feel like cowering at the moment.

I'll cower very soon, but not just yet.

"I need some caffeine."

ANA

9:55 PM

Everything is spiraling out of control. It's not whether everything is going to come crashing down around me, but when. My own brother is going to get us in worse trouble than we've ever been in, and the only thing standing in the way is a guy who believes in hobbits.

Duquette and I lean against a wall, sipping sodas and watching the parade of humanity ooze by. For the first time I get a look at his ludicrous smoking jacket–T-shirt combo. I can't help but laugh.

He smiles back. "What really worries me is wearing a red shirt around here."

"I don't get it."

His smile broadens. "So much to teach you."

I look away. It's hard to concentrate when he's smiling like that. How can he be so calm? In a few minutes or hours, everything is going to fall apart. My parents will kill me and Brinkham will kill him. And yet, here he is, joking like he doesn't have a care in the world. Why is he even doing this? What's in it for him? Is this all just some macho plan to impress me?

He stretches and then subtly leans to the side, rubbing his back. I remember how many times he's been hurt tonight. How he told me about his father and I told him about Nichole.

He's being nice to me . . . because he's nice. Obnoxious and annoying and with a terrible excuse for a beard, but nice.

"Hey, Zak?"

He straightens up. "Yeah?"

"Um, I want to thank you for all you've done tonight. You know. Just in case I don't get a chance again, I wanted to tell you—"

He frowns. "Knock it off."

"Knock what off?"

"Talking like I'm about to charge an enemy machine gun nest. We're spending tomorrow together, remember? Not to mention next week at school."

I thought I'd get to keep seeing Nichole. Nothing is certain.

"Let me say it anyway, Zak. Thank you. For everything. A sane person would have abandoned me long ago."

He grins again with that same annoyingly optimistic attitude. "Call me Duke. Hey, um, Ana, maybe when all this blows over, you and I could . . ."

He then stops talking, though his mouth continues to move.

"What?"

"I said maybe you'd like to . . ." He trails off.

"Gosh, Zak, I'd love to *mumble mumble* with you."

He clears his throat, smiles, and starts again. "Maybe we could get together and do something a lot more low-key. A movie or grab a bite to eat or something."

His self-assured grin never falters, but the rest of his face is nervous. That makes me happy. Makes me feel superior to Baldy and Strawberry.

"Zak, thanks, but I can't. I'm not allowed to date."

He instantly tries to backpedal. "I didn't mean like that," he blurts unconvincingly. "Just a couple of *friends*"—he pauses, as if I'll object to being called that—"hanging out."

I shake my head. "Sorry. Mom and Dad have it in their head that if I do anything with a boy, he'll end up dragging me off to some den of depravity."

I think he's going to argue, but at that moment a

man in a suit of armor stumbles to his knees, yanks off his helmet, and proceeds to loudly vomit into it.

Zak looks away. "Kind of a paranoid attitude, don't you think?"

We laugh. Zak helps Sir Pukes-a-Lot to his feet. After he staggers off, the two of us just kind of stand there. I feel a chill in the air. Zak won't look at me.

Don't be like that. I'm sure I'm not the first girl to turn you down.

And it's not like I have any choice. Not like I could sneak out and see you. That's exactly what Nichole did.

It's not like I actually want a date with Duquette and his weird movies and whatever. To sit somewhere and talk. To hear about his family issues. To tell him more about Nichole. Have him help me get some things straight in my head.

"Zak?"

"Hmm?"

"Where do we go from here?"

As soon as I say it, I realize my words could be misinterpreted. I almost clarify that I'm talking about our search for my brother. But I don't.

Zak shrugs. I note that the gesture makes him grimace. I wonder how much physical pain he's hiding. "I dunno. I guess we show up at the Vampire Ball and hope Strawberry wasn't hallucinating again."

"And until then? Should we keep looking around?"

"I'd rather not. James called, said Conan has been drinking and rounding up a barbarian horde to mangle me."

I reach out and slap Duquette in the back of his stupid head. Hard.

"Ow!"

"You idiot! And you've just been hanging out here with me? What if that lunatic had showed up?" I reach out and swat him again.

"Stop that!"

"That guy tried to kill you! And now he's drunk? Do you have some kind of a death wish?"

He stares at me dumbly. I hit him again.

"What was that for?"

"I dunno. Violence in the Middle East. Global warming. Whatever." I smile sweetly. He rubs the back of his head and glares.

"Well, I wouldn't mind taking a load off until the dance. Somewhere no one will notice me. You wanna learn how to play Illuminati?"

"No."

"We could see a movie . . . no, wait . . ." He checks his phone. "Maybe you'd like to escort me to Mark and John's wedding. No one will bother us there, and there's going to be cake."

The very thought of attending the ceremony depresses me. They seem like nice guys, after all, but I can't sit around for an hour, watching two people I don't know get married, while my brother's wandering around, ruining my life.

"Zak, I—"

"Hey, it's that SOB who chased Eric's girlfriend!"

He's a gangly guy, dressed in furs and leggings. I don't recognize him, but he's staring at Zak with anger.

"Eric!" He turns and hollers down a hall. "Get over here! It's that guy who tried to kidnap Lisa!"

I look at Zak. "Friends of your Viking pal?"

He nods, still slouched on the bench.

"They wouldn't follow us into a wedding, would they?"

"Probably not."

We stand, bump fists, and then take off sprinting down the corridor.

We've made it back to where Zak first accosted Boba Fett. We either outran the horde or lost them at the start.

"I'd ask if we're underdressed, but something tells me we're not."

People are filing into the ballroom. Many are wearing dresses and suits, but others are more creatively attired. There are Ewoks, Stormtroopers, Klingons, and one girl in that Princess Leia bikini.

Zak offers me his arm. I take it.

We're greeted by two ushers, dressed as Mr. Spock and Obi-Wan Kenobi.

"Are you with the Horowitzes or the Danvers?"

"Friends of both," answers Zak.

The Vulcan directs us to an empty row near the back. "Live long and prosper."

"And may the Force be with you . . . always."

Zak looks a little uncomfortable, this might be a bit much, even for him. Soon we are seated.

"I haven't been to a wedding since Mom and Roger jumped the broom. You ever been to one?"

"No, I . . ." And then the memory hits me. The reminder slaps me in the face. That note from Nichole. Her beautiful handwriting on the save-the-date card.

"Hey, Ana, is something wrong?"

I shake my head. *Think of something else, Ana.*

"Hey?"

He won't shut up. He's sitting there, staring at me, all concerned, with those big brown eyes, wanting me to talk to him. He's probably the first person since . . . maybe since Nichole left, who's ever wanted to have a serious conversation about me. Just about me.

The idea shocks me so much that I almost smack him again, for lack of a better reaction.

"Zak, have you ever done anything you're really ashamed of?"

He opens his mouth, then stops. "Um, nothing I'm going to tell you about just yet."

"After Nichole left, I think Mom and Dad expected her to call, to beg to come home, to discuss adoption. But she never did. And the longer she was away, the more worried they got. And one day she sent us a letter, saying she and Pete had settled down in Olympia, and when our parents were willing to talk, they could come visit." I stop to take a breath. "And they refused. You see, they had a plan for Nichole, and her being a pregnant teen living with some guy wasn't part of it."

What I don't tell Zak is how I begged and begged my parents to at least let me go see her, but they were stone.

Even when their grandchild was born. Being right was still more important. Not just my parents, but to Nichole, too. They were all willing to tear up my family, rather than to budge one inch.

"At any rate, Nicole started writing to me. She didn't have a computer, but still managed to shoot me an email every so often. Things were tight for her, but I think she and Pete survived on love for each other and hate for everything else. And after my nephew was born, they kept asking me to come down. You can guess how my parents reacted to that.

"But last year . . . last year, they decided they were going to finally tie the knot. They'd saved some money, things were going well. So they sent me an invitation. Actually . . . Nichole called me. Asked me to be her maid of honor."

I'm breathing heavily, like you do when you're trying not to be sick. Trying to keep back the awful memories. But I have to tell him the whole story.

"And I didn't go, Zak. I told Nichole that Mom and Dad had a fit and wouldn't let me out of their sight."

It takes a great deal of willpower to face him. "Ever hear of anything more pathetic?"

As usual, he tries to cheer me up. "Ana, it's not your fault. You said yourself your folks aren't totally rational."

And I should leave it at that. Zak seems to like me for some reason. There's no point in telling him my shame.

But he told me about his dad. I owe him a painful memory.

"They didn't know about the wedding, Zak. They weren't invited. Nichole didn't want them there."

"So . . ." He leaves the syllable hanging.

"So if I were going, it would be on my own. Sneaking out and everything. I had it all planned out. I was supposed to go to a debate tournament that weekend. Instead, a friend of Nichole's was going to drop me off at the bus station. But, if I did that . . ."

As I struggle to put the next part into words, Zak finishes my thought for me. "Your parents would have found out about it. And you would have gotten in trouble for the first time." He's not smiling, but his eyes have a warm, sympathetic look.

"I would have had to face them, tell them I broke the rules, and deal with the fallout. And who knows, maybe that would have changed some things. Let them realize how stubborn they were being. But . . . I couldn't do it. I was too scared. I went to the tournament instead. Missed my sister's wedding. I still haven't met my nephew. All because I couldn't stand up to my parents."

There. I said it. I missed a once-in-a-lifetime family event because I didn't want to get yelled at.

Zak scratches his hair. "No one can blame you . . ."

"Don't sugarcoat it!" The ballroom is now very crowded and several guests look at me. "If you'd been in my shoes, you would have gone. You would have hitchhiked if you had to. I know I don't have any excuses."

Zak breaks eye contact and sits there, jiggling his legs for an annoyingly long time. He then turns and faces me. I brace myself for a namby-pamby answer that excuses my behavior. He turns to me.

"Ana, you're one of the most intelligent people I know, and I know a lot of smart people. And someday I'm going to see you on TV and say 'Hey, I know her, we used to . . .'" He trails off. "'Hang out.' But, Ana, your mother can't hold your hand when you're being sworn into the Supreme Court or whatever you're planning on doing. And if you just let your folks use you to win a fight with your sister, then you're not going to have much to look forward to. Maybe it's time for you to make a stand. Hell, Clayton's kind of made that decision for you."

Easy for him to say. He's not playing for the stakes I am. "Zak, I don't think you quite realize what it's like for me. Let me put it this way. You were obviously very close to your father. But did you ever really screw up? Ever just do something dumb and you knew there'd be hell to pay later?"

"Sure."

"And did you worry that he'd stop considering you as his son afterward?"

"Of course not . . ." He freezes, realizing where I'm going with this.

"Well, I think about that every day. I live in fear of a bad grade or a detention, or getting in a fight with them. And I'm almost done. After I graduate, things will be different. I'll be in college."

"So you'll just have to hang tight for a couple more months, I guess," says Zak, though not enthusiastically.

"Yeah." But even as I respond, I know I'm lying to both of us. Because even in college, I'll still be living at home. Going to a school that they picked for me. With a curfew and monitored phone calls, and parents who are waiting for me to screw up. Eighteen years of being a perfect kid, and college will just be another four years of high school.

I feel a tear start to form.

"Ana?"

"Shh. The ceremony is about to start." I place my hand on his.

We sit there, hand-in-hand. I don't know what Zak's thinking. Me, I'm thinking about the future. And Nichole. And how I've been blaming everything on my parents because it's easy. And about this not-bad-looking goober who takes me on adventures.

ZAK

10:25 PM

I blew it. I should have said something cool, but I completely screwed the pooch.

This is the best time I've ever had at a con, just because she's with me, and I keep expecting her to ask me to stop following her around, but she never does, and I want to help her with her family problems, but what the hell do you say to a story like that, and all the time I just want to tell her . . .

ALL WORK AND NO PLAY MAKES JACK A DULL BOY

ALL WORK AND NO PLAY MAKES JACK A DULL BOY

ALL WORK AND NO PLAY MAKES JACK A DULL BOY

With a great deal of self-control, I squash the panic attack. Something tells me I'm going to need to keep my head come midnight, when we get our last chance to capture Clayton.

An organ chord silences the whispering crowd. The musician breaks into the theme from *Star Trek*, then seamlessly flows into "The Imperial March."

"So nice when people can make a mixed marriage work," I whisper.

"Is one of them Jewish?"

"No, but John's a *Star Trek* fan and Mark likes *Star Wars* . . ."

"Shh."

John and Mark appear from opposite wings, wearing matching tuxes. They join hands at the front of the room and smile at each other. Normally, their physical demonstrations give me the heebie-jeebies (yes, I know, not that there's anything wrong with that, but it does, okay?), but tonight I'm touched by how much in love they obviously are.

The minister takes to the podium. Like all members of his sect, he carries an unlit briar pipe clenched in his teeth.

"Dearly beloved, we are gathered here tonight in the

sight of the United Federation of Planets and the Rebel Alliance to join these two men in holy matrimony." He says all this with the easy patter of a game-show host. The pipe never leaves his mouth.

"The good book says that what God has put together, let no man put asunder. Well, God couldn't make it tonight, but He sent me to close the deal."

That Bible verse rings a bell. Where had I heard it? Somewhere unpleasant. The Grand Inquisition? No . . .

Six months ago. The almost-empty chapel at the United Methodist Church. Reverend Weiss reading that same verse in front of my mother and Roger.

Mom looked very pretty, in a new dress and clutching some silk flowers. Roger, stuffed into the same shirt and tie he wore to work every day, and a jacket that was too small. They stared at each other like a couple of flirting drunks.

I sat in the first pew, sickened by the spectacle. And with the world's fakest grin smeared across my face like the jaw trap from Saw. There were only about fifteen spectators. Some people from Mom's and Roger's work, me, and my grandparents.

Not just my mom's parents. My dad's parents. The ones who had buried their son just a few years ago. And now they'd come here to watch his widow remarry. I hoped they'd avoid this tragic farce, but no, they flew out from L.A. just to be there.

I sat, uncomfortable in my new suit, silently bending a

prayer book and trying not to scream.

Two months she'd known him. Two months.

I waited for the minister to get to the part where you're supposed to say something if you object, knowing full well I'd keep my mouth shut. As it turned out, they apparently only say that line at sitcom weddings.

The minister officially blessed Roger's eternal position on our couch. I averted my eyes as Mom kissed him. The others applauded and we shuffled toward the receiving line.

I was the last one through. I kissed Mom on the cheek and nodded to Roger. He stopped me.

"Zak, I want to thank you for being here. This is the greatest day of my life, and, well, I hope I'll get a chance to get to know you more. I'd really like that."

I smiled. Then things seemed to go in slow motion as I pulled back my fist and clubbed him, full-force, in his fat, smiling face. He didn't expect it and went sprawling.

Mom screamed. The minister tried to grab me, but it was too late. I leaped on top of Roger and begin pummeling him in his mouth, his nose, his eyes. He moaned helplessly as blood poured from his ears, all the while the lifeless face of the altar Jesus stared down at me in mocking condemnation . . .

I should be a writer. That's a much better ending than what really happened, when I limply shook Roger's hand and left to get a slice of cake.

Ana jabs me with her bony elbow.

"You're growling," she whispers. "Be quiet."

I settle down.

The minister has reached a crescendo. "And do you, Mark David Danvers, take this man, to be your lawful—and by lawful I'm referring to the laws of the State of Washington and not the rest of the United States, not yet—wedded husband, to have and to hold, in sickness and in health, until death's icy hand comes for one of you?"

"I do."

"Then, by the power vested in me by whatever gods are tuned in, I now pronounce you married!"

They don't kiss. Instead, they hold hands and just stare at each other for a long moment.

"I love you," says John.

"I know," replies Mark.

Everyone sighs and they kiss.

I glance over at Ana to explain the vows, but she's dabbing a tear from her eye.

"God, you can tell they're in love. The way they looked at each other."

Yeah, I noticed too. That look of utter devotion.

Same joojooflopping way Mom and Roger looked at each other. *Still* look at each other.

I touch Ana's shoulder. "I need cake."

✱ ✱ ✱

We mill around the small buffet table. Ana is looking at one of the cakes, which has an image of the Death Star emblazoned on it.

"Is that supposed to be a moon?" she asks.

"THAT'S NO MOON!" everyone around her, myself included, loudly replies.

Ana's eyes narrow into the annoyed expression I'm so familiar with.

"Duquette, you're just a font of useless knowledge, aren't you?"

I'm a touch offended. "Said the captain of the quiz bowl team."

"That's different."

"How is it different?"

"It just . . . *is*," she stammers.

"Great comeback. Seriously, you're as bad I am. I watched you at the tournament today—you know more random facts than I do. Face it, you wouldn't do quiz bowl if you didn't love trivia."

She's quiet for a long time. Did I say something wrong?

"I hate quiz bowl, Zak," she whispers. "Always have." She laughs, but she's not kidding.

"What?"

"I hate it, Zak. Every week I waste hours practicing and memorizing pointless information, and now I've dragged my brother into it. I've dragged *you* into it!"

I'm too dumbfounded to be articulate. The girl who chastised me earlier about how important the tournament was . . . she didn't want to be there either?

"But you're so good at it! Brinkham thinks you walk on water."

She snorts. "I do it because it looks good on a scholarship application. They want people with a lot of interests. That's why I do it. Same with archery. It could have been fun, but now it's just another stupid thing I have to do." She reaches out to touch the bow slung over her back, but stops. "It doesn't matter. It'll all be over in May. So how about you? What are your plans after graduation?"

I shrug, more interested in her revelations. "The junior college, I guess."

"You guess?" She has a look of horror on her face. "You haven't applied yet?"

"What's the rush? It's community college. Not like there's a waiting list."

"But classes might fill up. Zak, you have to take care of all that."

"I'll get to it sometime." *Geez, how'd we get on this subject? I feel like I'm on a date with Mrs. Brinkham.*

I see just a flash of Ana, the quiz bowl captain. "Are you kidding me, Duquette? And don't you have to meet with an advisor? And what about your books? And getting your transcript in?"

"I'll look it up when we get back. Hey, where did that guy get the cocktail wieners?"

Ana flicks one of the mints off my plate. With an archer's precision, she nearly lodges it up my nostril.

"Ouch."

"Focus, Jedi. What are you planning on studying?"

"Computers."

"More specifically?"

Now I'm on a date with my mom. "C'mon, Ana, why all the school talk?"

"Why? Because tonight I saw this really interesting guy fight a samurai, crawl through the ventilation system, and beat a bunch of excellent quiz bowl players without trying. And I'd hate to see him end up some sad, overweight, middle-aged fanboy who never did anything with his life."

"I'll turn into a happy overweight fanboy, thank you very much." Like the two grooms, I'm not at all ashamed of my lifestyle. So why is Ana's disdain rattling me?

"Duquette, are you that anxious to live with Roger for another couple of years? Have you even looked at other colleges?"

"Sorry, Ana, but the scholarship committees aren't exactly banging down my door."

She cocks her head. "Listen. Did the fire alarms just go off?"

"I don't think so."

"Oh. I could have sworn I heard something going *eeee-eeee-eeee*," she says, imitating a high-pitched whine.

"What do you want from me, Ana?"

She steps closer to me. Very close. I hear mints tumbling off my plate, but I can't look away from Ana's face. I notice, for the first time, the little lines around her eyes. Laugh lines. Or, more likely, stress lines.

"Duquette, look around you. Any one of these people might wind up in the newspaper one day, but with them, it'll say something like 'hundreds of cats' or 'arrested for stalking.' You, I expect a little something more than the junior college and a cubicle."

"Look who's talking. I'm guessing you could do a lot better than going to U Dub. So which one of us is really slumming it?"

I think I've pushed things too far, but she just tosses her hair. Or tries to. It's so kinky it doesn't really flip.

"Here's the thing, Zak . . ."

She then takes her wedge of cake and shoves it into my mouth. I have to take a drink to keep from choking.

"It's almost midnight. Our last chance to find my brother. C'mon."

Coughing and sputtering, I swallow the cake. I still

have a thing or two I want to say.

Ana turns and looks at me. And winks.

Just a little thing. She probably doesn't mean anything by it.

But I close my mouth and follow her.

ANA

12:07 AM

Dozens of stretchers line this hall. At first I think it's fallout from the earlier battle, but then I see the signs: VAMPIRE BALL BLOOD DRIVE.

"That's clever," I tell Zak, impressed at the unexpected charity.

"What is?"

"You know, having a blood drive with the vampires. Nice connection."

Zak stops walking. After a moment, he smiles. "You know, they've been doing that as long as I've been coming here, and I never made the connection. Huh."

I wait until I'm at his back and then facepalm. For

an intelligent guy, Duquette can be amazingly dense at times. If he'd just stop and think occasionally, and didn't always make a joke out of every stupid thing, and shaved and dressed up a little . . . oh, it's hopeless.

We enter the ballroom. It's tiny, no bigger than the room where we met Arnold. The lights, of course, are down very low. In a dim corner, a DJ plays something slow and Hungarian. The vampires lurk in shadowy corners, dressed in nineteenth-century finery: men in top hats, ruffled collars, and suspenders; women in ball gowns with corsets that jam their cleavage up under their chins. Everyone is wearing eye shadow and face powder to make them appear undead (at least, I'm assuming it's makeup). To my relief, no one is sparkling.

It's impossible to recognize anyone in the dim light. "You see anyone who could be Clayton?" I ask Zak.

"Yeah, but I'm not about to make that mistake twice. Let's hang out by the door and keep our eyes open."

The undead begin to pair off. They remind me of wraiths, smokily waltzing in the gloom. People glance at us. With my cloak and Zak's T-shirt, we're kind of underdressed. Again, I don't fit in.

"Do you come to this every year?" I ask Zak.

"No." For once, there's no elaborate story. We continue to stand there, quietly and awkwardly.

Another slow song comes on. People shift partners.

They silently move in time to the beat, with a rustle of silk and the tap of spatted shoes. Kind of reminds me of a high school formal.

Not that I've ever been to one. There was that time last year, when Landon asked me to the junior prom, and I told him no. I had no choice. I wouldn't have been permitted to go to a dance with a date. So he asked Sonya, and the rest is history.

"Hey, Ana, check it out."

A chubby girl in a loosely laced corset stands near the door. Even in the dim light, I recognize her florescent red hair. Strawberry. She's lurking near the entrance with her hands clasped in front of her. When a boy enters the dance her face breaks into a smile, then instantly collapses.

"She's still waiting for your brother. Did he stand her up?"

I knew it wasn't going to be this easy to find Clayton. "So if he's not coming here, where is he?"

Duquette isn't listening—he's still staring at his ex. "She looks so sad. Maybe I should go ask her to dance." He takes a step away from me.

Oh, no you don't.

I snake my arm out and grab him by the wrist. Heedless of his bruised ribs, I pull him toward me. I place his hand on my side. Then I smile at him.

Zak smiles back, but he looks kind of frightened as well. "Or I could stay here and dance with you." He takes my other hand and begins to lead.

It's immediately apparent he doesn't have a bit of rhythm. He kind of swirls us around the dance floor in time to some much faster beat than the waltz coming out of the speakers. He grins at me and I smile back.

What the hell made me grab him like that? I guess I didn't want him to go dancing off with Strawberry when we're supposed to be finding Clayton. I need to keep him focused on the search, not remembering the good times he had with the living baby doll.

Speaking of which, I glance around the ballroom, trying to see if Clayton ever arrived. Zak's twirling is giving me whiplash and my longbow keeps poking me in the side of the head, but I see that Strawberry is still alone. I notice Arnold is here. He bows to a woman in a huge domino mask, who allows him to take her hand. There's a woman from the wedding. A guy from the SCA battle. But no Clayton.

Zak bumps into another dancer and lets out a groan. I'm reminded how physically grueling this evening has been for him.

"Do you want to stop, Zak?"

"I'm fine. Just a minor spinal injury."

Maybe I shouldn't have asked him to dance. Maybe

he isn't enjoying himself.

The music ends and Zak slowly pulls away. When the next song starts, I wonder if he'll want to dance again. Or maybe he'd rather keep searching for Clayton. It's his choice. What do I care?

"Mind if I cut in?"

It's Gypsy, that bald-headed girl from registration. She's now wearing a dress that shows off her willowy neck, the cute freckles on her shoulders, and her ample cleavage. All things I don't have.

And I don't have Zak, either. She's leading him away. At least she's trying to. I think he's momentarily stunned.

"C'mon, Duke, you promised me a dance." Already, she's trying to put her arms around his neck. She doesn't look in my direction.

And so what if he wants to dance with Uncle Fester? She's known him a long time, and it's obvious she has a thing for him and I'll be damned if I'm going to just let her waltz off with him.

I've elbowed my way between them before I lose my nerve.

"Excuse me!" snaps Chrome Dome.

I refuse to back down. "You're excused. But I'm with Zak at the moment. Have a good evening."

Her forehead wrinkles all the way to the back of her neck. She's about to say something, but instead we both turn to Zak. This is his decision.

For a horrible moment I think he's going to choose the human bowling ball, and I've just made a fool of myself. Instead, to my great relief, he takes my hand. "Another time, Gypsy."

We're back on the dance floor. He's grinning. I fully expect him to make a wise-ass comment about having two women after him. But he just smiles. Wow, that smile.

I do a quick survey of the room, but my brother's still not here. Strawberry's gone, too. I look back at my partner. He's still smiling. I should tell him we should leave. I should tell him we're wasting our time here.

Instead, I keep dancing. Only we're not really dancing. We're both just kind of standing here, slightly swaying, our faces not too far from each other.

Zak moves slightly closer to me. I can just feel his hot breath on my mouth.

Oh, God, he's going to kiss me.

Wow. That smarmy, self-centered jackass. Just because I let him dance with me a couple of times, he thinks he has the right to smash his lips up against mine?

But . . . he doesn't. He just kind of hovers there for a minute, then leans away.

Oh, God, he's NOT going to kiss me. Here we are, together on the dance floor, me chasing away other girls, and now he's just going to stand there. What the hell?

Okay, maybe I did slap him and scream at him and

call him an idiot. But that was *hours* ago.

He moves closer again, his smile shy.

C'mon, Zak. Make up your mind.

Our noses are nearly touching. His hand moves a strand of hair back behind my ear.

What are you waiting for, Duquette?

And he takes the plunge. It's awkward and it's beautiful.

My first kiss.

ZAK

12:30 AM

She let me kiss her. Son of a gun, Ana Watson is letting me kiss her.

Oh, hell, she's kissing me back. We're kissing.

It's so warm and soft and beautiful. I never want it to end.

Speaking of which . . .

I pull away before things become too awkward. I have to take this slow, I can't risk coming on too strong. Not with Ana. I can't risk scaring her off.

She bites her lower lip and ducks her head, while still looking up at me shyly. She's utterly cute. I wish I could tell her that. I wish I could tell her that I think she's amazing. I wish I could run my fingers through that forest of frizzy dark hair. I wish I could kiss her again.

Instead, I lay my head next to hers and we stand there, not dancing, holding each other.

To think, I almost spent the evening playing cards.

Should I say something? Savor the moment? Tell Ana we need to keep looking for her Clayton? Tell Ana that I feel . . . what?

Someone's phone rings. Ana pulls away from me with an apologetic smile, which collapses when she sees who the text is from.

"It's my brother!"

We both lean in to read the message:

LOOK BEHIND YOU

We slowly turn toward the door, scanning the room for Clayton. I don't see him. Just a bunch of vampires. I notice Arnold, the T-shirt guy, attempt to kiss his dance partner, and I chuckle when she leans away. And there's Kevin, a con security guy. And . . .

Uh-oh.

Kevin. He worked the Mazes and Monsters game. Ana gasps. She pulls her hood up over her head, but I'm sure we've been spotted.

"That guy was at the tournament," she hisses. "He must have seen me pull the alarm."

He's wheezing his way over to us, but there's only one door and he's blocking our exit.

Ana is attempting to hide behind me. Geez, if she thinks her parents are going to flip out because she lost Clayton, imagine what they'll do if she gets busted by the con police.

Do something, Duquette! Think!

No, that always gets me into trouble. Time to act.

Arnold is next to me. He's talking to his dance partner, a masked woman who seems to be trying to edge away. I lean in and put an arm around both their shoulders.

"Um, hello?" says the woman, with a pronounced Indian accent.

"You!" hisses Arnold, who has clearly had enough of me.

I glance over at Ana. Kevin has cornered her. She's rapidly shaking her hood. I'm out of time.

I remove my hand from the girl's shoulder. "Arnold, forgive me. It's for the greater good."

I then drive my fist into his flabby gut. He collapses to his knees with an agonized wheeze, a disbelieving look on his face.

It's the first time I've ever violently punched anyone, and I feel terrible. But my ploy is working. Half the people in the ballroom turn to look at us. Including Kevin.

Arnold rises to his feet, a dangerous look on his face.

I may have landed my only blow of this fight. But the commotion will be enough to distract Kevin and give Ana a chance to escape.

Arnold raises his fists. I'm going to have to let him have a free punch. Hopefully it won't be in the nose.

"Get your hands off of him!"

I don't see her face, but judging from the accent, it's Arnold's date. A second later, she leaps onto my back, raking my cheeks with her nails. I stagger forward. Arnold's not expecting this, and my forehead connects with the bridge of his nose. He yelps and tumbles backward into the DJ's table. The music skips, then stops.

"Fight, fight, fight!" I scream as the girl pulls me to the ground by my hair. Our flailing legs trip up several children of the night. People shout, confused. Someone hits the lights, transforming the smoking European tomb into conference room B11. Kevin is waddling in my direction. Ana stands indecisively near the doorway. I gesture for her to leave. I try to stand, but someone leg tackles me. Down I go. Arnold, his date, Kevin, and some seriously pissed-off vampires tower over me.

And I left my garlic in my other pants.

"Hey, lady! Put your shirt back on!"

It's Ana's voice. Arnold and Kevin turn toward her.

"Both of you girls! It's not that kind of con! Don't take off your clothes!"

I scuttle backward like a crab. Ana is standing by the door. Every man in the room is shoving toward the exit, desperate to see what Ana is describing. As soon as Kevin is distracted, I rush over to her. Clutching hands, we . . .

We have nowhere to go. The crowd is blocking the exit. And as soon as they realize there's no orgy going on in the hallway, we're sunk.

"Come with me if you want to live."

A short man in a trench coat has appeared behind us. His voice has a buzzing, mechanical quality. He's wearing a top hat, which obscures his face.

"What?"

He places an artificial voice box against his neck. "This way. Now." Without waiting to see if we're following, he rushes behind the DJ's chair and pulls back a decorative curtain.

There's a hidden door marked HOUSEKEEPING.

There's no time to think. I yank it open and practically drag Ana through with me. Just before the door swings shut, our guide tips his hat to me.

Clayton. That little creep was watching us the whole time.

Ana is momentarily stunned by the sight of her brother, but I know we don't have a moment to lose. Leading her by the hand, I go tearing through a maze of stacked chairs. It takes me a few seconds to get my bearings, but I finally lead us to a stairwell. Down we go.

After three flights we reach the subbasement. A heavy door blocks the way. I approach the keypad and enter the code: 12345.

We enter the Bowels. The Pit. Shelob's Lair. The Undercomplex.

Actually, it's nothing but a lot of storage cages, the generator, access to the plumbing, and other mundane crap. But looking into the emergency-lit tunnels and cubbies, it does seem kind of magical. I remember the countless games of flashlight tag, live action role-playing, and scavenger hunts I've participated in down here.

Ana removes the hood. "Are we safe? No one followed us, right?"

I listen, but the only sound is the buzzing of the generator, interrupted by a trickling sound when someone flushes upstairs.

"We're fine."

"Well, what about Clayton? Do you think that guard—"

"No. He'll be okay."

We sit on a bench. I rub my neck where Arnold's date scratched me. When I pull my hand away, my fingers are dotted with blood.

"Pretty fast thinking there, Ana. Nothing empties a room like the prospect of a naked girl."

"I saw it in a movie once." She stares straight ahead, holding her bow between her knees.

"I thought we were dead back there. When—"

She turns to me, frowning. "Why did you punch him?"

"Who?"

"Arnold!" Her voice is screechy, angry. "What the hell did you hit him for?"

"You were about to get arrested! I had to create a distraction!"

"By beating up that poor guy?" Her voice is judgmental. "What the hell, Duquette?"

"Excuse me? I did that to save your ass! What do you care about him, anyway?"

She opens her mouth but doesn't say anything for a moment, as if she can't believe what I just said. "He's a nice guy. He gave you that shirt, and that's how you repay him?"

"He'll live. I made him look like a brawler in front of that girl."

Ana shakes her head. "Not everyone's a meathead like you."

"So I'm a meathead now? And hey, while we're on the subject, why the hell does he have your blouse?"

Ana turns away from me. "Just don't talk to me. Just . . . don't."

She folds her arms and I'm looking at her back. I

almost get up and storm off. Almost.

Really, Ana Watson? After all we've been through, you're going to get pissy now? Who cares about Arnold? Does it even matter that I did that for you? You think I want to be hanging around in this basement with you? You act like you like me, you act like you hate me. Do you know how nervous I was when I kissed you? I think I deserve better. I think—

Slowly, without facing me, Ana's hand creeps toward me. It stops, halfway across the bench, palm up.

Does she want me to touch her? I can't see her face. What do I do? I wish I had a D20 to roll to help me decide.

Risking everything, I place my hand on top of hers. Still not facing me, she closes her fingers around mine.

"Ana?"

"Shut up, Duquette. I'm not done being angry with you."

We just sit there in the silence, holding hands, not talking, not looking at each other.

But holding hands.

Over the years, I've taken eight girls down here to the basement, or equivalent places at other conventions. Eight for eight at first base, and one time, second.

Sitting here on this bench, with Ana Watson pissed off at me but gripping my fingers . . . it's better. So much better.

ANA

1:16 AM

It's not supposed to end like this. I can't stop thinking about that kiss out on the dance floor. Yes, I have
nothing to compare it to, but that moment with Zak—
it was so unexpected and confusing and great. And
instead of being able to enjoy the moment, instead of
being able to relax for one second, that stupid security
guard barges in, Zak turns into a barbarian jerk, my
brother shows up dressed like Mr. Hyde, and now we're
hiding in a dungeon.

Because that's how Ana Watson's first kiss goes. Of course.

It would be nice to stay down here for a while, to
avoid the police, the Vikings, Boba Fett, the Tribute, and

Cyrax, but it's not feasible. Besides, I'm still angry with Zak for punching Arnold. I release his hand.

"Zak? We've missed curfew."

He nods grimly.

"Do you have money for a cab?"

"No. You?"

I shake my head. "Do you know anyone who could drive us back to the hotel?"

He nods. Of course he does. Because he's Zak Duquette and he always has a plan.

"I know a guy. He's not here, but he always gets up crazy early. He'll take us."

I stand. Zak follows.

"This way, Ana. The tunnel goes under the building. It'll take us back to the lobby. I'll call from there."

We manage to walk silently for thirty seconds before Zak opens his mouth again. "You know, all is not lost. There's actually an easy way out of our situation."

I want to believe him. I want to think that Zak Duquette has a solution to our dilemma that doesn't involve time travel or constructing robot doppelgängers.

"Yes?"

He grins at me, his old smarmy smile. "It's so easy, I can't believe we didn't think of it earlier. I'll just tell Mrs. Brinkham this was all my fault."

"What?"

His smile widens. "It's perfect. I'll just say I dragged Clayton here and then you followed me to try to get him to come back. She'll believe that. It'll cover you and your brother. Problem solved!"

I swear, I almost slap him again.

"Duquette, are you stupid?"

His face falls.

"Do you honestly think I'm going to blame you for this mess? Do you think I'd just throw you to the wolves because it's easy?" He must really not think much of me.

Zak shrugs. "Listen, Ana, you've been telling me all evening about how your parents are going to crucify you. Well, this way they won't. My mom won't care if I get in a little trouble, and if I fail health, so what? It's not like I'm going to Harvard."

I try to grab him by his lapels, but they're just painted on his shirt. "Do you think that I think that you think—" I take a breath and start over. "You think I have that little regard for you? That you're not important?"

His face takes on a confused expression.

"You're an idiot, Duquette, but this is not your fault. And when we see Mrs. Brinkham, I'm going to face her, look her right in the eye"—I smile weakly—"and blame everything on Clayton."

He starts to say something, but I turn and walk away. His request to play the hero really rattled me. Does he honestly see me as that self-serving? Does he really believe all he's done for me tonight means so little?

I slow down and let him catch up. We glance at each other and quickly look away. God, just when I'm starting to tolerate him, everything goes nuts.

Maybe I'll get to see him again. Not at school, but maybe I can take him up on his offer to hang out some-time. I'll just explain things to Mom and Dad. They'll understand.

Yeah, that's a very probable outcome. About as real-istic as one of Zak's movies. Whatever we almost had, it's gone.

Which is too bad, because he occasionally has a charming, heroic side.

"Jesus, look at this damn mess!"

Sometimes.

Zak's pointing to a pile of fast-food bags and other trash someone has left all over the floor. A Washingcon pamphlet shows that the mess was not made by a hotel worker.

"Raised in a barn." To my surprise, he kneels down and begins gathering up the garbage.

"Zak, leave it. That's not your job."

He continues stuffing wrappers into a McDonald's bag. "Ana, Washingcon isn't exactly your typical con-vention. Warren tells me that the owners here would be happy if we stopped coming. And if they get enough complaints, they'll have an excuse to kick us out. Then we'd have to meet in another city, like Portland. I'd really hate that." He overstuffs the bag and the greasy bottom tears out.

I bend down to help him. "This convention really is the center of your universe, isn't it?" I shudder to think what kind of Faustian bargain Brinkham forced out of him to get him to miss this.

Zak gathers the trash into a big, greasy ball and stuffs it into a bin. "When my father died," he says, with his back to me, "I didn't leave the house for two months, except to go to school. Sometimes not even then. But when Washingcon came around, I went. It helped me get on with things. This . . . this is my happy place." He faces me. "Stupid, huh?"

I don't think it's stupid at all. "I wish I had a happy place."

We look at each other for a long moment. I think we're both waiting for the other one to make some sort of a move. Zak eventually winks, then gestures to a brown vinyl backpack that someone has forgotten on the ground.

"Check it out." He picks something from the floor next to the bag. It's the stub of a hand-rolled "cigarette." That explains the slightly sweet odor in the air.

"Have you ever smoked one?" I ask.

He grins. "Once. Last year. Down here, actually."

I'm not sure how I feel about that. "What was it like?"

"I . . ." He laughs. "I coughed so hard I threw up."

I immediately kiss him. Quickly, but hard.

"Whoa!" he says, staggering slightly. "What was that for?"

Because you didn't lie and say, "Dude, I was so effing wasted!" like a lot of guys would have.

I reach out and lightly punch his shoulder. "No reason."

"Hey!" barks a voice. "What are you doing down here?"

A man in coveralls is staring at us from a side corridor. He's young but has weather-beaten features, like someone who's lived too hard too quickly. His beady eyes regard us with suspicion.

"Forgot my bag," says Zak with bored confidence. He picks up the abandoned backpack, takes my hand, and leads me onward.

Zak guides me through a twisting, turning back corridor until we come to a freight elevator. It's a short ride back to the first floor, and we giggle the whole way. Not at anything specific. I think we're both giddy from almost getting caught, the lack of sleep, and, well, other things.

Soon, we're back in the main building. Though

there are a lot fewer people now, the party is seriously heating up. Literally. There's so much body heat, it's like five hundred degrees out here. Men have stripped off their shirts. So have women, revealing their corsets, underthings, and armor. A man in an executioner's mask pours out liquor from a wooden keg into a satyr's leather drinking vessel.

Zak nudges me. In a secluded corner, two con-goers lean against the wall, seriously making out. I let out a gasp when I recognize Arnold and the masked girl from the dance.

"Told you it would work out for him. I made him look like a wounded warrior."

"Oh, shut up."

He laughs. "Let me drop this off at the front desk," he says, hoisting the small backpack.

I look wistfully at my bow. "You should get rid of this too, I guess."

Zak's digging through the bag, thumbing through crumpled stacks of graph paper.

"What are you doing?"

"Trying to find out who this belongs to. Maybe I know 'em."

It wouldn't surprise me. If the pope showed up here and shook Zak's hand, I think everyone would be asking, "Who's that with Duke?"

"Hey, Zak, are you going to call your friend about a ride soon?"

"Yeah, I'll . . ." He stops speaking, mesmerized by something in at the bottom of the bag.

"What?"

His pasty face grows even paler. Something is upsetting the unflappable Zak Duquette. Good lord, there's not a human head in there, is there?

"Zak?"

He doesn't answer. Doesn't look at me. I gingerly peak over the lip of the backpack.

Nestled among some old shirts is a plastic bag, filled with fine white powder. It's not large, but it's large enough.

It's funny, but I don't freak out. It's like I'm watching some movie, and it's two other people who've just made a serious error in judgment.

Zak obviously doesn't see it that way. The pack begins to tremble in his hands.

"Ana, that's cocaine!" he loud-whispers.

"You don't know that."

"What the hell else could it be?"

"I don't know. Heroin?"

This does not calm Duquette down. He stands there, staring at the bag in his hand, sweat beading on his forehead. I've never seen him lose his cool like this, and it doesn't do much to keep me relaxed.

"Ana, do you know what will happen if someone catches me with this shit?"

"They're not going to catch you." Clearly, I'm going to have to take control of this situation. I pick up the stray clothes and papers from the floor and stuff them back in the satchel. Zak stands rigid, his eyes wide.

"Prison, Ana! I can't go to prison! Do you know what happens to guys like me in there? You've seen *Shawshank Redemption*, right?"

"Duquette, get a grip! Right now."

He stops trembling, but he's clutching the bag so tightly his knuckles grow white. I finish repacking and fasten the top.

"This doesn't concern us. See the registration desk over there? Just go over to them, tell them someone forgot this in the bathroom, and it'll be their problem. Not ours. Got it?"

He just stares at me. I shake him. "Zak! Just go over there and leave the bag. This isn't our problem. It'll be like we never saw it. It never happened."

"Right," he squeaks. As subtly as a man carrying a live bomb, he turns to go.

And then two dark hands snake out and grab us by the shoulders.

"Come with me. Both of you."

ZAK

1:46 AM

I know it's Warren, even before I turn around and see the mask. And it's pretty obvious what this is all about.

"In the office. Now." He's not happy.

Ana looks sick, but I'm actually kind of happy he found us. Warren and me, we go way back. With a little schmoozing, a little reminder of the times Warren himself bent the rules, I'll have Ana off the hook in no time. Then we can ditch this bag and end this ridiculous night.

He takes us through a door marked SECURITY and into a tiny room lined with TV monitors. Ana grimly takes a seat. I flop down next to her. Warren sits opposite, staring at us with his unreadable mask.

Might as well get this over with. "So what's this all about?" I ask, somewhat distracted by the sight of a harem girl dancing on camera three.

"Your friend pulled a fire alarm at the Mazes and Monsters tournament, Zakory. Don't bother denying it, the security cameras captured the whole thing."

I smile, as if we're all going to have a good laugh about this one day. "Warren, Warren, Warren. I seem to remember a certain fellow—I'm looking at him right now—who once peed on a police cruiser. We've all done crazy things at con."

I swear, his alien eyes narrow for a second.

Unflapped, I continue. "Now, Cyrax was getting in Ana's face. He wouldn't let her leave the room. She kind of panicked, but can you blame her? If anyone should be in trouble, it's Cyrax. Right, Ana?"

She doesn't answer. She just stares at her lap. Warren says nothing. I wonder why everyone's so serious.

"C'mon, Warren. It was just a couple of sirens. No harm, no foul."

He doesn't respond. Instead, he lifts a remote and points it at a monitor. There's a grainy, black-and-white picture of the card tournament. I recognize Cyrax. I'm pleased to see Ana drive a fist into his gut.

"See! He's not letting her leave. Not her fault. Not . . ."

Video Ana reaches out and pulls the fire alarm. Cyrax backs off, Ana runs . . .

Why are all the card players jumping to their feet? What's falling from the ceiling?

Warren turns to me. "When Ana pulled the alarm, she set off the sprinklers."

I feel like I've been kicked in the gut. I remember James carefully sliding his cards into their plastic sleeves, only ever taking them out for battle. I turn to my companion.

"You left out that detail, Ana." I can't believe she didn't tell me the whole story. She made it sound like a stupid misunderstanding. All those cards. Not to mention the rugs, the tables, everything.

She looks up at me, an agonized, guilty expression on her face. "I'm sorry, Zak. I didn't know the sprinklers would go off."

"You should have told me!"

"Duke, be quiet," says Warren. "I'll deal with you later."

I'm suddenly irritated by his authoritative tone. If he wants to be taken seriously, he could take that mask off.

Ana is cowed, but not beaten. "I'm sorry. I really am. But that guy wouldn't let me leave and no one was helping me. I panicked, but I had no choice."

"You could have called security. Miss Watson, the

convention center will now withhold our two-thousand-dollar security deposit, and we'll probably end up owing more than that. Not to mention the hundreds of cards that were ruined. Not to mention there was no winner to the tournament. Not to mention—"

I bang my fist down on the desk. While I'm not pleased with Ana's half-truths, I have to take her side. "Not to mention, that idiot was holding Ana hostage! Would you listen to yourself? She had to do something to get away!"

"Zak," warns Ana, gesturing to the bag of contraband on my lap. "Calm down."

I take a deep breath. I know Warren's in a world of hurt over those sprinklers, but surely he doesn't plan to sacrifice Ana.

He shakes his mask. "I'm sorry. I'm going to have to turn Ana over to the authorities. It's out of my hands."

"But—"

"It's out of my hands," emphasizes Warren.

Ana has gone absolutely pale. I worry that she's in shock. Her green eyes are horrified circles. All her nightmares are coming true.

Warren has the evidence against my friend right on the screen. He's going to call the cops. They'll take her downtown. They'll call her parents.

Ana bows her head, probably picturing this, and

worse. Plus, on top of everything, we'll lose the quiz bowl tournament later.

Game over, man. Game over.

"Warren," I begin. "C'mon. Old times."

Because of that stupid mask, I can't read his expression.

"I'm sorry, Duke, but this isn't about you. If you want to help your friend, call her parents and let them know what's happening."

Ana looks like she's about to faint. I think that's what pushes me over the edge.

"You wanna call the cops, Warren? Fine. You do that. But when you do, I'm going to show them this little surprise I found in the basement."

My dramatic actions take a hit when I have to dig through a bunch of old clothes before I can retrieve the Baggie. I throw it onto the desk. The package of white powder skids across and lands just in front of Warren. He jumps back in his chair, startled, then points his dead alien eyes at me.

"Duquette!" screams Ana, in horror.

"How do you like that? Found it downstairs. That's worth over five thousand." Assuming *Grand Theft Auto* was telling the truth. "Someone's probably going nuts trying to find that. So let's call the police. I'd love to show them what goes on here."

Warren keeps shifting his gaze—I think—between me and the bag in front of him. Ana just sits in her chair.

"They'll turn this place upside down, trying to find out who that belongs to. They'll bring in the dogs. Bust every underage drinker and dope smoker in this place. You think the convention center people are pissed now? Wait till they stage a huge friggin' drug raid. You think they'll ever let us come back?"

"Calm down, Duke."

"No, Warren. You wanted to make a big deal out of this, well, I'll make a bigger deal. Maybe I tell the cops there's more where this came from. Maybe they'll search every room in the hotel. Maybe I'll call the news stations, let 'em report on the big drug raid." I pause to wipe the saliva off my chin.

"Duke!" barks Warren.

"Choice is yours. Ana walks, or I shut down Washing-con. Maybe for good."

Wow. Did I really just say that?"

"Zak, don't . . . ," says Ana, but I cut her off with a slashing movement. It's all down to Warren. I hope I haven't pushed things too far.

After a long pause, he puts the Baggie into a drawer. "Both of you. Get out of my sight." His voice is wrathful. "I want you gone from here by sunrise."

We both stand, trembling.

"And don't come back. Either of you. Not tomorrow, not next year, not ever."

Wow. Lifetime ban from Washingcon. They said it could happen, but like the girl who lost her arm out the school bus window and the boy who only got coal from Santa, I always assumed that was just a story to scare children.

Ana just sits there, slightly trembling. I gently take her by the arm and lead her out of the office. I wait until the door closes behind us. Wait until we're halfway across the lobby. Then I start to run.

"Zak, wait!"

I don't stop. Because I have been banned from Washingcon for life. I can never come back.

I need to be alone.

ANA

2:30 AM

Zak's easier to follow than the plot of a vampire novel, but I don't catch up with him. I'm the last person he needs to be with right now. I trail him to the hotel part of the convention center. He ducks into the dining room where they serve breakfast in the morning. I don't enter, but wait about five minutes so he can regain control. I then join him in the darkened room.

Chairs are stacked upside down on every table but one. Zak sits there in the gloom, his face buried in his arms, looking like he's passed-out drunk. He lifts his head slightly as I approach. For a second I can just see his eyes, reflecting the light from the lobby. He reminds me of the Once-ler.

He says nothing. And there's nothing I can say. Not in words.

Zak, I would have been dead if my parents had to pick me up at the police station. I know the sprinklers were all my fault, but thanks for shifting the blame. Thanks for giving up the most important thing in your life.

Instead, I stand behind him. I place my hands on his shoulders and begin massaging his neck and back. I've seen Sonya do this to Landon when he's upset. It always seems to calm him down.

"Ana?" mumbles Zak, after a bit.

"Yes?"

"That really hurts. Please stop."

I instantly quit. I lower a chair and sit down beside him.

I wonder if he wants me to leave. I wonder if, when he finally sits up, he'll ask me to go. Permanently. I mean, it's not every day you ruin a guy's life. If he wants to tell me off, he deserves to.

Slowly, he lifts himself to an upright position. It's impossible to tell in the dim light, but his eyes look kind of reddish.

Nice, Ana. You meet a decent guy who likes you, who'd give up everything for you, and you utterly break him. You should be proud.

"Zak, I—"

He shakes his head. "Don't apologize. You didn't do anything wrong."

"But—"

"I'm sick of Warren acting like he's the Jesus of Washingcon. If Cyrax was harassing you and not letting you leave, then he's the one who should be hauled downtown, not you."

"It wasn't your fight, Zak. I know what this meant to you."

"It is my fight, Ana." He suddenly stands and begins walking out of the room, but slowly enough for me to follow.

Back at the con, things are still going strong. People sing, drink, juggle. I'm still amazed at this world I never knew existed. One I was almost part of.

"Hey, it ain't so bad," says Zak, with the mirthful expression of an undertaker. "Now I'll have time to work on all those side projects I've been meaning to tackle. That doomsday laser isn't going to build itself."

"You can practice your hand-to-hand combat skills."

The edge of his mouth lifts up just a bit. Maybe I'll get to see that smile again.

"Or maybe work on my screenplay. You'll have to play the female lead, though."

His smile is just about there.

230

"Okay. But no nudity."

"C'mon, Ana, it's for art."

"Let me look at the script first."

He turns to me, and his mouth grows broader. He's going to smile. Zak Duquette is going to smile at me again, and everything will be okay.

And then his entire face collapses. Every muscle slumps into a frown. His eyes lose their sheen. His back hunches.

Because I destroyed him. I ruined him. We've been friends one day, and I've taken everything important from him.

Slowly, we walk toward the exit.

"Zak? For what it's worth, my life would have been over if I'd been arrested. Thank you."

And then, my phone rings. I almost don't hear it over the wheezing of a passing Darth Vader.

Who'd be calling me in the middle of the night?

Zak, as usual, is quick to realize the danger.

"Don't answer that, unless it's Clayton. You're sound asleep at the hotel, or sitting in a hospital emergency room."

With a sense of doom, I look at the number.

"It's my father."

Zak grimaces. We both stare at the device until it stops ringing. A few seconds later, it rings again, the tone that indicates I have a voice mail.

I call it up on speakerphone, but my finger freezes just before I can activate it. Gently, Zak takes my hand and pushes it downward.

"Ana! This is your father. Mrs. Brinkham just called me, said you and Clayton were visiting your grandfather in the hospital. I don't know what kind of shenanigans you two are up to, but rest assured, it's over. I've informed your teacher you have lied to her. The both of you better get back to the hotel immediately. Your mother will be there in the morning to pick you up from the tournament."

I'm clutching Zak by the arm for support. Literally, for support. I feel like I'm about to fall over. But the message isn't finished.

"I can't begin to tell you how disappointed we are. Especially in you, Ana."

I put the phone in my pocket, then face Duquette.

"Well, that's it. I'm . . ." *Ah, heck with it.* "I'm screwed."

"C'mon, Ana. We'll think of something." Already, I can see the devious little gears in his mind turning.

"You don't understand, Zak. Dad has said that before. To Nichole. The night he threw her out."

"Oh, Ana . . ."

I sniffle. "Zak? Earlier, you said your father told you something that helps you get through rough times. What was it?" Lord knows I could use some cheering up right now.

Zak's eyes look away. He stands there for a moment, remembering.

"It was really the last time I talked to him, Ana. He fell into a coma that night. But we talked for a long time that day. And I'll never forget this. He looked at me . . . looked at me . . ."

Zak takes a moment to compose himself.

"Looked at me and said, 'Son. Sometimes life just goddamn sucks, don't it?'"

I wait for the rest of the story, for the inspiring words. And then I realizes that's it.

And the worst part of it is, Mr. Duquette was right. Life does suck. A lot.

And I start to laugh. At the absurdity of being at a comic book convention in the middle of the night. That my brother is running around here like a crazy person. That I'm actually in danger of being arrested. That the first guy I've ever kissed is the last guy I thought I'd ever want to be friends with. I laugh and laugh.

And then I wrap my arms around Duquette's neck, bury my face in his shoulder, and cry.

And for a few minutes we stand there, hold each other, and pretend that both our worlds haven't ended.

ZAK

2:51 AM

Ana holds me, quietly sobbing. And there's not a thing I can do to make things better.

I used to believe in happy endings. I used to buy into the Technicolor happily ever after. No matter how grim things look, Indiana Jones will always defeat the Nazis. Han and Lando will blow up the Death Star, and John McClane will wisecrack the terrorists to death. I always believed that.

Until Dad got sick. Then I realized it was all happy Hollywood horseshit.

Like right now, for instance. I've been blacklisted from Washingcon, and the girl that I was really starting to like, the girl who was way out of my league but who was still kind of into me, is going to be killed by her parents.

All too soon, Ana disengages her face from my chest. She wipes her nose on the sleeve of her cloak, an action that is somehow incredibly sweet.

"Zak? You said you could find us a ride?"

Ah, back to the cold, humorless outside world. I've been banished, and we have to leave.

"Yeah, he gets up at four thirty, he can probably get here by six."

"Do you want to wait in the parking lot? I don't want to run into any security guards."

Waiting outside in the cold for three hours. That sounds like a downer. But she's right, we need to get out of here. Unless . . .

They probably wouldn't think to look for us *there*. And it beats hanging around in the cold and dark.

"Ana? Since it's my last night here, I was wondering if maybe you'd like to . . ."

"To what?"

"Wanna filk?"

ANA

3:05 AM

Puff the magic maggot lived in the trash . . .

There are about forty of us crammed into a tiny conference room. Half the people hold guitars. Every person has a beer, a flagon, a plastic cup, or some other drinking vessel. The room is almost hazy with the stench of alcohol. The wooden veneer of the conference table has started to warp and bubble from spilled drinks. That minister from the wedding is passed out in the seat across from me. If it wasn't for the occasional puffs of smoke from his pipe, I'd worry that he wasn't breathing.

Everyone is singing. Zak tells me "filking" is kind of a folk song circle, an old con tradition. And though I don't recognize a single tune, every person here knows all the lyrics. Of course.

Duquette stands in the hall, a finger in his ear, talking to someone on his phone. I'm getting kind of annoyed at him for dragging me to this place. Then I remember how, because of me, this will be his last night here ever. I can't blame him for wanting to have a little bit of fun before we leave.

Though I kind of wish we were spending these last few hours alone. Just him and me.

Zak pockets his phone and joins me. "He'll be by around six."

"Who?"

He's not listening. At least not to me. A guy, who must weigh four hundred pounds, is belting out a dirty, double-entendre song, and Zak is paying attention to him. Everyone is paying attention to him. He's fat, hairy, and ugly, and he has more friends than I ever will.

"Duquette!" I snap.

"Sorry." His grin vanishes as he remembers how much trouble we're in. Or at least that he's not supposed to be having a good time right now.

"Ana, you want to leave?" There's no whining in his voice—he sounds generally concerned.

"We don't have to."

"Ah, it's noisy in here. There's a Denny's across the

way. I'll buy you a cup of something."

His last night here ever, his last couple of hours at the con, and he's willing to leave early, just because he can tell I'm uncomfortable.

But then again, this may be our last chance to be alone together for a while. I'd rather spend that time at an all-night diner than listening to these strangers singing about their fetishes.

"Thanks, Zak."

We stand. He takes my arm. I can't decide if that's sweet or annoying.

Just before we reach the door, the fat guy finishes his routine. "Hey, Duke! Duke, you ain't leaving us, are you?" He has a British accent, which I'm pretty sure is false.

"Um . . ." Zak points to me, himself, and the door.

"Duke! Not without a song! C'mon!"

And soon, the entire room is clamoring. "Duke! Duke! Duke!"

He looks sheepishly at me.

"Go on, Zak."

He smiles at me with gratitude, and we return to the room. I sit down next to a round-faced girl with glasses and a Sherlock Holmes hat.

"Have you heard Duke sing before? He's hilarious."

I shake my head. I've seen Zak do a lot more than

sing tonight, which makes me unique among this crowd. Then again, he's only really known me for one weekend. For all I know, tonight was just another crazy con for him.

He strolls to the center of the room and takes the mic from the human blimp. Everyone applauds. Zak grins. That same smile I like, but it's directed at everyone. His people.

"So who here's from out of town?" For some reason, everybody cracks up.

Everyone gets the inside jokes here. Except me.

"Doug, did they let you out early? Hey, Hope, looking good!"

Sherlock girl ducks her head and giggles. I find her irritating.

After working the crowd for a little bit, Duquette breaks into song. And right away, it's obvious he can't sing. I mean, he just doesn't have the voice. He's singing "Piano Man," but with different parody words, and he doesn't come anywhere close to the key or the beat. It's terrible.

But no one seems to notice. Because he's funny. He's at ease. He's popular.

And right then I realize that despite all that happened tonight, he's going to land on his feet. This may be his favorite con, but there are others he goes to. And in a couple of years, someone else will be doing Warren's job, and all will be forgiven. Zak will come back and be kissing some other girl and telling her how special she is.

Zak slowly circles the room, glad-handing the guys, winking at the girls. He doesn't look at me.

The song ends and his flunkies cheer again. A bra flies from the audience and Zak grabs it. I would have been so pissed off if a woman had thrown it.

I irritably pluck the string of my bow, waiting for him to be done. He tries to return the microphone, but fatso just shoves it back. A guy with a synthesizer on his lap strikes a chord. The audience cheers. They all break into a fast-paced song, with different sections of the crowd singing the catchphrases of various *Star Trek* characters. Zak runs the whole show, of course. His face is split in a joyous grin. He's completely forgotten about Clayton, the cocaine, the quiz bowl, the Viking . . . and me.

"And now the guys: HE'S DEAD, JIM!"

This will be Duquette's life. Forever. He'll get some kind of tech support job and go to cons like this every weekend. He'll live with his mom until he finally blows up at Roger and moves into an apartment. He'll keep dating geek girls until he marries some chick named Moonbeam, gains a hundred pounds, and takes over Warren's job.

240

He'll never have an ounce of responsibility, but he'll still live happily ever after.

"And now the ladies: BEAM ME UP, SCOTTY!"

Not me, though. I'll spend all summer paying for this one night. Even though Duquette's right, this stupid night is all Clayton's fault. I haven't done anything wrong. Except for possessing cocaine.

"This side of the room: FIRE PHOTON TORPEDOES!"

And I'll go to college, and study every night, and get some kind of job that requires eighty hour weeks and lots of meetings. I'll rarely see Nichole and Clayton. I'll marry some good-looking, safe guy and have two kids. I'll make my parents proud. I'll never go to one of these stupid conventions again.

Never see Zak again.

"Now this side: THAT'S HIGHLY ILLOGICAL!"

Because that's the way the world works, isn't it? You can work hard and be miserable, or do nothing and be happy. I wish I'd realized that before I wasted all those years on the former.

"BOLDLY GO!"

The song ends, with everyone in the room laughing. Duquette still isn't looking at me. I stand up, grab my bow, and head for the door. I need some air.

Sherlock girl, who was standing during the last song, blocks my way. "Don't go yet!"

I attempt to shove past her.

"Hey, you have to give us a song first! It's the rules. C'mon . . ." She checks my badge. "Ana."

Duquette has materialized at my side. "Not tonight, Hope." He attempts to edge past her.

"Hey, one song!" yells Doug, the fat guy.

"Not now!" I growl. Zak winces.

Everyone starts booing me. Why are people booing me? Why is nothing I do ever good enough? I have to leave.

"Hey, hang on. You owe us a tune. How about the 'Peanut Butter Jelly' song?"

"'Peanut Butter Jelly!'" squeals the crowd. Someone begins to pound on the table. "'Peanut Butter Jelly!'"

They remind me of a bunch of shrieking mental patients. I want nothing so much as to leave this building, to stand out on the cold night air and to get away from this insanity. I make for the door.

"C'mon, Ana," says Hope. "Live a little. Don't you want to have fun for once?"

That does it. I turn and walk back to the table. The filkers begin to cheer. I smile briefly, grab the edge of the table, and shove it forward. It crashes to the floor in a rain of sheet music, drinks, and costume accessories.

The room falls silent.

I step over the collapsed table, march past Duquette and out of the room.

ZAK

3:20 AM

They're going to be talking about that at Washingcon for years now. One minute Ana is sitting there all quiet and sad, the next minute she's throwing stuff like a Little League dad.

What the hell was I thinking, taking her there? She obviously needed to be somewhere quiet, less stressful. And what in Dobbs's name was I doing, singing like that? I might as well have told her I didn't care that she was upset.

L'esprit de l'escalier.

I had to stay in the filk room for a few minutes, to apologize and help pick up. Fortunately, nothing was broken and most everyone found the incident to be more funny than not. Actually, I was the only one who was really worried.

Ana will probably never speak to me again. Why the hell didn't I take her to Denny's? Why do I always screw everything up? Why didn't I write that stupid health paper in the first place?

My phone sings. Praise Zeus, it's a text from Ana.

IN THE BACK PARKING LOT.

On the other side of the complex, of course. I rush through acres of halls, hoping to reach Ana before she does anything else psycho.

The lot is empty, except for some employees' cars. It's raining again, lightly but steadily.

"Ana?"

"Over here, Zak."

I'm horrified to see her lying, spread-eagled, on the asphalt, her bow propped against a trash can. I rush over, fearful that something horrible has happened.

Ana stares up at me with a big grin. Her cloak is wet with rainwater. She waves her arms and legs. "I'm making gravel angels!" she squeals, in an almost babylike voice. "Join me!"

Uh-oh. She's flipped. Lost it. I've heard about this. Sometimes a smart kid just suddenly snaps and goes nuts. I have to get her back inside.

"Oh, stop freaking out," she says, in a normal tone. "I'm fine."

She doesn't get up, though. Unsure of what else to do, I squeeze between the cars and lay down opposite her, the tops of our heads almost touching. The ground is hard and wet. Water drips into my face and runs into my ears.

Much to my surprise, Ana lifts her head, scoots back, and rests it on my shoulder. I do the same thing to her. We're using each other as a pillow. The rain no longer runs into my nose, and the parking lot isn't so uncomfortable.

"Ana? You okay?"

"I don't want to discuss it."

"Don't, Ana. Talk to me. I think I've earned that."

There's a long silence, broken only by the steady, monotonous drizzle.

"You really want to know what's bothering me?"

I nod into her shoulder.

"Okay. When I was five I asked Santa for a puppy and got a Barbie instead. When I was eight, Nichole got a new bike and I had to ride her old one. Clayton has been pulling that cutesy Boy Wonder routine for years, and I'm sick of it. I have no real friends. I spent two months campaigning for a congressman who I thought was big into education and after he was elected, he votes to slash school funding. Nichole keeps telling me I'll develop, and here I am at eighteen and I'm only an A-cup. I'm not allowed to drive or even leave the house without an itinerary. Mr. Klein wrote me a letter of recommendation for college, but it was bland and noncommittal. I almost got arrested tonight, and you go off and karaoke, you butthead. It's raining. Everyone wants to spell my first name with two Ns. It's the twenty-first century and most of the world lives in poverty. And my brother is still missing."

I lay there, taking all this in.

"Just an A-cup? Really?"

"Duquette!"

"Sorry." A pause. "But none of that's what's really freaking you out."

She suddenly sits up, causing my head to fall to the ground with a painful crash. "No, Zak. What really bothers me is I never do anything fun, never do anything for myself. And maybe I can't lay that all on my parents, you know? And in a couple of months . . . forget it."

I sit up and face her. "No, what?"

We're sitting there, cross-legged, staring at each other in the drizzle. "It doesn't matter. I don't own you."

What did she mean by that? "Ana, I can't read your mind. Just say it."

Ana waves her hands around, as if trying to mold an abstract thought into words.

247

"Zak, in a few months we'll both be going off to different schools."

Unbelievable. I'm getting the breakup talk in the middle of our first date.

"And even if I find a way out of the insanity with my family, you'll still be here with all your buddies and your cons, and all your little girlfriends."

"My what?"

Her green eyes bore into me. "Strawberry, Gypsy, some chick from the filk circle. And I'm sure there are others."

Maybe one or ten, but I know better than to bring that up. "Ana, what's that got to do with anything?"

She gives me the sad smile of someone delivering unpleasant news. "I don't belong here, Zak. I don't fit in. Tonight was special, but I know you'd have had more fun with—"

She's going loopy on me again. I make the rash decision to share a memory I've almost completely repressed. "Ana, a couple of months ago I ran into Gypsy at the movies. She was with some friends. When I said hi, she pretended not to know me. Just acted like I was some weirdo she'd never met. And if it hadn't been for you, I still would have danced with her tonight. I'm that pathetic. Trust me, I'm glad I was with you. I had a wonderful time."

She laughs out loud. "No, you didn't."

"You're right. This was hellish. Worst con ever. And it's your fault. But I'm still happy you came." *Tone it down, Duke.* "I mean, yesterday I thought you were this stuck-up ice queen. I'm glad I got to see this side of you."

Fortunately, she laughs. "Yeah, well, I always thought you were a brain-damaged slacker."

"Maybe we were both right."

She takes both my hands in hers. "No, we were both wrong."

I so want to kiss her right then, but I can't bring myself to end the moment.

"Zak, thanks for a memorable night."

"I, um, hope it's not the last. If we go out again, I promise less drugs and violence."

"Deal. Of course, tomorrow we're both dead." She smiles sadly.

"That's the logical prediction. But my theory is that things can't possibly get any worse for us. We're going to get through this. Watch."

"That's a pretty improbable theory, Zak."

"Doesn't mean it can't happen."

She lets go of my hands. "Where's the nearest ladies' room?"

"Um, through the handicap entrance there."

Ana stands, pats my head, and collects her bow. Just

then, her phone rings. She glances at it.

"Mrs. Brinkham." She then turns off her phone . . . all the way off. "You coming, Zak?"

"In a minute. And call me Duke."

She starts for the building. "Hey, Zak, I'm sorry about freaking out back there. It was a long time coming. Hope no one was too mad."

"Ana, you wigged out over the 'Peanut Butter Jelly' song. Congratulations. You're one of us now. You'll get your Spock ears in the mail."

She leaves with a big smile on her face. I watch her until she's safely inside, then lean against a Nissan. Maybe she actually will want to see me again. And maybe we'll find Clayton and make it back safely. And her parents won't be too mad. Or Mrs. Brinkham.

Maybe.

I suddenly realize I'm not alone. There's a guy standing near me, staring. This must be his car.

"Sorry, I—" I look at him. He's a tall, scruffy-looking guy of about forty. He's wearing a flannel shirt and the ghost of a smile. And he has a gun. A revolver. He's pointing it at me. And while there are lots of phony pistols at Washingcon, this one looks really, really . . . real.

"Hello," I say, for lack of body armor.

"Hello," he replies in a lazy, friendly voice. He levels the gun. "I believe you have something of mine."

ANA

4:01 AM

I plunge my face into the icy water of the sink, but it does little to wake me up. I'm about to fall over from fatigue. I'm sure I'll do great at the tournament. Provided my mom even lets me stay. And provided Clayton shows up. If that twit doesn't report for the morning meeting, I'm going to kill him.

I recall what Zak told me. How he wants to keep seeing me. When I'll be a college freshman. When maybe I'll finally have the nerve to tell my parents that they can't dictate my schedule anymore.

Then again, maybe Duquette's just talking. Once he meets my parents, maybe he'll decide he wants to date someone less complicated. Guess we'll just wait and see.

I replace my hood and leave the bathroom. I'm at the end of a long, darkened hall, far from the regular festivities. I wait.

And wait. And wait. I check the men's room, but it's empty. I look back out in the parking lot. The rain has stopped, but Zak's not there. I turn my phone back on, but there's no call from him. I dial his number, but he doesn't answer.

My head is swimming. Surely, he didn't wander off. I mean, we're leaving in a couple of hours, right? He didn't run into some friends for one last party, did he? He would have at least called me.

I wait some more. Then I decided I'm sick of waiting. I go back to the lobby, keeping an eye out for the police. It's nearly empty, with just a couple of helmetless Storm-troopers slumped against a wall. The con is at its nadir. No one is around.

Don't do this, Duquette. Not now.

I stumble toward a bench. If Zak doesn't call me and tell me where he is in the next half hour, then . . .

"Ana Banana! Ana Banana!"

The population of the earth is about seven billion. If I had to rank the people I most want to see right now, Strawberry would come in seven billionth.

"Ana Banana!" She rushes up to me. Her freckles

252

have smeared and one of her pigtails has come undone. "I have the most *dreadful* news!"

"Not now, Strawberry."

"But the most un-smiley thing is happening!" She clutches her hands in front of her chest. "Gray skies are—"

I do not want to sit around talking to Duquette's psycho ex. "I'm busy!"

"But—"

"Go away!"

I turn my back to her, and am floored when she suddenly grabs me by the hair and won't let go. I'm painfully twisted back to face Strawberry. Her face is contorted with rage.

"Listen, you stupid slut," she barks in a deep, almost masculine voice. "Duke's in trouble!" Her voice echoes through the cavernous lobby. She lets go.

"What? What kind of trouble?"

Strawberry's eyes are wide with fear. "I . . . saw them going up the stairs. Duke and some guy. They didn't know I saw them. Ana, he had a pistol jammed in Duke's back."

"Strawberry, you're just seeing things. It was some kind of squirt gun, they must have just been playing around." Even as I say the words, I can't convince myself. Zak wouldn't have ditched me unless something serious was happening.

"They weren't pretending, Ana Banana. Duke . . . he looked terrified. My phone's back in my hotel room." She starts to sob. "Oh, this is so not jolly! This isn't jolly at all!"

How on earth has Duquette gone from quiz bowl alternate to hostage in less than twelve hours?

That Baggie of coke. Someone knows we took it. Someone needs it back, real bad.

"Listen, Strawberry—"

My phone rings. With a horrible sense of foreboding, I pull it out. Zak has sent me a video file. Strawberry huddles close to me as I play it.

The tiny screen is black. I hear the voice of an unfamiliar man.

> **Man:** It's not working.
> **Zak:** The light's on, it's fine.
> **Man:** No it's . . . okay, here we go.

The image shifts rapidly, out of focus, as the phone is moved. It finally zooms in on a human face. It's Zak. He's up against a brick wall, smiling at whoever's filming.

Strawberry and I both let out a horrified yelp. Zak's forehead is cut and bleeding, and his right eye is swelling shut.

> **Zak:** Hey, Ana, something came up. Go ahead and leave without—

The image goes blurry as the phone is moved rapidly.

It's impossible to tell what's going on. Suddenly there's the sound of a blow and Zak, screaming briefly.

My entire body grows numb. I clench hands with Strawberry, praying this is just some stupid joke from Zak.

The camera focuses again. Zak is lying on a concrete floor, clutching a bleeding mouth.

> Man: You have some property of mine.
> Deliver it to the roof of Building A in
> one hour. If you do not show up, or if
> you call the police . . .

The image shifts again. Then a booted foot snakes out and catches Zak in the ribs.

Zak, Strawberry, and I scream in unison.

> Man: One hour.

The screen goes black. There's a pause, but the film doesn't end.

> Man: Wait, now how do I send it?
> Zak: (laboriously) Tap the send icon.
> Man: I don't see it.
> Zak: Give it here.

The message ends.

Strawberry collapses to her knees and begins to hyperventilate, but I hardly notice.

Everything in my life—Clayton, my parents, Nichole—vanishes.

Zak is in trouble. Real trouble. Worse than anything either of us have experienced.

There's no one I can go to for help, no one who can take care of this for us.

I have to save him. It's all down to me.

Oh, dear God, it's all down to me.

ZAK

4:20 AM

It's so very cold up here on the roof, but at least it's stopped raining. I lean against a furnace exhaust port for warmth. With my one eye that still opens, I see my captor, sitting silently on an exposed pipe, softly illuminated by a security light.

He's not a bad-looking guy, considering. Older, unkempt, but kind of has a handsome, outdoorsy vibe going on. He just sits there, staring at me. With his pistol in one hand and my phone in the other, he stays there, motionless, incessantly whistling "The Entertainer." He doesn't smile.

Well, I'm going to die. Of course, I've thought that

before. Several times this evening, actually. But my luck can't hold out forever.

I am so disgusted with myself for letting him call Ana. But when he demanded that I find someone to retrieve his bag, I panicked. Then he started hitting me with his gun, and I couldn't think. Hopefully, Ana will be smart enough to call the police or to just run off.

Surely she won't be dumb enough to come up here.

I rub my sore face. Still, he stares. This guy is desperate and violent. I should keep my mouth shut. But quite frankly, I'm sick of the mind games. I need to know what his plans are. I have to break the silence.

"So, you're a drug dealer?" I ask.

He nods.

"How's that working out for you?"

A smile twitches at his mouth. "Not too bad. The hours aren't the greatest, but it pays well. Been doing it since I dropped out of UW Tacoma about fifteen years ago."

"Hey, I have a friend who's going there in the fall." *This is going well. We're talking. We're bonding. Maybe he won't sink me in the harbor.*

The guy pockets my phone, then scratches his belly. "How about you, kid? You in school?"

"Senior. I'll probably start at the junior college next semester."

"Probably? Shouldn't you have enrolled already?"

And now a psycho drug dealer is on my case about my education. I change the subject.

"So, is this your first time at Washingcon?"

The man stands and stretches, his pistol pointed toward Puget Sound. "You know, a lot of guys would be blubbering and begging right now."

I shrug, playing cool to hide my raw terror. "Would that help?"

"Nope. And yes, this is my first time here, and I have to say, this is a weird place. But it's crowded and was a nice location to drop off my product. You should have left it alone, kid. What the hell were you thinking?"

"It was just a misunderstanding. I thought someone had forgotten their bag."

"Lucky for me, I had someone watching. He realized you weren't the pickup man and followed you."

Okay, now's the time to grovel. "I really, really didn't mean to interfere. You don't know how sorry I am." And how desperately, desperately frightened I am. I've never been in this deep.

"You're going to be very sorry if your friend doesn't come through."

Jesus, Ana, please be gone. "Can I ask you a favor?"

"Kid, do you ever shut up?"

"Not really. Which is probably why you're the third— third?—person to beat me up tonight. But seriously.

None of this is Ana's fault. If she can't get your stuff back, take it out on me, not her."

He scratches himself again. I notice he does that frequently. "This Ana, is she your girlfriend?"

I ponder that for a moment. "It's complicated."

"Freakin' kids today!" he suddenly bellows. "All this 'it's complicated,' or 'friends with benefits,' or 'friend zone' and shit. Piece of advice, kid, you're in or you're out. Act like a damn man, not some kind of sad little puppy."

Surprisingly, I'm indignant. "She saw me naked earlier tonight."

"Good start. And listen, unless she tries something stupid, I'm not going to bother her."

I know, just know, I should keep my trap shut, but I ask anyway. "And me?"

He grins and laughs. "I follow the traditions of the great Luigi Vampa." He continues before I can ask. "Character in *The Count of Monte Cristo*. Outlaw. Whenever he'd kidnap someone, he'd give their friends a timeframe to bring in the ransom. And if they were late . . ."

I swallow hard. "Yeah?"

"He'd give them another hour." He sits back down.

"Good man."

"And then he'd kill the hostage."

He resumes whistling.

ANA

Strawberry clutches my hand and whimpers as I lead her back toward the security office. I have to get that bag back. If I can retrieve it, that guy will release Zak. We'll all be fine.

Unless Warren threw it away or turned it in. Or if the office is locked. Or if there's someone in there. Or if we get it back to the dealer, and he's still not satisfied.

We're almost to the office. I disengage from Strawberry. "Straw . . . Jen, look at me."

She looks up, facing me with her round little innocent eyes. Her lower lip quivers. "What do you suppose that awful man will do to darling Duke?"

I really, really want to smack her, but I need her help.

"Something bad. Listen, I have to break into the security office and steal something. I need you to stand lookout."

"Oh, Ana Banana, I don't think that's a berry creamalicious idea!"

A convention full of space commandos, ninjas, and Romulans, and this is who I team up with.

"Just follow me. This is for . . . for Duke. Please."

She nods. We approach the security office. There's a light on visible behind the frosted glass. As we watch, a very young janitor emerges and dumps a wastebasket into his wheeled trash cart.

"Now!" I whisper. "Distract that guy!"

Thankfully, she doesn't argue. Leaping and prancing like a psychotic ballerina, she hurls herself toward the startled custodian.

"Dance for the morning!" she yells. "It's going to be a sunshiny, sparkly gumdrop of a day! Dance with me!"

"Er, hello," says the man, his face a mix of amusement and fright.

"Dance with me"—she glances at his coveralls—"Duane! Duaney Wayney bo baney!" Grabbing him by the arms, she forcefully waltzes away with him, his wastebasket clattering across the floor.

Now's my chance. I dart through the door, into the

tiny alcove of an office. Around me, screens broadcast images of various rooms of the con. I glance at the monitors, hoping to catch a glimpse of Zak. Except for a few tables of sleepy people playing dice games, no one is about.

I dive toward the desk and begin to yank open drawers. Fortunately, none are locked.

It's not there. I search the desk twice, but the bag of cocaine is gone. I poke through a file cabinet and another desk, but I realize with a rising sense of hopelessness that Warren has disposed of the drugs.

I peak around the door, but the hall is empty. I slink out, and look around. The janitor's cart is still here, but my companion is gone.

"Strawberry?" I call.

There's a clank and a grunt from a door marked SUPPLIES. It swings open and the janitor stumbles out, regarding me with a shocked expression. Ducking his head, he locks the security office and leaves the area quickly.

Peeking into the closet, I see Strawberry, tucking in her top. She glances at me with a wry smile.

"Tee-hee."

We flee the hallway. When I see a door marked STAIRWAY: ROOF ACCESS, I stop.

"Did you find what you were looking for?" she asks,

pulling her disheveled hair into a ponytail.

"It's gone."

She pouts. "Is it time to call the police?"

I consider that. It would be so easy—just dial 911 and let someone else take care of my problems. Or I could track down Warren. Or Kevin. Or I could call my parents.

But I remember that terrible video, of that man kicking Zak. He's a desperate person, and if he realizes I've ratted him out, he's going to panic. Which would be bad for Zak. Very bad.

"Jen, listen to me." My voice seems to cut through her haze and she looks at me with less of a lobotomized expression than usual. "Go to the front entrance. Stay there. If you don't hear from me or Zak by five thirty, call the police. Tell them everything."

"What . . . what are you going to do?"

I take a deep breath and take the quiver from my shoulder. Removing my remaining blunt arrows, I reach into the bottom and pull out a small cloth sack. Something that came with the arrows, but I didn't think I'd use until I was out on the range.

Strawberry gasps as I begin to affix the hunting tips onto the arrows. The tiny barbed heads glint in the light of buzzing overhead fluorescents.

"Ana?"

I expect more of her ludicrous baby talk. Instead, she reaches out and wraps me in a huge, fruit-scented hug. "Please be careful."

"I will."

I replace my quiver. With my bow in hand, I vanish into the stairwell.

The roof door is propped open. It's cold and windy up here. I hide in the doorway until I can get a sense of where I am.

I scan the rooftop, searching for my friend among the exhaust ports, pipes, and electrical substations. Am I even in the right place?

What the hell am I doing up here? I should call the police. It's out of my hands. I'll end up screwing all this up anyway. I'm no superhero. I should go back, find the police, find Warren, tell them what's going on, and then just sit back while that psycho kills my friend.

I nock an arrow. I have to do this. I cannot let Zak down.

I huddle against an electrical transformer, trying to locate this lunatic. If I can get the drop on him, get him in my sights, I can order him to release Zak. Just point the arrow at him, and he'd have to see there was no other way out. Because if he didn't . . . because if he pointed his gun at me . . .

These are real arrows. Hunting tips. Designed to shred the insides of a deer. If it came down to it, could I really shoot that guy?

Concentrate, Ana. This is for everything.

Did a shadow move over there? Something . . . yes . . .

I creep forward, which is rather hard to do while keeping a bow drawn back. Just a few more feet.

"No! Ana! Look out!"

I whirl, but it's too late. He's right behind me. The man from the video. His gun is in his waistband, but it doesn't matter. He's so close to me, the tip of my arrow touches his belly. At this distance, it wouldn't hurt him at all.

He smiles at me. It's a warm, big brother type of smile. Gently, he takes the bow from my hand. He cocks an eyebrow at me. "Really?" His tone is almost humorous. I could almost believe this whole thing is some sort of joke.

Almost.

"Leave her alone!" As Zak staggers up behind this man, I know there is nothing funny about this situation. He's limping, holding his side. Even in the darkness, I can see the blood on his forehead, and his bruised eye. And yet he's stumbling forward, charging this guy.

The man throws my bow across the roof and draws his gun. He aims it at me.

"Get over there with your boyfriend."

Trembling, with my hands raised, I join Zak.

I've failed. I've ruined everything. Whatever happens now, it's my fault.

"Ana!" shouts Zak, as he staggers toward me. "What the hell are you doing here?" His voice is furious.

"I couldn't just leave you!" I yell back. Did he honestly think I'd abandon him up here?

The man with the gun chimes in. "Well, nice try, but it looks like you brought a bow to a gunfight. I take it from your Robin Hood act that you don't have my property?"

I look at Zak, as if he'll somehow tell me what to say. But I'm the one who screwed up. "I'm sorry. I couldn't find it."

The man growls. "Kid, tell your girlfriend what Luigi Vampa did when the ransom wasn't paid."

Why on earth were they discussing The Count of Monte Cristo?

And then I remember the book, just as Zak answers.

"He'd . . . he'd kill the hostage."

I look at the man, and Zak, and the gun with horrifying realization. Surely he wouldn't . . . not because of a stupid bag of . . .

Not Zak . . . dear God, not Zak.

Zak, surprisingly, only looks vaguely annoyed.

267

"Let Ana go. That was the deal."

The man nods. "Okay. But I don't want her following us." He removes something from his pocket. They look like a pair of those zip ties. "Tie her to that pole."

I take a step back. "Zak, what about you?"

"Shhh, Ana." Then, out of the man's line of sight, he winks at me.

He has a plan. Of course Duquette has a plan. It's going to be okay. Everything's going to be fine.

Standing with his back to the gun, Zak loops both restraints around my wrists. He leaves them so loose, I have to keep my arms level so they don't slip off.

Excellent. As soon as they leave, I'll sneak out and get the police here. It's all going to be okay.

Zak smiles at me and steps away. Unfortunately, the drug runner just laughs. Shoving my friend to the side, he yanks the ends of the zips until they are digging into my wrists. I can't move, I can't escape. Then, keeping Zak at bay with the gun, he pats me down. Small mercy, he doesn't feel me up, but he does take my phone.

"C'mon, kid, we're going for a ride." He takes Zak by the arm and starts leading him to the exit.

Zak looks back at me. He's not smug. He's not confident. He's out of plans.

This isn't happening. Surely the man will just rough him up a little . . . there's no way he'd really . . . really . . .

"Ana!" Zak suddenly shouts. Heedless of the gun, he runs toward me.

"Zak?" My voice catches, a tear streams down my cheek.

"I just wanted to tell you . . ." I think he's about to cry as well.

"Yes, Zak?"

"I . . . I . . ."

"Yes?"

"Be careful." He quickly turns away. The drug runner frowns.

"Freakin' kids today!" He looks at me. "He's all into you, but he doesn't have the balls to say it. Now move it!" He drags Zak to the stairs. I lose sight of them. I hear the door slam.

Falling to my knees, I begin to cry. *Zak, oh, Zak . . .*

Oh, hell no. No way. Zak Duquette is my friend and I'm damned if I'm going to sit here and blubber while some SOB takes him from me. Not after tonight. He's leaving with me. I'll shoot that monster if I have to, but I'm not going to let him hurt Zak.

Ignoring the three painful years of dental braces, I clamp teeth down on the thin plastic restraints and being to gnaw. They're tough and unyielding, but I don't care. I'll sacrifice every tooth in my head, but I'm not staying up on this roof.

I'm coming for you, Zak.

I pull my head back to spit out a fragment of plastic. I then scream as a knife blade lunges toward me.

It's a pocketknife. It slices straight through the restraints.

I look up in shock at the boy in the trench coat and the familiar, glaring red-and-orange T-shirt.

"C'mon, Ana," says Clayton. "We don't have a lot of time."

ZAK

5:17 AM

Luigi Vampa jams his gun in my back as we descend the stairs. I hardly notice. He's right. Why didn't I say something to Ana before I left? Something sweet and romantic, to let her know that even though we really just met, I think she's amazing?

Sadly, it's looking like I might not get another chance to see her.

We pass into the main building. My captor presses up against my back, so the gun won't be visible. This is ridiculous. Is he really going to kill me? Of course not. He just wants to teach me a lesson. He'll probably just beat me up some more. Not like I can't handle that. It's really been just one of those nights.

We cross the lobby, but it's empty. Empty. Thousands of people at this con, and no one's here. I know it's bloody early, but still . . .

Luigi continues to jam his gun in my back. I consider making a break for it, but I fear that will inspire him to do something rash. I hold my cool and pray that we'll run into someone in the parking lot.

I'm shoved into a side exit, a little hallway that leads outside. I'm beginning to lose my optimism. No one is going to be driving anywhere at this hour.

One person. I need one person to see us, and I can call for help. Anyone.

"YOU!"

A shadow falls on us. Someone is thundering down the stairs. Someone huge. We both turn.

It's the Viking. He clomps down the steps, leveling his gnarly finger at me, his eyes red and narrow. Behind me, I can hear Luigi take a surprised step backward.

"You!" As the Viking fe-fi-fo-fums his way toward me, all I can do is smile. True, I'm about to have my arms broken, but sadly, that's the happier option. My screams of pain will alert a crowd, and Luigi will be helpless to exact revenge. Or, if I'm very lucky, I can use Conan as a human shield.

I face him, eye to nipple. Luigi tries to pull me away,

but the barbarian roughly shoves him aside, oblivious to the gun. I'm trapped between a man who wants to kill me and a man who just wants to hurt me.

"You!" he repeats. I'm nearly knocked over by the stench of alcohol wafting off him.

I dash to the left, maneuvering him between me and the drug dealer. And blocking the exit door, unfortunately. I slink toward the stairs, but the Viking's hand restrains me.

"Looks like we have some unfinished business," I say with a forced smile. "Let's go out into the parking lot and settle this."

He stares at me, unfocused. "I got somethin' to say to you."

"Um, can it wait?"

He clamps his other hand on my shoulder and pulls me toward him. I can just see Luigi edging toward the exit.

"You . . ." We're so close we're almost kissing. "I . . . I'm sorry."

"Excuse me?"

He wraps his hairy meathooks around me. "I'm sorry. I'm sorry I hit you. I'm sorry . . ."

And then he starts blubbering. As he forcibly embraces me, I'm treated to an incoherent rant about how he and Boba Fett girl had been on the outs and tonight was supposed to be different and he might have lost her forever and how he was sure his mother had always wanted a girl and that he just knew he was going to get laid off from his job as a teacher's aide and the band was going nowhere and he was sorry he took it all out on me.

He's really drunk. As I struggle to free myself, I notice Luigi watching the spectacle with a smile.

"She's too good for me!" bellows the Hulk, tears and snot staining my shirt. "God, man, I'm sorry. Tell your girlfriend I'm sorry."

I finally free myself. "No! Let's fight! I . . ."

He's not listening. He's lumbering back to the stairs. "I'm sorry, man. I gotta go talk to her. Lisa! Lisa!"

"Can I at least buy you a cup of . . ."

He's gone. And when I feel the familiar pressure of the gun barrel in my spine, well, I can't say I'm totally surprised.

"Freakin' kids."

Luigi leads me through a back exit and manhandles me out the door and into the parking lot. The sun is just starting to show on the horizon. One by one, the overhead lights are blinking off.

It's a sizeable lot for downtown. There are about fifty cars parked back here. I know from past cons that at least some of them will have people sleeping in them, but I have no way of knowing which.

Time to play the sympathy card. It's all I got left.

"You know . . . my father used to come here with me. He's . . . he's dead now."

"So's my father," grunts my captor.

There. We have something in common. "I sure miss my dad."

"I didn't miss mine."

I think of his gun and don't ask for clarification.

Luigi leads me to a nondescript compact and, much to my horror, pops the trunk.

"Climb in."

Oh, this isn't good. This is bad. Han-in-carbonite bad. Indy-in-the-snake-pit bad. Spock-in-the-reactor-core bad.

And this isn't a movie.

I hesitate. Something tells me if I wind up in that trunk, I'm never coming out.

Well, Dad, looks like maybe I will get to spend another Washingcon with you.

And then the rear windshield of Luigi's car explodes.

I'm slow on the uptake, but not my captor. He's already dropped to one knee, his pistol ready, braced with both hands.

And there's Ana. She's already loaded another arrow. She stands there in the early morning light, her bow drawn back, looking utterly badass and sexy . . . and doomed.

"That was a warning," she barks. "I didn't have to miss."

Luigi responds by driving his elbow into my testicles, causing me to double over. He presses the gun against my neck.

"Little girl, you just made a serious mistake." His jovial threats are gone. He's very unhappy. He's going to start firing. And I'm going to have to watch Ana die.

Cold comfort, but I'll probably only have a few seconds to reflect on that.

"Ana! Run! Get out of here!"

She stands there like some sort of wood sprite, the wind whipping her frizzy hair. "Let him go."

There's a click as he cocks his gun. I feel the barrel tremble against my neck. It's because I'm silently crying.

And then there's another, electronic click, from off to our right.

Luigi whirls. And there's . . . Clayton? He's still wearing that trench coat. Behind him, Strawberry clings to his arm like a monkey.

He's holding out his phone. He's just snapped a picture. He hands the device to Luigi, who takes it with one hand, still poking me with his very cocked weapon.

It's a beautiful photograph. Luigi's face is clearly captured, as well as mine. And the gun. Clayton even managed to catch the car's license plate.

"I just sent that to a friend across town," says Clayton, more calmly than I'd have thought possible. "If he doesn't hear from me in twenty minutes, he'll send it to the police."

Luigi tosses the phone to Clayton, then yanks me to my feet. "Delete it," he commands.

"I can't. It's gone. Out of my control."

"Is that true?" Luigi whispers. I nod. There's a moment of silence, broken when the drug dealer drives a boot into my kidney. Strawberry screams as I go sprawling at Ana's feet.

Ana doesn't blink. "Drop your gun."

He stands there for a confused moment, then smiles and tucks his pistol into his belt. "Now you put down yours."

Before I can scream, "IT'S A TRAP!" Ana lowers the arrow. Then I really do scream as Luigi draws his gun and fires it at me three times. I only stop screaming when I realize no bullets are coming out and I look like an idiot.

Our captor smiles, but it's the same angry smile the Viking gave me at the battle. "I was never going to shoot you, kid."

"Eeep."

"I was just gonna break your legs and leave you in the woods."

"Eeeee . . ."

Two rows down, a car door opens. Luigi quickly sticks his gun back in his belt. "If that picture shows up anywhere . . . if any of you decide you want to tell your friends about what happened here . . . I will find each and every one of you." He levels a finger at me. "Zakory Duquette." His finger shifts. "Ana and Clayton Watson." He points to Strawberry and pauses.

"Jennifer Callahan," she chirps. "My friends call me Strawberry."

Luigi glances down at me with questioning eyes. I shrug. He reaches for his car door.

"You four are very, *very* lucky."

"Sir?" asks Ana.

"What?"

"Can we have our phones back?"

For a moment I think she's pushed things too far, but he just laughs. "You've got chutzpah, missy. If you ever consider a career in pharmaceuticals, look me up."

"Thanks, but I start at UWT in the fall."

"Hey, that's where I went. Go Huskies!" He hands Ana our phones and climbs into his car. Rocks spray into my face as he tears out.

"Wow," says Strawberry. "You always meet the most interesting people here."

Ana helps me up from my supine position. I can only stare at her beautiful face. She risked everything for me. Faced down a heavily armed drug runner.

That's one for the old college application.

"Ana, I—"

"Shut up, Duquette."

We kiss, long and hard.

ANA

5:59 AM

Clayton clears his throat four or five times before Zak and I disengage. I don't care. Duquette's alive. He's in one piece, more or less. I saved him.

Huh. I did, didn't I? I completely defused a hostage situation and bested a crazy guy with a gun. Would not have expected that, twelve hours ago.

Zak is staring at me with his dopey grin and I'm content to stand there and return it.

"AHEM!"

Fine. We both turn to my brother.

"Mr. Watson," says Zak. "We find you at last."

"*I* found him," corrects Strawberry. "He went up and released Ana."

"All fine and good," says Zak, "But why the hell were you here in the first place? We've been looking for you all night!"

Clayton shrugs, which infuriates me. "You said this was a fun place to go, so I snuck out. I was going to come back before curfew, but then I met Strawberry and she wanted to go to the dance, so—"

I could slap him. "Clayton! Do you have any idea how much trouble we are in?"

"No, that's the cool thing! I called Mrs. Brinkham and told her Grandpa was in the hospital, and that Duke took us to see him. She totally fell for it! Now we'll just get cleaned up and go back."

I grab him by his stupid coat. "It didn't work! Mrs. Brinkham called Dad, and everything fell apart. Mom's coming to the tournament and we are screwed!"

His face doesn't go pale. His features don't mold into a mask of fear and regret. He does not start begging for forgiveness.

"Well, it's all my fault. I'll take the blame."

Until now, I thought "seeing red" was just a figure of speech. But I swear, for a moment, everything goes slightly crimson.

"Clayton, don't you remember what they did to our sister?"

And then he crosses the line. "Don't you think it's time you stopped hiding behind Nichole?"

I'm ready to punch him, to kick his scrawny little butt. But then I notice Zak, pointedly looking at his phone, and Strawberry, staring at her bell-toed shoes.

"We will discuss this later," I hiss. "Right now, we have to get back to the hotel. Zak, did you call for a ride?"

"Huh? Oh, yeah. He should be here any minute."

"I have to get going," says Strawberry, irritatingly chipper. "Thanks for the most bananariffic evening, everyone! And don't forget to call me, honey."

I'm about to grab her by the cherry blossoms and explain that Zak will no longer be calling her, when I realize that's not who she was talking to. She's looking at my brother.

"I will, Strawberry. See you soon." She and Clayton kiss. Briefly, almost chastely, but they do. Strawberry giggles and waves, then jiggles off toward the center.

Zak cocks an eyebrow but doesn't say anything.

I start walking toward the front of the building. I'm so incredibly furious with my brother, I forget about Zak and our adventures. All I can concentrate on is how much trouble we're all in.

"Hey, Ana? I saw you at the SCA thing. That was pretty awesome . . ."

I turn and throw Clayton against a nearby trailer. "Will you stop acting like coming here was a good thing?" I scream. "Do you have any idea what we went through tonight?"

"Ana," begins Zak. "Calm down."

I ignore him. "Clayton, thanks to you, Zak nearly died tonight! Do you think this is funny?"

My brother struggles free and looks me in the eye. I never realized it, but he's actually as tall as me.

"Ana, all I did was watch some movies and sing karaoke. You two are the ones who decided to get in bad with the local cartels! And someone told me you pulled a fire alarm at a card game. What's up with that?"

I wince. The more I think about it, the more embarrassed I am. "Well, I didn't know it was going to set off the sprinklers, okay? I was just trying to create a diversion."

"Well, you ruined a lot of people's cards," snaps Clayton. "A lot of people are . . . are . . ."

We are not alone. A half-dozen zombies have silently encircled us from behind the trailer, hemming the three of us in. Their makeup is very well done, with realistic compound fractures and everything.

"I thought I recognized you," says a man with half his

face missing. I squint. Under the blood and bone fragments, I see the pallid features of Cyrax.

Zak steps forward, the lies and excuses ready to spring from his lips. *No, you're mistaken, you misheard, isn't that your ear on the ground there?*

Unfortunately, Clayton, despite his posturing, is still very much a child.

"She didn't mean to! It was just an accident."

A low, guttural groan rises from the legions of the undead, a sound I really don't think should be able to come from human vocal cords. Cyrax grabs Zak by the shirt.

"You . . . owe . . . us . . . five . . . hundred . . . bucks . . ." I'm not sure if he's pausing for effect, or if it's just hard to form words without functioning lungs.

Zak, forever acting without thinking, drives an uppercut into the zombie's jaw. His head tilts back, then forward. Thanks to the makeup, it's impossible to tell if he's really injured, but I get the impression the punch didn't affect him at all. Cyrax reaches out with his free hand and grabs Duquette's other wrist. Zak begins to wince, trying to break free.

I move to intervene. A girl zombie blocks my path. She's cute, despite her visible intestines. Before I can say anything, she whips out a can of pepper spray and points it at my face.

Zak either is not aware of the spray or is beyond caring. He's still trying to wrench away from Cyrax. Clayton tries to move in front of me, but someone grabs him by the collar.

"We'll pay you back," stammers Zak. "Just not right now."

And then they are upon us. Arms raised, eyes rolled back, the zombies shamble forward, moaning and lurching. We have nowhere to run. This is the end.

"Whoa there, partners!" says a strange voice. "Everyone just calm down."

We all turn. A middle-aged man stands there, carelessly sipping from a paper cup of coffee. He's dressed conservatively, decked out in a college sweater and jeans. He smiles at Duquette. "You're not answering your phone, Zak."

Zak returns the smile. "Hi, Roger."

ZAK

6:22 AM

There is a moment of silence, broken only by the miserable moaning of the undead.

"Oh, uh, guys, this is Roger, my mom's husband. Roger, this is Ana, Clayton, and um, an angry mob."

"Charmed." He sips his coffee. "So did I hear something about money?"

Cyrax turns to Roger. "This girl!" he yells, forgetting to stay in character. "She destroyed my cards!"

"Your car?"

"My cards!" Seeing Roger's blank expression, he explains. "M-and-M cards. It's a game. They cost a fortune."

Roger tuts. He then takes out his wallet and counts

some bills. "I have . . . one hundred twenty dollars. Would that make things right?"

He shakes his skull. "Those cards cost more than five hundred."

Roger looks to me for confirmation. I shrug, then nod.

"Well, I don't have that much, and even if I did, I wouldn't hand it over. But think about this. In a couple of years, you'll be sick of that game, and you'll try to sell off your cards. But everyone else will be sick of it too, so you'll only make maybe fifty bucks. So here are your choices: I can put this money away and we can settle this like men, with fists flying. And when it's over, we'll all be bloody and bruised—us more than you, judging by the numbers—and you'll still have no money. Or you can walk away richer and"—his voice falls to a whisper—"maybe show a girl a good time this weekend."

I look over at the girl corpse. She winks at me, but it may just be that only one eye closes.

Cyrax looks at Roger, then back at his friends.

"Brains!" shouts one of them.

He takes the money and tucks it into his rib cage. He turns to Ana. "We'll meet again."

"Is that a threat?" she snaps.

"No. But next year I'll be back. Work on your attack deck, you owe me a rematch."

Slowly, the horde shambles away.

I stare at my stepfather with a mounting sense of less hate.

Ana rushes forward. "Thank you so much, Mr. . . . . "

"Call me Roger," he says, with annoying familiarity.

"Roger, thank you. I'll pay you back this week. Zak and I go to the same school, I'll give the money to him soon."

"I appreciate that. I'm sure you're good for it."

He turns to me and shakes his coffee cup. It's empty. "Zak, I just saw a man dressed like a Mexican wrestler dancing with a girl dressed like one of those *Star Trek* robots. Were you aware this sort of thing goes on?"

"Of course."

"Is your *mother* aware?"

"Lord, no."

He laughs. "I need a refill. C'mon."

He leads us to the hotel and into the little breakfast area, the place where I had my breakdown after Warren kicked me out. In an hour, they'll begin serving a continental breakfast to the registered guests. I've snitched bagels here many mornings.

Right now, the room is dark and the chairs still sit on top of the tables, but one coffee urn still appears to be on.

He turns to Ana and Clayton. "Could you give us a couple of minutes?"

We're alone now. Roger pours two cups of joe. Though I've never drunk coffee in my life, I take a drink. It's absolutely vile, worse than Romulan ale.

I take down two chairs and we sit.

"We're about to have a man-to-man talk, aren't we?" I ask with resignation.

"I think you owe me that much."

"Before you say anything, we're going to pay you back. If Ana can't, I will."

"You don't have to."

"I want to." I really do. And not because I dislike being in his debt. It's just kind of the right thing to do.

"So, what did you do to your face?" he asks.

I finger my swollen eye and cut forehead. *Such stories . . .*

"We had a discussion about the *Star Trek* reboot. It got pretty intense."

To my surprise, Roger laughs heartily. "Zak, when you called me earlier, I wasn't expecting to find you about to get effed up in a parking lot. There's only three reasons why that happens to someone. Now, you're too smart to use drugs and too young to have gambling debts, so I'm guessing there was a female involved."

I nod, declining to explain my brief but exciting role as a drug mule.

"Is it that frizzy-haired girl?"

"Ana? Yeah."

"She's cute."

"Yeah . . ." But, then again, so is Gypsy. And Strawberry, in her own way. Cute wasn't the reason I faced a gun, a sword, a boot to the groin, and multiple fists tonight. "She's brilliant. Brave. Great at archery. She's just . . . amazing."

Roger smiles, a faraway look in his eyes. "I know what you mean. When I first met your mother . . ." He suddenly stops. "Sorry, you probably don't want to hear about that."

Maybe it's the repeated head injuries I've suffered, but I tell him to go on. He almost takes a drink of coffee, but stops.

"I was divorced twice before I was thirty-five. Nasty business. Swore I'd never do it again. Then I met your mom. And, well, you know how fast things moved."

"I'm well aware of that," I say, maybe too bitterly.

He looks at me but says nothing. "The thing is, Zak, when you marry a widow, there's always another man in the house."

I'm a little stunned. I had no idea Roger had ever given a thought to my father, the real head of our family.

"Sylvia's great," he continues. "It's just that sometimes . . . well, I know she still loves your dad. That if she had a choice, she'd be with him. That's not an easy thing to deal with."

Now would be a great time to feed his insecurities and give him a laundry list of reasons how he'll never measure up to my father.

But I don't. There's something I have to say, and I have to say it before I lose the nerve.

"Roger, you do have pretty big shoes to fill. And yeah, ever since you came around, I've always kind of had a fantasy that one day you'd . . . you know."

"Leave?"

"Die in a wood chipper accident."

Again, the eyebrow flash, but he doesn't interrupt. I take another disgusting swig of the coffee. It's somewhat crunchy.

"The thing is, you . . . you make Mom happy. Really happy." I can't face him, I look away. "And, well, good. For that. Yeah."

It was no "welcome to the family" but it was a hell of a lot nicer than anything I've ever said to him. It's all I can manage right now. Baby steps.

Roger seems to understand. "Thanks. You ready to hit the road?"

"Yeah." But there's one more thing I have to say. I remain seated and face my stepfather.

"My friend, Ana, she's going to get in a lot of trouble

for coming here. She's worried her parents are going to throw her out of her house."

Roger looks at me with concern. "Will they?"

I wish I knew. "I'm not sure. I think she's overreacting, but I need to keep an eye on her. But here's the thing." I force myself to maintain eye contact.

"Ana's afraid of her real father. And you're not my real father, not by any stretch. But when I called you in the middle of the night, you could have told me to piss off or ratted me out to Mom, but you didn't. You drove all the way out here to pick us up. So . . . thanks. Seriously."

This time, it's Roger who looks away. Damn if we're not having a moment. "Hey, no biggie. It's been a while since I had to lie to someone's mom about where they were all night."

We both raise our glasses and take a swig. My stomach almost backfires, but I'm determined to be as manly as my stepfather.

Roger, on the other hand, immediately spits his back into the cup. "Dear God, this is terrible! How the hell did you swallow it?"

We stand and walk back to the lobby.

"You know, Roger, maybe we'd have an easier time of things if you didn't always try to hang out with me."

"You think that was my idea? Sylvia insisted I try to do stuff with you."

"Hey, me too!" Looks like we were both miserable, just to make Mom happy.

We're about to enter the lobby, but Roger pauses. "Zak, why did you call me tonight, instead of your mother?"

"Easy. Mom would have worried. I didn't think you would."

He looks at me intently. "You're wrong."

There's nothing else to say but thanks, which I mumble.

"Don't mention it. It's just a good thing I usually go to the gym this early, so your mom won't wonder where I am."

"Roger? Why did you come out here? You didn't have to."

Roger is about to drop his coffee cup into the trash, but stops. He holds it over his mouth and begins to breathe heavily.

"BECAUSE—DUKE, I AM YOUR FATHER."

ANA

6:50 AM

I sit on a bench next to my brother, repeatedly dozing off and jerking awake. Clayton continues to talk about his adventures, his monologue forming a background of white noise.

Clayton broke the rules. Not only that, but he's not sorry. He lied to my parents, just like any thirteen-year-old would do. He's willing to take the consequences.

The question is, am I? Or am I just going to beg for forgiveness and go back to the way things were?

I hear Duquette's stepfather as they return from their meeting.

"And how many decorator plates does one woman need?"

Zak laughs. "No kidding. It got so bad there for a while, I thought we were going to have to organize an intervention."

They both chuckle. *This is the evil stepfather Duquette has been ranting about all night? They seem all buddy-buddy now.*

I try to imaging joking around with my parents like that, but it's such a foreign idea, I give up.

"C'mon, guys, Roger is going to drive us back to the hotel. We should make it in time for stale biscuits and gluey gravy."

I stand up, groaning. Everything aches. The idea of throwing on a dress, plastering a smile on my face, and spending four hours at the tournament makes me want to whimper.

I notice that Zak is limping. And his right eye is almost bruised shut. I keep forgetting he's had an even rougher night than I have. As we leave the building, I link my arm through his. He gives me that puppy-dog smile.

Roger leaves to pull his car around. I stand there with Zak as we lean on each other for support. The night is just over and the rain clouds are dispersing. It's shaping up to be a sunny day in Seattle. I take a deep breath, savoring the damp air. Maybe everything is going to be okay.

"Are you two heading out?"

We turn. A tall, skinny black guy in a suit stands there. I don't recognize him. He has a pencil thin mustache, perfect teeth, and sparkling eyes. Easily the most handsome man at the conference.

Actually, aside from Zak and the drug dealer, the only good-looking guy I've seen all night.

"What the hell happened to your face, Duke?" asks the stranger.

"Poor genetics." Zak pries his swollen eye open with his fingers. "Sorry, pal, have we . . ."

It hits us both at the same time. "Warren?"

The suit, the shoes, the perfect hands. It's him, minus the mask.

Warren does not acknowledge his coming out. "I need a word with you two."

Good Lord, what now?

"I apparently owe you an apology," he continues. "I checked the security cameras. Seems one of the convention center janitors was making a little money on the side, down in the basement. He dropped off that Baggie for something, and then you two Smurfs blundered in and swiped it. I turned it all over to the police."

I remember what Zak's captor said would happen if we told on him. "Um, did you see who was supposed to make the pickup?"

Warren shakes his head. "I doubt he'll come around again anyway. The cops are going to put a couple of undercover guys here tonight, but you two probably scared everyone off. That makes me happy. So, thank you."

Zak smiles. "Does this mean . . . ?"

Warren does not return the grin. "Yes, Duquette, in light of things, you are unbanished."

Zak's face seems to glow, like a happy little sun.

I'm willing to leave well enough alone but Zak has one more question. "How about Ana?"

Warren stares at me, and there's no love lost. "I don't know. Are we going to have any more abuse of the fire alarms?"

"No, sir."

"Very well. Our insurance should cover the damages, and the convention center is pretty embarrassed about their employee's extracurricular activities. I think we can sweep the whole thing under the rug. I've told the police as much."

"Thank you, Warren. Um . . ." I sadly hand him my bow. "Will you drop this off at the lost and found?"

He solemnly takes my weapon. "You're on probation.

Don't make me regret this. Now get some sleep you two, you look terrible." He starts to go. "Oh, hey, Clayton. You coming to *Rocky Horror* next week?"

Clayton laughs. "If Strawberry brings me a bra to wear."

Warren leaves while Zak and I stare at my brother with great fatigue and wonderment. A car horn wakes us from our stupor and we slump toward Roger's car. Clayton climbs in the front. Zak opens the rear door for me, then falls in after.

As we pull out of the parking lot, I slump in my seat. That was one hell of a night. The craziest thing I've ever experienced, by far. I think it was wild, even by Zak's standards.

And despite everything, the three of us got out alive and mostly unharmed. No matter what my parents do, we're always going to have the con. I lean over to thank Zak, to tell him how much everything he did tonight meant to me.

"Zak, I . . ."

He's sound asleep.

ZAK

7:27 AM

Everything hurts. Everything. Each ache reminds me of a different injury, from my sore balls where Boba Fett kicked me, to my black cye where Luigi Vampa pistol-whipped me.

I look at my companions as we walk from the car toward our hotel. Ana's still wearing that weird cloak, Clayton's still got that long jacket on, but they otherwise appear normal. Me, all my clothes are in tatters. I'm thirsty, tired, and guilty of felony drug possession.

And it was so worth it. Especially the parts with Ana. Lord, what a night.

A bank clock tells me it's not yet 7:30. We've got

plenty of time to freshen up before we're supposed to meet Brinkham at eight. I try to come up with a way to spin this evening's activities in a way that won't get us in too much trouble. Or at least place all the blame on Clayton.

Roger stops when we reach the hotel doors. "I guess this is where I say good-bye."

"Already?" says Ana. "You're not coming to the tournament?"

"Yeah," says Clayton. "Stay for a couple of rounds."

Roger looks at me quizzically. Again, I'm overcome by a wave of unhate.

"At least come in and have some real coffee."

He nods at me and I smile back. It's amazing how much you can grow to like a guy when he drives the getaway car.

A woman carrying a box of doughnuts and a bottle of water walks past us. I hold open the door as she enters the hotel, and we follow.

As we come into the lobby, I'm surprised to see that she's still standing there, looking at us. I'm even more surprised when my brain focuses in on the face.

It's Mrs. Brinkham.

She's still staring. More than half her team has just walked in off the street, looking like they've been out all night partying. She sets down her doughnuts.

"Ana? Clayton? Zakory? What's going on?"

I instantly shoot a finger toward Roger. "The nice stranger said he'd give us candy if we got into his van."

"Zak!" shout Roger, Ana, and Clayton.

I smile. "This is my . . . my stepfather, Roger. He's in town on business and took us out for an early breakfast. Roger, this is Mrs. Brinkham, our quiz bowl sponsor."

"Ma'am." He half salutes her.

She's not buying it. "Ana, I received a very disturbing call last night. Your father says your grandfather is in fine health. So I have to wonder, where the hell were you three last night?"

I attempt damage control. "Just a little misunderstanding, Mrs. B."

But then Clayton steps forward. "It's all my fault. I snuck out. Ana and Duke tried to find me, and then we didn't have enough cab fare to get back. We had to wait for Duke's father to pick us up. I'm sorry I lied about my grandfather. I didn't want Ana and Duke to get in trouble. But it was all me."

I'm kind of touched by the kid's honesty, but Mrs. Brinkham looks anything but convinced. "What did you do to your face, Zakory?"

I shrug. "Football game." Roger coughs, though it sounds like a suppressed laugh.

My teacher shakes her head. "Zakory, I should have

known you wouldn't take this tournament seriously. Though I have to say I'm surprised at you, Ana and—"

Ana interrupts. "We were with a responsible adult, everyone's fine, and we're back in time for the tournament. So let's not make a big deal about this, okay?"

I'm impressed at how Ana is suddenly no longer afraid of anything. Though out of all of us, she's the least guilty.

"It most certainly is not okay, young lady! The three of you get up to your rooms. I will be calling your parents."

"Um, right here," mumbles Roger.

"And you, sir, ought to be ashamed of yourself—"

"Hey, Roger didn't do anything!" I yelp. *Since when am I so protective of him?*

"Zakory, I will deal with you later."

"It's not his fault, Mrs. Brinkham," says Ana. "Stop blaming him."

"Ma'am, the kids are okay. What's the big deal?"

"Hey guys," chirps the desk clerk. "Could you keep it down?"

"Get back to your rooms now, before I decide we're going to forfeit!"

"I didn't want to be here in the first place!"

"Seriously, lady, I know you were worried, but—"

"I never should have let you on the team, Zakory."

"He saved our butts yesterday!"

"C'mon, folks, people are still trying to sleep—"

"You don't want me on the team? Fine!"

"Don't take that tone—"

"QUIET!" It's a loud, buzzing, mechanical voice.

We all turn. Clayton, who's been watching the exchange in silence, has barked out the order through that artificial voice box. He stands there, alone, staring at all of us with kind of a weary, disappointed look on his face.

"Where'd you get that thing?" I ask.

"Everyone, please calm down," says Clayton through his mouth. "Listen."

He then gets his foot caught on the tail of the coat he's wearing. He tries to right himself, slips, and tumbles, face-first, into a marble-topped table.

We all rush over. Ana kneels by her brother.

"Clayton?"

He sits up with a groan. Blood trickles out of his mouth.

"Are you okay?"

"Yeah, I'm . . . uh-oh."

He pulls his upper lip back. There's a large gap where a tooth used to be.

Our heads turn to the floor, where the long white incisor sits in a puddle of red. He didn't break it—he managed to knock the whole thing right out of its socket.

Mrs. Brinkham and the clerk are both groaning, probably imagining a lawsuit. Ana is grabbing at her hair. Clayton still looks stunned.

"Don't panic."

It's Roger. He bends down and picks up the tooth. "If we get him to an emergency room, they can reset it. You." He points to the clerk. "Get some milk."

"Excuse me?"

"Are you deaf? Milk! A big glass, right now! And a Baggie of ice."

Moaning, the man runs off in the direction of the dining room.

Clayton, who seems the least concerned of all of us, spits out a wad of blood. "Why milk?"

"Believe it or not, it's the best thing for preserving missing teeth, severed fingers, or torn-out eyeballs."

Ana looks at him oddly.

"I do the books for half the hospitals in Tacoma. I've picked up a trick or two. C'mon, on your feet, boy."

"You're an accountant?" I ask.

Roger is helping Clayton stand, but he pauses to look at me. "You really didn't know that?"

My mother married both an insurance man and an accountant. Did she have some kind of fetish?

Roger is talking to Mrs. Brinkham. "I'll take him to

the hospital. And I'll call his parents, tell them about the accident. None of this is your fault, I'll make that clear."

She nods, miserably.

"I'm going with you," says Ana.

"No," mumbles Clayton through the hand he's holding against his jaw. "We'd really have to forfeit without both of us. You stay."

"But . . ."

"Stay. Talk to Mom. Tell her it was all my fault."

The clerk returns with a milk carton and a glass of ice. Roger drops in the tooth and adds the milk as a chaser. He takes Clayton by the arm and walks toward the door.

"It's going to be okay!" he repeats.

"Be careful, Clay," calls Ana.

Her brother turns and smiles a gap-toothed grin. "What, me worry?"

Then they're gone.

Mrs. Brinkham stands and glares at us. Oh, how I miss the flustered, clumsy health teacher I thought I knew.

"You understand that if it were not for Landon and Sonya, we'd be returning home right now."

We both nod.

"Good. Go get dressed. Rest assured, we will discuss this later."

Ana and I begin to slink out of the lobby, but she has something else to say.

"Answer me this, and truthfully. Did you guys really stay out of trouble last night?"

"Mrs. Brinkham," answers Ana. "We were at a comic book convention. Snooze city."

Our sponsor nods, relieved. We climb into the elevator. Ana hits the button.

"And as it turns out," I add, as the doors close, "the gun wasn't even loaded."

I can hear her screaming my name as the car rises.

ANA

11:51 AM

"George Orwell."

Zak is mumbling so much I'm afraid the judge will ask him to repeat himself, but he simply awards us another ten points.

The timer buzzes. Against all odds, we've done it. We've made it to the very final round. Without Clayton.

The other team captain growls a forced congratulation and the judge calls for a ten-minute break. Zak's head instantly flops onto the tabletop, and within seconds, he's snoring.

I sheepishly grin at Sonya and Landon, who have answered three questions between them this whole morning. They look at me with quiet respect. Mrs. Brinkham has done little to keep her anger bottled up inside, and they can tell we lied about going out last night. To them, we're badasses.

It's hysterical to think that exactly one night ago, I would have felt the same way.

I move a curl of hair off Zak's face and resist the urge to kiss his cheek. Even with that stream of drool running out of his mouth, he's kind of cute. I'll have a talk with him about the goatee later.

Our next opponents boldly walk in. It's St. Pius, a wealthy Catholic school. All their team members are dressed in identical navy blue uniforms. They join hands in a prayer circle.

I nudge Zak. He awakes with a start and nearly falls out of his chair.

"Son of a bitch!"

After a moment he regains his bearings and realizes that everyone is staring at him. He smiles at the opposing team's sponsor. "Sorry, Sister."

In the front row, Mrs. Brinkham facepalms.

Everybody takes their places. A girl on the other team wishes me good luck. I nearly give her the finger before I realize she's sincere. This lack of sleep is doing strange things to my head. I take a deep breath.

One of the judges launches into his spiel. This round

is for the championship. This one is for everything. For the win. To make Mrs. Brinkham slightly less pissed off.

We can do this. I can do this. I'm awake. I'm focused. I'm . . .

Screwed.

Just as they're closing the door, three people sneak in. I'm pleased to see Zak's stepfather, followed by Clayton. He grins at me, showing that they've somehow successfully put his tooth back.

And here's Mom.

Yep, she ices in right behind my brother. Prim, upright, and frowning dangerously. I think the nun from the other team looks more laid back.

I knew I'd have to face her, but I was kind of expecting the confrontation to be this afternoon. Nope, just like Dad threatened, she's driven out here to punish me. The fact that Clayton was injured is just icing on the cake.

She sits in the front row. Our eyes meet. She shows absolutely no reaction. I wonder if I'm already dead to her.

"Hey, Ana, how about a kiss for luck?" Zak is already leaning toward me. Mortified, I shove his face away. He looks at me, confused, then turns to the audience. His face lights up when he sees Roger and Clayton, then crumbles when he realizes who the glowering woman with them must be.

It's all over. There's nothing left for me to do. Nothing left but . . .

TO WIN.

To hell with everything. I came here to be a champion, and that's what I'm going to do. What we're all going to do. And no matter how much trouble I'm in, Mom can't deny the fact that I'm a winner. That I'm a daughter to be proud of. I can be brave. I can do this.

Why won't she smile at me? Why won't she wish me luck?

The game begins. The St. Pius kids are fearless, buzzing in before the questions have finished. They take a quick lead. Zak, for once looking like he's actually on the team, fights back. Sonya answers one wrong.

Screw this. I press my buzzer.

"The Thirty Years' War."

"Correct."

It's on. The questions come in a blitzkrieg, but none of us back down. The judge has to struggle to keep up as both teams rapidly fire off answers. Mom stares at me, unblinking, the whole time.

And then the timer sounds. I don't want to, but I look at the scoreboard.

One hundred seventy to one hundred seventy. Dead even.

The moderator clears his throat. One final tie-breaker. The entire game rests on this one answer.

"Which Alexandre Dumas novel featured a bandit named Luigi Vampa?"

My God, is it really going to be this easy?

I face Zak, who is grinning at me. The ironic thing is, if it hadn't been for that drug dealer, I probably wouldn't have remembered the villain from *The Count of Monte Cristo.*

I stab the buzzer at the same time as Zak. But neither of our indicator lights illuminate. Instead, Landon's goes on.

"*The Three Musketeers!*"

"Incorrect."

The other team rings in.

"*The Count of Monte Cristo?*" answers an opponent, clearly guessing.

"Correct."

Well, that's it. We've lost. We're losers. I'm a loser. We're a losing team. And now I can go face my mother in defeat and accept whatever punishment she . . .

I turn to Zak, who looks more concerned than disappointed.

The hell I will.

I stand, nod to the other team, and join my mother.

"Ana . . ."

"Let's talk. In private."

We leave the room. I turn back for one moment.

Duquette is watching me. He winks and then taps his chest with his fist right above his heart.

I can do this.

We do not speak until we've located a small, empty conference room. Neither of us sit.

"So what went on last night?" demands Mom.

I mentally review the wildly improbable things that happened to all of us. "What did Clayton tell you?"

"He said that he snuck off to some sort of comic book thing, and that you had to spend all night looking for him."

I was touched by my brother's honesty. "Yes. Clayton was just curious. Please don't be mad at him."

"I'll deal with Clayton later. You're the one who has really disappointed your father and me."

Here it comes. "How is any of this my fault?"

She shakes her head, sadly. "Ana, you know we didn't think Clayton should go on this overnight trip. We trusted you to watch out for him. It's only through the grace of God that nothing happened to you or your brother."

Oh, if only you knew.

"Mom, Clayton walked out of his hotel room without telling anyone. How could I have seen that coming?"

I think I've scored a point, but I've underestimated

my mother's capacity for blame. "You should have told Mrs. Brinkham. Or called me. You had no business running around Seattle with God knows what sort of people. I really expected more of you, Ana."

Yesterday, I would have taken all the blame and apologized. But that was yesterday. "Maybe I screwed up. But maybe I just didn't want Clayton to get in trouble. It's not like he was out drinking or something. He wanted to go to a comic book convention. We messed up, okay? But it's not a big deal."

She shakes her head. "The fact that you don't see the problem here just drives home how immature you are being. Ana, if you can't show responsibility in a situation like this, then how can we expect you to do so away at college? After you've had time to think, we need to sit down with your father and map out a plan for your future."

I know what that means. Another year living at home. Another year of the rules. Another year of being a slave.

Mom is turning to leave. In her mind, the conversation is over.

"I'll plan my own life, thank you very much!"

Mom just manages to hide her shock. "Young lady, I can see you're tired and upset. We'll go home, you'll get some rest, and we'll talk things through in the morning."

So now I'm being sent to bed for back-talking? I

313

think back to how Zak said I only had myself to blame for letting Mom and Dad walk all over me.

"We'll discuss it right now! I'm eighteen years old! I'm at the top of my class! I've been accepted into four colleges! What the hell more do you want from me?"

"Ana—"

"I am not a baby. Neither is Clayton, if you haven't noticed. Maybe if you let him out of the house once in a while, he wouldn't have snuck off last night! Maybe if I wasn't so darn afraid of screwing up, I *would* have called you." I'm aware of how whiney I sound, but I can't stop. I wish I wasn't so exhausted so I could make a less emotional argument.

"Stop that right now!" snaps my mother. I'm obviously getting to her—she rarely raises her voice.

"Or what?" I hesitate, then say it. "Or you'll kick me out too?"

Mom's face goes white.

"You know what it's like living like that, Mom? Knowing that if I ever mess up, out the door with me?"

"Ana, please—"

"Please what? You disowned your daughter because she screwed up. Well, she's my sister, and you robbed me of her."

"Don't bring that up now."

"Say her name! Say your daughter's name! You

haven't said it years! Say it now, or by God, you will lose another kid!"

I'm not prepared for my mother's hand. It flies up. I don't have time to duck, but it stops, an instant before it strikes my cheek. We both stand there, stunned. No matter what happens next, we've crossed a line. Things will never be the same.

Mom turns her back on me and walks to the corner of the room. For a long minute she stands there. I want to go to her. I really do.

When she turns around, I can tell she's been crying. She faces me.

"Nichole. My daughter's name is Nichole. My grandson's name is Levi. And if you think we've forgotten about either of them, then you're not as smart as you think you are, Ana."

"What do you mean?" I'm already second-guessing myself, but it's too late. "You kicked her out right when she needed us the most."

Mom winces for a moment. "Yes. We did. We were angry and scared. But did you know we called her back the next day? Did you know we invited her and her boyfriend to come talk with us? Make some plans?"

I'm shocked. According to Nichole, she ceased to exist the minute the stick turned pink. "So you started planning her life for her. Big shock."

"You need to watch yourself. She was younger than you at the time, with no job and no money. She wanted to keep the baby. We were willing to get behind that. But she needed our help."

"And?" I'm almost afraid of the answer.

"And she still insisted on moving in with that . . . with Peter. We would have invited the both of them into our house, but she wanted nothing more than to live on her own. And we all said some things we shouldn't have. Things you can't take back. All of us."

I can't remember the last time I saw Mom show an emotion other than disappointment. And here she is, practically in tears.

"So you just gave up on her?" I ask.

"No! Don't you understand? We didn't! But every time we communicated, we both got caught up in what the other one was doing wrong. We were all too stubborn to admit our mistakes. All of us, not just Nichole. I . . . I tried to see her when the baby was born. She told me she'd have security throw me out of the hospital."

I'm so stunned, I sit down. Every time I talk to Nichole, she portrays herself as the unwanted child, the martyr. I guess there are two sides to every story.

So maybe I'm not in danger of getting thrown out. Maybe I never really was.

"Mom . . . I didn't know. But I'm not Nichole, and

316

neither is Clayton. You can't keep us locked away at home because of one mistake my sister made."

"I've lost one child. I'm not going through that again."

I have to phrase this next bit very carefully. "You have to give us some space. Especially Clayton. Or it might be out of your hands."

Her eyes narrow, but she doesn't respond.

"Let us make our own mistakes, okay? You'd have been proud of both of us last night. We're back here in one piece—well, not Clayton, but that was an unfortunate accident—and we almost won today."

Mom shakes her head. "I refuse to believe you were only concerned about your family this weekend. I saw that boy making kissy faces at you in there."

"So what? I'm a senior. I've never been kissed. Well, until last night."

That almost gets a smile. "I'm sorry, Ana. There are some things I can't talk to you about."

"Try me."

"You really want to know?"

I swallow hard. "Talk to me."

"Ana, when Nichole was about seventeen, I . . . I found some condoms in her purse. I wasn't snooping," she adds. Big talk, coming from the woman who checks my phone records. "And I was going to say something, but I didn't. I knew she was smart, knew she was responsible, and I decided it was her life. There was nothing I could do. And look where it got us. We've lost our daughter and our grandson." I think she's about to cry again.

"Mom . . . do you believe if you'd grounded her for a month, then she wouldn't have had sex?"

Mom shakes her head.

"You did what you did. But I can't keep paying for my sister's mistakes. Sometimes it's like you don't even love me."

Mom looks so horrified that I'm sorry I said it. "How can you even think that?"

"You never say you're proud of me. You never hug me."

"I hug you every day!"

"Yes. At six thirty a.m., every day as I leave for school. And only then."

I can almost picture my Mom's thoughts, as she tries to prove me wrong. And she can't.

"Oh, Ana."

"Mom . . . we do have a lot to discuss. And I know I made some bad choices last night. But when we do talk, let's do it for real, okay?"

"Okay." She dabs at her eyes with a tissue. Neither of us move.

"Ana?"

318

And then we hug. Awkwardly at first, then tightly. And we're both crying.

"So proud of you, Ana. So proud. You did so well today. And that one chemistry question was bullshit."

I pull away, shocked. "Mom!"

"Well, it was. Now let's get out of here, or you'll miss your ride back."

She's letting me go back with the team?

As we leave, I take Mom's hand. It's sort of like holding Zak's hand: unfamiliar, but very comforting.

"Mom? I'd like to visit Nichole this summer. I really want to see her. I miss her."

Mom nods. "We'll see." But for once, that's not a dismissive comment.

"Hey, Mom?"

"Yes?"

"I'm grounded forever, aren't I?"

I'm gearing for the affirmative, but Mom just kind of gives me a sideways glance. "I don't know. You are eighteen. And you've never actually been punished before."

It occurs to me that I've essentially been grounded since Nichole left, but I don't say anything.

"I'll discuss things with your father. Now, what's up with you and that boy on the team? Was he that strange kid I talked to on the phone last night?"

I giggle. "His name's Zak. He was the one who helped

me track down Clayton. He saved us a lot of trouble."

"Hmm."

"C'mon. He's smart, funny, and a really nice guy. You'll like him."

"We'll see."

I've seen him naked, too.

ZAK

1:13 PM

"And then, right when the guy is about to tear my head off, Ana shoves this blunt arrow right up his nose. You should have heard him howl."

Roger stares at me over his coffee cup. We sit on a bench in the hotel lobby, my overnight bag between us.

"Zak, one night when I was in high school, me and some friends snuck into my principal's office and covered it in toilet paper. I've always considered myself a guy who had some wild times in his teens. After hearing you talk about last night, I realize I was an amateur."

I smile. "It was an unusual con. You should have been

hanging with the sci-fi geeks. We know how to have a good time."

"Obviously."

I'm putting on a cheery face, but I'm worried about Ana. I have a horrible feeling that once she talks to her mother, I may never see her again, until we're both eighty and run into each other at our spouses' graves.

Roger stands and stretches. "I have to make tracks, Zak. Your mom will be worried."

"Hey, thanks again. You really came through for us."

"My pleasure."

"Hey, um, Roger? Maybe some time, you and me, we can catch a flick or something?"

"Sure. Maybe one of those *Star Trek* movies you like. I just love that Yoda guy."

"You're killing me, man."

Roger grins, pleased at his joke. "Right back at you. See you tonight." He raises his cup to me, and leaves.

Wow. I'm actually going to have to buy him a birthday present this year. Eh, it's worth it.

Mrs. Brinkham arrives, carrying her suitcase and a lot of hate. She stops directly in front of me. I stand. Not so much out of respect, but fear I may have to defend myself.

"I just talked to Clayton's mother. Thankfully, she is

not going to make a big issue over this morning."

"Score!"

"I would wipe that smirk off my face, Duquette. Three of my students vanished last night. I could have lost my job."

I'm chagrinned. "I'm really very sorry. Ana and I were both just worried about Clayton and didn't want to see the police involved." *So blame him for all this.*

"You know, Zak, a lot of teachers would have overlooked your plagiarism. Or at least let you redo that assignment. I hate that attitude. It shows students that you don't have to try very hard, that you can get away with anything. That's why I made that deal with you. I knew you were smarter than that."

"Do you regret it?"

"Lord, yes." I can't tell if she's being sarcastic.

"We didn't do too bad in the tournament, though."

"No, you didn't." She shakes her head. "I have to go check out."

"Hey, Mrs. B? You're my staff advisor, right?"

"Yes?" she asks warily.

"Maybe next week we could get together and talk about . . . you know, my long-term goals? Help me register for college classes and stuff?"

She stares at me. "Why the sudden interest?"

I shrug. "Maybe you're right. Maybe it's time I planned ahead."

She gives me the thinnest of smiles and heads to the front desk.

And maybe I know a girl who's headed for more than community college and a tech department job. Maybe I want to show her, I can make plans too.

And there she is. As she comes out of the elevator, I can tell she's been crying.

"Ana . . ."

She smiles at me. "It's okay."

"What . . ."

"We talked. It's okay. Things are fine."

I know not to press. Instead, I take her hand. There's so much I want to tell her, but I don't have the words. But it's nice just looking into her reddish-green eyes and seeing them smile back at me.

"I had a good time last night, Zak."

"Please, call me Duke," I ask her for the hundredth time.

"No."

Why is she so insistent on that? "Ana, literally everyone calls me Duke. You're the only one of my friends that calls me Zak."

"Yes, I am. And I think that just maybe, I've earned the right to call you what I want. Zak."

She smiles at me and I'm no longer annoyed. Our faces get closer.

"You two." Mrs. Brinkham has returned. Ana and I quickly pull apart. "We're leaving. Your brother is already in the van. Are you coming with us, or going with your parents?"

"We're . . ."

Ana interrupts me. "We're going with our parents. We'll see you on Monday."

Mrs. Brinkham nods. "Very well. And Zakory, if you ever get the urge to cut my class again, please feel free to do so."

"Ana," I say when she's gone. "Roger already left."

"So did my mom."

I don't understand. "So how are we getting home?"

"Who's going home? Doesn't this con go on through Sunday?"

"Yes . . . but so what? We have no money, no car, no way of getting back." She's gone slap happy.

Ana smiles sweetly, turns, and begins to walk away. She then twirls and faces me. "Shockingly, I'm not grounded, at least not yet. I told Mom Sonya invited me to stay over at her place, kind of an end of the quiz bowl season celebration. Sonya loaned me fifty bucks, and said she'd cover for me. So I don't know about you, but I'm going back to the convention. I'm going to have a good time. If you're too scared, you can still catch Mrs. B."

She walks out of the lobby.

Numbly, I get up and chase after her.

My God, what have I started?

ACKNOWLEDGMENTS

This book could not have happened without the help of a lot of people. Firstly, I'd like to thank Claudia Gabel for always believing in me, even when I'm difficult to work with. Also, big thanks to Melissa Miller, who really helped me get my thoughts in order.

Huge thanks to my writers' group and other friends who were willing to read this manuscript over and over again: Kate Basi, Jenny Bragdon, Ida Fogle, Paula Garner, Debi George, Mark George, Mike George, Heidi Stallman, Elaine Stewart, and Amy Whitley. Special thanks to my Seattle connections, Antony John and Brent Hartinger. Big hugs to Hope Mullinax and Rachel Proffitt, the con-queens.

Biggest ever thanks to my wife, Sandra, and my daughter, Sophie, who put up with me wandering around the house talking to myself when the muse is upon me. Love you both.

Finally, long overdue thanks to the following people:

Mrs. Dawkins, third grade, Hawthorne Elementary; Mr. Harley Marshall, fifth grade, Progress South Elementary; Ms. Pat Turpin, speech, Fort Zumwalt South High School; Ms. Kelly Barban, creative writing, Fort Zumwalt South High School; Ms. Elaine Somers-Rogers, English 20, University of Missouri.

Those people helped inspire in me a lifelong love of writing. Also, big raspberries to Ms. U, sixth-grade language arts, and Ms. T, seventh-grade language arts, South Middle School, who almost killed it.

Read on for a sneak peek of
Brian Katcher's next offbeat and
smile-inducing novel,

DEACON LOCKE WENT TO PROM.

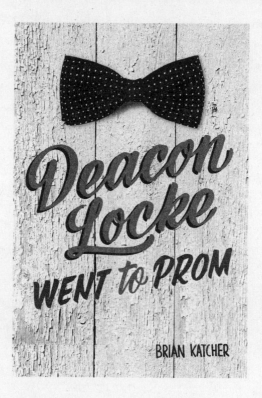

CHAPTER ONE

Look, I'm not a weirdo.

Not a weirdo. Good one, Deacon. Something only a weirdo would say. Let's try that again.

Okay, so you know how you, like, see a guy jumping over a school bus on a motorcycle, and you think, "That's something I could never do"?

I was kind of like that. Except instead of a motorcycle, it was talking. And instead of a school bus, it was girls.

I mean, it's not that I didn't want to talk to them. They smell nice and are pretty and . . .

Wow. Totally sounds like a weirdo.

Once more. My name is Deacon Locke. Last year, when I was a senior at Fayetteville High School, I achieved a bit of national prominence when . . .

1

No, that's boring. And last year was anything but boring.

Suspense! Romance! Intrigue! Broken bones and fistfights!

No, no, no, no.

My name is Deacon. This is the story of how I went to my senior prom.

With my grandmother.

But I'm not a weirdo.

The fancy couple in the stock photo are grinning so wide, their mouths almost look deformed. It's like something out of a propaganda banner: *Join the Glorious Soviet Army!*

They're not wearing Red Army uniforms, of course. The boy is wearing a tux, the girl, some sort of dress.

STEPPING OUT IN STYLE
Fayetteville High School Senior Prom
Tickets on sale now.

Stepping out in style. Who the hell comes up with these themes? There's probably an official, administration-approved list somewhere. Even I could come up with better names. *Infectious Waste Disposal*, for instance. *96-Hour Psychiatric Hold. The Slums of Bangkok.*

Those would also make good names for college bands, by the way.

Maybe my cynical nature is the reason I've never been to a school dance. And not because the idea of asking out a girl fills me with crippling panic. It's not that. So put that thought out of your mind. Because that's not what it is.

I check the date on the poster. May 6. One month from today. If I'm going to go to this dance, I have to get a date. Like, this week. I'm not going to chicken out this time. Not like homecoming. Or junior prom. Or the spring formal. Or homecoming last year. Or that sock hop thing.

I find Kelli in the back parking lot, directing the loading of boxes of canned goods into the back of a truck. Even in the mild Arkansas spring, she's dressed in heavy black jeans and a tight sweater that shows off her curves. Though she's barely five feet tall, she has a commanding presence. Her minions leap to obey her commands as to how the loot from the food drive is to be stacked and stowed.

Just seeing her there, I'm overcome with an intense feeling of . . .

Uh . . .

Well, not love. Like, maybe. Compatibility. Familiarity.

"Deacon! Come over here!"

There's no other option but obedience.

Kelli blows her nose into a sodden Kleenex, then points to a cart. It's loaded to the gills with pumpkin-pie filling, evaporated milk, Spam, and the other canned-food rejects people give to the poor. "You wanna give us a hand?" Her eyes smile at me through her round John Lennon glasses.

I bend down and grip the cart by both ends, lifting it slightly to get a sense of the weight.

"Deacon?"

Trying not to grunt, I hoist it chest high. I stagger, but don't fall.

"Deacon!"

I nearly topple over backward but manage to stay upright. I shove the cart into the back of the truck.

I turn to see Kelli and her flunkies staring at me.

"Um, thanks. But I just wanted you to pull the ramp out for us."

I quickly grab the toggle and extend the truck's built-in ramp. In retrospect, that makes a lot more sense.

"Thanks. We'll take it from here." She shoots me a tolerant smile, showing off her overbite.

Last year I heard a guy making comments about her teeth, how they would make it difficult for her to perform a certain biological act (I shan't elaborate further). Later, I took him aside and explained how I felt such comments were unworthy of a gentleman. He's avoided us both ever since.

I sit down on the nearby bike rack, which groans slightly, and watch as Kelli's crew makes short work of the remaining cans. For someone so small, she sure takes up a lot of space. I'll never forget the first time I ran into her.

Watch where you're going, you big stupid asshole!

We've talked every day since then. Eaten together. Studied together.

Never did a single thing outside of school together.

She's my closest friend here. I guess, technically, my only friend at Fayetteville High. But I'm the new guy. I only enrolled two years ago.

The other workers wander off. I watch them leave with a sense of foreboding. It's now or never.

Of course, there's always tomorrow. . . .

No! I'm not going to wimp out this time! My great-grandfather was a Scotsman! My grandfather lost his leg in Vietnam! I can ask a friend to go to a dance with me.

Kelli is busy filling out some paperwork on a clipboard. I walk up behind her.

"You're blocking the sun, Deacon."

I force a laugh. It sounds forced. "The sun is over a million miles in diameter. You honestly think I could block that?"

She sets down her clipboard and looks up. And up. "You? Yeah, I think you could."

I shift uncomfortably. While I'm not the *tallest* guy in school, I . . .

Okay, I am the tallest guy. And not by a little bit.

But then Kelli smiles at me. Her dimples appear. They're so deep they look like a bullet passed through each of her cheeks.

Good one, Deacon. Open with that.

"Kelli . . ."

"Are you okay? You look like you're going to barf or something."

Here goes nothing. "We're about to graduate."

She nods. "Yes, I'm aware of that."

I always feel dumb when I talk to her. Maybe that's why I like her. Since she's impossible to impress, there's no pressure to try.

"And I . . . there's something I'd like to ask you." I've armed the bomb. There's no turning back.

"What's that?"

"Well . . ." *God, why is it so hot out here?* "I wanted to ask . . ."

"No," she cuts in. "What's that?"

She points at something over my shoulder. I turn, grateful for the reprieve.

I can see what's grabbed her attention. Over in the

soccer fields, a knight in shining armor has ridden up on a horse. Seriously. A knight.

Okay, he's actually riding a pony, led by a middle-aged man. And the knight's armor is made out of tinfoil-coated cardboard and a spray-painted bike helmet. But still. The girls' soccer team stops their practicing. One player shrieks and covers her mouth with her hands.

The knight is helped down from the saddle by the horse wrangler. He then falls to one knee. We're sitting too far away to hear what he asks, but the girl's resounding *YES!* echoes off the scoreboards.

As often happens, I don't understand what's going on, and I look to Kelli for an answer. She seems to read my mind.

"A promposal. It's trending."

"Huh?"

She shakes her head and rolls her eyes, which happens at least once during all our conversations. "He's asking her to the prom. Big, fancy spectacle. A lot of people are doing it."

Huh. Now that I think about it, there *have* been a quite a few costumed serenades in the halls this week. That explains a lot.

The girl has now joined her date on the back of the animal, while the man leads them around the outskirts of the field.

"Hey, Kelli?"

"Yeah?"

I close my eyes, curl my toes, and swallow. "I was wondering."

"What?"

"Would you like to . . . would you like to . . ."

"Spit it out, Deacon."

"Want to go pet the horse?"

She looks up at me and shows me her dimples. "Hell, yes! C'mon!"

She jogs ahead. I follow.

Somewhere, the ghost of my grandfather laughs at me.

"I'm home!" I bellow.

"Deacon Locke, I swear to God if you slam that screen door again I will personally carve out your eyeballs and feed them to the crows!"

"Missed you too, Jean."

It's funny. I've known my grandmother my whole life, but I never once called her grandma, or granny, or nana. She's always been Jean to me.

I find her in the kitchen. While the heavenly smell of tonight's meatloaves wafts from the stove, Jean has taken a break from her cooking. I wince when I see she has her oil paints out and is wearing a smock over her housedress. Her hair and makeup, of course, are perfectly in place.

Not that I have a problem with her crafting obsession. It's just that a guy can only own so many bedazzled sweaters and crocheted toothpaste cozies. I paste on a smile, mentally composing a glowing review of whatever she's painted.

"What do you think?" She cocks her head.

I'm actually kind of floored. It's a portrait, and I instantly recognize the subject.

"Wow, that's amazing. The likeness . . . it's uncanny."

She beams up at me. "You really think so? I thought the mouth came out funny."

"Are you kidding? I'd know that guy anywhere. Ol' Johnny Cash."

Jean's face falls. "That's your grandfather, Deacon."

Whoops. Better laugh it off. "Johnny Cash was my grandfather? Then why aren't we rich?"

"Very funny." She shakes her head and closes her paint box. "Now tell me, how did it go today?"

Trying to ignore the question, I dig in the fridge for a snack. "The usual. School."

Jean removes her smock and folds it. "So did you ask that girl? What did she say? Do you need money for the tickets?"

I stick my head into the fridge and wince. Living

alone with Jean in this old farmhouse . . . I guess I tell her pretty much everything. She's a good listener. But I kind of wish I hadn't shared my plans about asking Kelli to prom. It was a spur-of-the-moment decision, and now that Jean knows, she'll never let me back out.

"I'll ask her tomorrow."

Jean closes the refrigerator door, just barely missing my head. "You've been saying that for days. What's your excuse this time?"

I'm having a hard time meeting her eyes, and not just because of the nearly two-foot height difference. "This horse came onto the soccer field—"

"The truth, Deacon. Even your father could have come up with a better story that that."

I laugh. "I'm serious. It was part of this guy's promposal."

Jean is about to check something on the stove, but pauses. "Don't throw your slang at me, I'm too old. Your aunt used to do that. I still have no idea what 'gag me with a spoon' means."

This is hard to explain. I don't even fully understand the concept. "A promposal is like a proposal. To prom. In costume."

She looks perplexed. "Why a costume?"

I pause. "I'm not sure."

Jean rolls her eyes. "Reality TV ruined your

generation. Back when I was your age, a boy would simply ask a young lady to the dance. We were honored to be asked and didn't expect more than a sincere smile."

I don't comment on this. Honestly, I can't buy the idea of every boy in the late sixties being a perfect gentleman. I think everyone secretly believes that their generation was the last to have manners and take risks. And the first to have sex. And that *Saturday Night Live* was funniest whenever they first started watching it.

I remember how I could barely even talk to Kelli, despite two years of friendship. Acquaintanceship. Going-to-the-same-schoolship.

"How about you pick up the phone and call her right now?" says Jean.

"Just let me handle it. Is supper ready?"

Jean is having none of my excuses. "We'll eat when we're done talking."

"Jean, you know that song 'Grandma Got Run Over by a Reindeer'? I really like that tune."

She shakes her head. "My favorite grandson—"

"Your only grandson."

"Going to miss what should be a great night, just because he won't get off his duff and ask someone."

This is kind of uncharacteristic for Jean. In her eyes, I can do no wrong. Why is prom such a sticking point with her?

"What's the big deal about some stupid dance? So I can sit around and stare at my date? I'm not exactly a dancer."

"You've no one to blame but yourself. Your father went to his prom, you know. Said he had a wonderful time."

Dad had told me about that night once, when I was still living with him. "Wasn't that when he wrecked Grandpa's pickup?"

She keeps talking as if I hadn't spoken. "You're going to be a college man in a few months. Those girls are going to expect you to be confident. Adult. How are you going to do that if you spend every night here with me?"

"Didn't realize hanging out with me was such a burden for you." That statement sounded a lot less whiny in my head.

Jean stands, wipes her hands on her towel, and walks over to me. She touches my arm.

"Deacon, having you live with me was one of the great joys of my life. But you're no longer a little boy. Well, you were never a *little* boy, but that's beside the point. This isn't about the prom. I just need to know that someday, when I'm not around—"

Why does every old person like to talk about death? Jesus.

"—that you'll be okay on your own. No more excuses.

12

Now, are you going to make an effort to get out more? Start bringing home girls I can disapprove of?"

I think of Kelli. Maybe it's all in my head. Of course it's all in my head. I'll ask her out tomorrow.

"Okay, Jean."

"And you'll make the most out of college, and not lock yourself up in your dorm every night?"

"Yes."

"But not waste your time partying, flunk out twice, and suddenly move to Arizona because that's where the rest of the band is?"

Funny, same thing happened to my father. "No."

"And you'll marry a nice girl and provide me with lots of great-grandchildren to play with."

"You're really pushing it."

We both laugh. I pick up the plates to take to the dining room. (In Jean's world, eating in the kitchen is reserved for breakfast and informal luncheons.) But then I stop. There's something I need to talk to her about.

"Hey, um, what happened to your taillights?"

She turns and stirs something on top of the stove. "What's that?"

"On your car. I'm pretty sure you had two of them when I left the house this morning."

She doesn't face me. "Someone must have hit me in

the parking lot at the Walmart. Drivers today, too busy interneting to pay attention."

I head to the dining room. A distracted driver. That's what she always says when I ask her about the new dents and missing parts on her car.

That driver must have really been distracted. He also managed to gouge a big gash in that pine tree out front.

Jean's driving has gotten a lot worse recently. There's been a couple of close calls at stoplights that scared the hell out of me. But every time I suggest she may not be up for driving anymore, she denies it. Gets defensive. Says I'm making a big deal about nothing.

Looks like I'm not the only one in this house who's worried about their future.